JUSTYCE SCALES
of THE OTHERLY
and OBSCURA

*To Lindsey
Stay beautiful &*

Norma Rrae

Copyright © 2022 Norma Rrae.

All rights reserved. No part of this book may be used or reproduced by any means, graphic, electronic, or mechanical, including photocopying, recording, taping or by any information storage retrieval system without the written permission of the author except in the case of brief quotations embodied in critical articles and reviews.

This is a work of fiction. All of the characters, names, incidents, organizations, and dialogue in this novel are either the products of the author's imagination or are used fictitiously.

Archway Publishing books may be ordered through booksellers or by contacting:

Archway Publishing
1663 Liberty Drive
Bloomington, IN 47403
www.archwaypublishing.com
844-669-3957

Because of the dynamic nature of the Internet, any web addresses or links contained in this book may have changed since publication and may no longer be valid. The views expressed in this work are solely those of the author and do not necessarily reflect the views of the publisher, and the publisher hereby disclaims any responsibility for them.

Any people depicted in stock imagery provided by Getty Images are models, and such images are being used for illustrative purposes only. Certain stock imagery © Getty Images.

ISBN: 978-1-6657-2281-0 (sc)
ISBN: 978-1-6657-2282-7 (hc)
ISBN: 978-1-6657-2280-3 (e)

Library of Congress Control Number: 2022907902

Print information available on the last page.

Archway Publishing rev. date: 06/21/2022

CHAPTER 1

T-minus twelve hours since her last daymare. Lucille Amberly Flask was feeling good. The camera in her hand helped her discern between reality and hallucination. A Canon Rebel T3i was the perfect birthday present from her mother, Ruth, to match the best birthday adventure—a trip to Liard Hot Springs.

Luci snapped pictures of velvet-like wooden statues as they sped past in the green Volkswagen Beetle, road-trip paraphernalia packed into each side pocket of the small car.

Her mother pressed the brakes to slow to the speed limit as they entered Chetwynd, British Columbia. Luci wasn't sure how to say the name, so she didn't try. She knew the fastest way to make an intelligent person sound stupid was by pronouncing a word wrong.

The last town was Fort St John, and the next would be Prince George. Parksville was home, but they still had fifteen hours further to travel, as they weren't halfway.

The breath-taking beauty of the north filled half of Luci's camera memory. She experimented with taking pictures between her iPhone and the Rebel, comparing quality and features.

"This camera is lit," Luci said.

Her mother beamed, "I think that means something good? Oh! Make sure you get a picture of that statue," she said.

Luci tried to line up her mother's pointing finger to a single figure. Dozens of wood sculptures lined the single highway stretch that made the town. A wooden man stood on horse legs with a broad animal face and twisted horns. He held a wooden scroll in his hands and reminded Luci of *Pan's Labyrinth*, her favourite subtitled movie. A medusa-looking mermaid stood next to two dinosaurs frozen in a violent collision.

"Oh, this one here," Luci said. She snapped a photo of the fairy hanging from a vine littered with dandelion seeds. A smooth wooden parachute sat over the art. "Just like the fairy homes that you build."

"That *we* build," her mother said.

Luci laughed, "All I do is collect the building materials."

"That's the most important job. What's a fairy home without driftwood and discarded hermit shells fresh from the beach? That statue is all wrong, though," her mother said.

Luci thought it looked perfect. "How so?" she asked.

Her mother pushed the polygon glasses up her nose at a stoplight. "Well, dandelion seeds are already a parachute in themselves, called a pappus. The seed body is porous and creates a vortex, an invisible parachute for the wind to carry them. Did you know dandelions hold the record for the most travelled distance without using a motor or wings?" her mother said.

Luci snickered, "I guess that's why they're such irritating weeds."

"Yes, but also no. People waste hundreds of dollars to rid their yards of these nutritious plants. You can eat them raw or cooked. They have loads of Vitamin A, B, C, E and K. There's even iron, calcium, magnesium, and potassium in them. They're a very nutritious power punch disguised as an itty-bitty yellow weed," her mother said.

Luci watched her mother's face crease from her smile, with elegant laugh lines like ancient tree rings. Then she playfully punched her mother's arm. "Your nurse is showing again."

"Careful, I'm driving," her mother dramatically exclaimed. Then winked. "You could cause an accident."

Luci smirked. Then pointed. "Look at that statue. It's a grumpy cat like our Earl."

Her mother chuckled, "I wonder how your father is managing that silly Persian puss of ours."

Luci clicked several more photos out the passenger window. "He probably tied him in a work harness and hung him from the ceiling."

That comment brought an animated laugh from her mother.

"Seriously though," Luci continued, "everything's beautiful here. Thank you for bringing me up here, Mom."

"It was nothing. Besides, the beauty of the hot spring was well worth the drive."

"Hmm, yes, but maybe a different campsite next time. One without the toilet paper padlocked in the outhouses." Luci said.

Her mother squared her shoulders and sat straight in the driver's seat. "It's to stop the bears, not the teens," she said, mimicking the park ranger's reply.

"His food recommendation was worth the conversation, though," Luci said.

Her mother laughed, agreed, then added, "The food at Toad River, mmmm."

"Yes, thank you for stopping there too. The hats covering the ceiling were epic!"

"Luci-two, I don't know why you keep saying thanks. It's your sweet sixteen, and that's a big deal. It deserves a big adventure." Her mother smiled and glanced from the road for a second. The sun shimmered on the grey in her blonde hair like hoar frost along branches.

"I know, Mom, it's just, with the camera too …" Luci blushed. "I don't feel like I deserve that much."

"What do you mean? You're a good kid, good grades, you always come home after school. I think you're a great kid."

Luci thought of her daymares that disrupted almost every outing, including yesterday at Liard. She didn't want to ruin the mood, so she said nothing—then or now. Her mother shot her a quick look, then back to the road. They sat quietly. The road twisted up a mountain causing the old car to slow with the incline.

An overhead highway sign warned of snow-packed sections and icy conditions. Unlike Parksville in March, where there wasn't snow worth a snowball, the weather in the north was unpredictable. Luci's mother had driven them through all four seasons to get to the hot springs. She admired her mother's driving skills, and now that she was sixteen, she couldn't wait to write her learner's test. But right now, she looked forward to getting home. Next weekend her friends would come over for pizza, movies, and lots of candy. The house would be vacant for them, mother's promise. Her father, Brent, and little brother, Lane, would be fishing for his ninth birthday. What better way to build a family than three members sharing the same extraordinary day, March 23?

"How old's Dad turning?" Luci asked.

"Fifty-two, he's still got three years on me. Maybe for my fiftieth, we can come to Liard again," her mother said.

"Yeah, for sure," Luci said, imagining all the pictures she would get. "That would be summertime. Wilds know what full bloom would look like!"

A perfect shot caught her attention. Luci centred the side mirror where the reflection of a charcoal mountain sat like a picture in a picture. The mountain's layered rock looked like millennia-pressed books hiding secrets. She snapped the picture.

"Aren't you glad you chose this trip over rock climbing with your father?" her mother asked.

"Yeah, Lane is big enough now. He can go. I mean, it's fun and all," Luci said, "but Dad's competitive. He's like a mountain goat. I can hardly keep up."

"I suppose he's a little intense," her mother said.

Luci smirked, thinking of all the Monopoly money found behind the bookshelf for weeks after their last family game night.

"A little? Don't you remember our last Monopoly game?" Luci asked.

"Yes, well, your father likes to win."

Luci turned in her seat to find a drink. "He doesn't let you quit," she said.

The back seat sat buried under luggage, shopping bags, and snacks. Luci dug through to grab a bag of candy and a couple of pops. "Do you want one?" she asked.

Her mother glanced at the haul and said, "Dr Pepper."

The car dropped into a valley where the weather changed dramatically. Cattails danced in gusts of wind, with dark clouds collecting overhead.

A green highway sign claimed Prince George was still 140 kilometres away. They passed a decrepit gas station with boarded windows and a door sealed by a plank of spray-painted wood.

Wind-torn billboards behind the failing building had their meanings stripped away by incredible weather.

Luci had an idea, "Want to play a game?"

"As long as it doesn't involve you driving." Her mother laughed at her joke.

"Ha, ha," Luci said sarcastically. "No, I was going to say, we should play a game with the broken billboards."

"You want to fill in the missing words from the destroyed slogans?" her mother asked.

Another three billboards flew past.

"Such a smart girl I have," her mother said. "OK, how do we know who wins?"

Luci lifted an eyebrow. "I see you're just as competitive as Dad."

"Well …" her mother trailed off.

"How about whoever gets tripped up loses."

"Deal. You start," her mother said.

A blue billboard approached, a classic yin-yang-looking symbol coloured red, blue, and white had four words left on the slogan. "Say it with Pepsi," Luci read, then considered the puzzle and added, "coming out your nose!"

They laughed.

"Meet the new smartphone," her mom read on the next board. "It'll take your *whole* paycheque," she added, then laughed until she snorted.

Luci giggled as her mother wiped laughter tears from her eyes. "I think you won," she said.

"Tim Hortons, every cup," her mother read the next one too, then added, "tells you the winning lottery numbers."

"Now you're just showing off," Luci joked. "Hey, a Tims is only forty minutes ahead," she read at the bottom of the same billboard. "An Iced Capp does sound pretty good."

"Good call," her mother said.

Norma Rrae

"Made with chocolate milk and whipped cream on top," Luci said. She could almost taste the silky coffee. The windshield wipers clicked on as light snow fell.

"Greenhouse for your soul," her mother read.

Luci didn't hear the punchline. Instead, her eyes trained on the wipers as they left black streaks on the windshield. Shadowy hands spread on the glass and melted into the car, heading straight for her mother's throat. Luci swallowed hard, thinking of what Dr Premiate had told her: keep your cool, remain calm, and collect reality.

Luci lifted the camera and snapped a photo.

"Woah, I wasn't ready," her mother said, but Luci paid no attention to her vanity.

Luci's hands shook as she turned the viewing screen on and examined the picture. No shadowy hands. Instead, a blurred image of her mother's face turning to greet the shutter. Luci fell into dark, miserable thoughts of daymares while her mother happily tapped her fingers on the steering wheel.

A new littering of billboards whizzed past, making Luci feel dizzy as she tried to read them to distract herself. Then an extra-large billboard appeared in the distance and caught her attention. The picture was of a girl's face with a website address scrolled at the bottom. It's a missing person's report.

The car sped closer.

The girl was near Luci's age with the same fiery red curls floating around her face as if she were in zero gravity. It was a strange photo for a missing person poster.

All the other billboards disappeared, and the missing girl took all her focus. Her mother said something Luci didn't hear.

The girl on the billboard resembled Luci.

The car was thirty feet away from the billboard. She saw two moles dead centre on the billboard girl's right cheek, identical to hers. Luci felt sick.

At twenty feet, she could make out the words under the face: *findjustyce.ca*.

At ten feet, she gasped. The girl didn't just look like Luci. The girl was Luci.

A mirror image of Lucille Flask as she was, sitting in the car. The way the open window caused her hair to float around her face.

Luci finally found her words and said, "What in the wilds?"

"What?"

"Mom, look at that billboard."

"Which one?" her mother asked.

The car sped down the highway and then past the billboard. She hadn't had the chance to capture a photo. How would she know if it was real or a daymare?

"That one that we just passed. The girl, she, uh," Luci stuttered.

"What?" Her mother glanced over. "You OK?"

Luci felt sick to her stomach, "On the billboard."

Her mother shrugged, "There's lots, Luci-two. Which one are you talking about?"

Luci's panic morphed into anger. "Stop calling me that! I'm not two years old," she snapped. "That billboard had my face on it." Her face felt hot, and that stupid piece of hair fell over her eye when she whipped around in the seat to look back at the billboard.

"Come on," her mother said, sounding exasperated, "what did Dr Premiate say about these daymares?"

Luci cringed at the comment. She muttered through clenched teeth, "This is different."

Her mother sighed, "Look, I thought we were having a good time?"

"We are. Can we just turn around? I want to go back. I need to see if that was my face on the billboard," Luci pleaded.

"Why would your face be on a billboard?"

"I don't know."

"It's getting dark soon, and now it's snowing. We don't have time to turn around. Remember your coping techniques? You need to tell yourself a different story," her mother said as if reading off the letter from her psychologist.

Acid bubbled in her throat. "Mom, that was my face. On a billboard."

"There are lots of girls—"

"No," Luci said, "it wasn't just any girl. It was me. My face!"

She felt an overwhelming urge to see the billboard for a second time. The slim face burned in her eyes like a flashbulb outline. "Can you turn around?" she asked.

"We'll stop in PG, and we can call Dr Premiate."

Luci's frustration boiled over. She simply wanted to take a picture of the billboard. Her camera lens had no brain patterns to alter reality. A picture would tell her the truth. Her voice came out with an unintended shrill plea, "Stop the car!"

"Sweetheart, please," her mother said. She reached over to reassure Luci, then snapped her attention back to the road and gasped.

Luci looked up.

A thick wall of fog cut the road in half.

Brakes squealed.

The car spun; metal screeched.

The car slammed to a hard stop.

Luci's head connected sharply with the dashboard.

Darkness.

A scream. Luci didn't know if it was her or her mother that screamed. Was that now, or had it been before? Luci blinked her eyes open, and the sting of a head wound smacked her in the face. She uncrumpled from the dash, fingers exploring a sore spot on her forehead. Bright-red blood flakes drifted down from her touch.

Time had passed. Luci guessed four hours with the fog gone and the sun high in the sky. Then she understood she'd been unconscious. A cold snake of fear crawled up her back and dug its razor fangs into her neck, forcing her to snap back to reality.

An intense pain banged in Luci's head, complicating everything: moving, breathing, even thinking.

Luci's breath hitched when she saw the driver's seat empty. It had to be a daymare. Her hands shook as she lifted the camera from her chest and clicked a photo. Her eyes were unfocused as if refusing to see that the viewscreen showed her mother was, indeed, missing.

The driver's door was closed, the car sideways on the highway's shoulder next to a cliff drop. At the bend in the empty road was a mountain topped with snow.

Luci's hands refused to obey when she tried to unclip her seat belt. Her fingers wouldn't follow commands as her heart beat erratically. Finally, she gave up on the seat belt and opened the door to scream, "Mom!"

Silence.

She screamed again.

"Help!"

She fumbled with the buckle and cried. And screamed for her mother.

Luci won the battle with the seat belt and stumbled out of the car. "Mom!"

Echo. Silence.

Her sloppy feet walked her nowhere. She yelled for her mother and wept. A smell of burned rubber, dirt, and desperation hung in the air. Luci moved in no particular direction, screaming "Mom" with each step. Every heartbeat was heavier than the last.

Luci tripped. Got up. Walked. She screamed until her throat

felt full of glass from calling for her mother. Her knees stung from the stumbling collision into concrete from her frantic search.

A lump of panic lodged behind her voice box. What if her mother was hurt?

No sirens or vehicles were approaching to help.

"Mom?"

She sobbed, fell, and didn't bother getting up again. Instead, she pulled her knees to her chest. "Where are you?"

Long minutes passed. With tears spent, Luci wiped her face to gather her senses. She looked up, cringing to see that she sat beneath the billboard, *findjustyce.ca*.

The enlarged picture of her face stared back. She groaned, lifted her camera, and snapped a reluctant picture. She wasn't sure she wanted to know if this was real or a daymare.

She checked the viewer and felt a rush of relief that she hadn't hallucinated the image. Instead, the picture was most definitely her face—as real as the cold the snowflakes brought. A daymare she'd finally conquered. Luci smiled. Then frowned. She dearly wished her mother was there to see that she wasn't crazy.

Luci's head swam with uncertainties. She didn't know where her mother was, and she positively couldn't comprehend why her picture was on the billboard. She glanced at the car. The passenger door sat open, but the driver's door was closed. Luci didn't recall her mother leaving the vehicle or hearing the door slam shut. It didn't make sense that her mom would go.

She must have been in shock, Luci decided.

A snap of cold wind stung the cut on Luci's temple. She needed help. She dug in her pocket and pulled out her phone. Spider web cracks covered the screen, sinking her chances of getting help. Luci tried to turn it on. Nothing. She warmed the phone with her cold hands and tried again.

"Garbage," she said.

Saying it out loud made her situation feel worse. Luci threw the phone down the lonely road, causing a petrifying pinging sound.

A silent fog rolled in like a ghost on a breeze. The damp mist returned with renewed force, pouring from clouds that weren't there a moment before. A curtain of fog rushed at her like a burst hydro dam. The blanket of white built with intensity along the ditches, then poured out to hide the pavement. The fog crawled along the highway, swallowing her cell phone's grave as she watched with wide eyes.

Luci regretted leaving the car when the mist clung to her clothing, making her shiver.

"Get back to the car," she told herself. She stood but cried out in frustration when she realized she could no longer see the vehicle.

"What have I done?"

Dread filled her veins with ice, and the fog ate her words. She'd walked away from the only safety she had, and the thick haze had gratefully accepted the car. Goosebumps covered her skin. Cold or fear, she wasn't sure.

Luci turned the opposite direction to see an undistinguishable landscape. Alone on Highway 97, her mother missing and possibly hurt, the girl collapsed to the ground, devastated by the situation.

She could no longer see the billboard. Instead, the fog sat around her like she were drowning in a glass of milk.

She yelled for her mother until her parched throat threatened to bleed.

The idea of her mother gone was suffocating. Luci didn't realize she was clenching her jaw until it throbbed. Her temple stung, and her throat burned. She hung her head, wanting to cry more, but fear drank the tears and left violent shakes behind. Desperately alone.

The air chilled to a frigid icebox temperature. Her skin so

cold it felt warm. Hot actually. She jumped up. She had to move or do something.

Luci tried to collect her thoughts. She needed the car.

She shuffled her feet in small circles until she found the edge of the highway. She followed the line for some time in one direction. This method should have theoretically taken her back to the car. But there were more fog walls. She listened for the sounds of a vehicle, her mother, or a hungry bear. Instead, there was silence, snow, and more fog.

Luci's legs felt like they filled with sand as she walked. Worry dragged her down even as fear drove her forward. A skiff of snow fell, making her regret the choice of light flat shoes for the supposed warm car ride. The snow covered her footprints as fast as she made them.

Luci turned around and walked twice as far back, looking for an indication of something. Anything. She found nothing: no footprints, no car, and no billboard. Only thick fog walls on every side, seeming to box her in.

She plunked down, exhausted, on the ground. The fresh snowflakes were so light they burst into the air like tiny feathers and drifted back down. Inventory check. She emptied her pockets: a pack of gum, a Chapstick, and some folded Kleenex—nothing useful. She craved water to bite her thirst or a hug to melt the worry. Maybe even a sweater to shield the cold. Luci sighed and stuffed a piece of gum in her mouth. Everything else went back in her pocket.

She clicked through photos of their trip on her camera. The smell of sulphur from the natural spring clung to her hair and brought her some comfort. A tear formed as she examined a picture of her mother mischievously grinning with her arm bent back holding a stone. A second after she had snapped the picture, her mother had released her ammo at a snow-covered branch above Luci's head. Thousands of ice crystals had rained down on her bare shoulders, causing her to yelp. Yesterday was fun. Today was a nightmare. And her actual birthday. Her lips formed the word Mom, but her broken soul prevented her from speaking, and instead, a whimper escaped her lips

Then someone, or something, hidden by fog, touched her shoulder.

CHAPTER 2

L uci scrambled away from the touch, scraping her elbows on the snowy gravel. All she saw was fog.

"Hello?"

The fog exposed nothing.

She choked out, "Mom?"

No response.

Instinct told her to run. Instead, imagination showed her body plunging over a cliff. Panic both solidified and liquified her feet.

Luci lowered her voice. "Mom, is that you?"

The answer was heavy breathing from what sounded like a mouth stuffed with cotton. Not her mother. Her head swivelled.

She saw nothing but suffocating fog. Luci franticly crawled backwards.

She tried to regulate her hyperventilating, but her lungs filled with teeming vapour. She held her breath, as painful as it was, to hear if the hidden guest was still there. There was only silence. Luci had never been so happy to hear nothing.

She let her shaky breath out and slowed her nerves. She adjusted the camera strap that felt like it was choking her.

Luci regretted her decision to binge-watch horror movies, but at least she knew monsters lived in the dark. The thick walls of fog would be the opposite, right? Then a scary thought, *The heavy breather brought the mist to cover its arrival.*

Luci rolled to her back, wincing. The material on her Wonder Woman long-sleeved shirt ripped open, exposing elbows torn down to bleeding pink flesh.

Hands around her camera, she forced her breathing into a rhythm and clicked the shutter. The flash illuminated a slight range, then faded. Maybe the breathing she'd heard was part of a daymare? If it weren't, the light would chase away the bogeyman, she concluded. She clicked photos in a full circle to illuminate the area. So far, nothing. Pointing the camera towards her toes, she snapped another blank photo. The shutter echoed. No toothy mouth screamed at her, no ghostly claws reached to her, and no murderer lunged for her throat. For a split second, she saw the road and nothing else. But then the nasal breathing started again.

There was someone here with her.

Luci moved to her right, away from the strained breathing sounds, and clicked the Rebel's flash. The light exposed her broken phone in the road, but nothing else. The mysterious company's breathing grew louder as if walking closer. She heard no snow-crunching footsteps.

Goosebumps rose on her arms. Luci snapped the shutter button repeatedly to light the surroundings.

She saw nothing.

Luci sighed, shook her head.

"Maybe I am going crazy," she muttered.

There appeared to be a spot where the fog thinned. Luci stood and walked across the highway towards the lighter-looking mist.

The thin mist, it turned out, was a shallow, dry cave that would offer protection on at least three sides of her. The chill from the fog was less here, but she couldn't hide from the breathing that was apparently in her head. It followed.

Luci sat with her arms hugged around her knees, rubbing her hands along her pants to create body heat. Her spine dug into the cave wall, and her knee pressed into the rock on the back wall.

She listened to the breathing. Crackles to inhale and huffs to exhale, each breath as painful to pull in as to push out. Luci imagined the intruder owned a hidden agony.

She looked at her camera. Would a picture ever pick up on the internal struggles?

She pointed the camera to the ceiling. *Click.*

A person hovered in the air.

Luci screamed.

She slammed hard against the cave wall, knocking the wind out of her chest. Her eyes spun.

"Don't go hurting yourself," a woman's voice said between heavy breaths.

No way, Luci thought.

She determined she'd lost her mind since there couldn't be a woman floating above her head. She clicked the flash again. The woman was indeed there, flying just beneath stalactites that threatened to impale them both. Luci glanced out of the cave. She wanted to run, but that was impossible, as she couldn't see anything. This just had to be a daymare. She clicked another photo to double-check.

Heavy breaths. "Can you stop doing that?"

Luci turned on the camera's viewing screen, which paused for dramatic effect. Then, the square blurred to life, revealing her company. It was a woman. Flying. She wore a broken porcelain doll mask and had splintered porcelain hands. Luci zoomed in on the flying woman's face, revealing deep ridges hiding puckered flesh and painful-looking scars. However, when she scrolled to the edge to find the seam, Luci realized it wasn't a mask. Instead, the woman's face was fragmented and cracked like a mask.

Piercing yellow eyes were captured in the fuzzy screen. Red lips like overcooked pottery set in a frown.

The woman's heavy breathing moved the fog around Luci's face when the girl looked up. Unable to say words, Luci squeaked some type of sound.

Between breaths, the woman asked, "What do you see?"

Luci jumped up. She shuddered when she brushed against the floating body.

She gulped, "Concord-grape hair swimming as if you're in the water."

"Hmm, I prefer to call the colour 'blood red of open veins'."

Luci decided the flying woman was tragically beautiful and very dark-minded. The girl muttered. "What is this?"

"I'm a who, not a what. The polite question is, then, who are you?" the woman said from behind the veil of fog.

Luci swallowed nerves that threatened to spill out. "I'm not going to ask who you are."

"Why not get curious?"

"My doctor says its best to not talk to my daymares."

"There's no doctor here," the woman said, "and I don't know what a daymare is, but you've been summoned to The Otherly."

Luci snapped another picture. Through the flash, she saw the woman shield her eyes with an arm that sagged as if made of bean bags.

"Can you stop with the bright flashes?"

She examined the viewing screen. "I'm trying to decide if you're real or not."

"I'm real alright. Come on. We need to go."

"What? No. I'm not going anywhere. I need to find my mother," Luci said.

"Funny story, your mother is the one who summoned you," the woman said.

Luci stepped forward. A swoosh of air told her the woman moved back to avoid a collision. "She did? Where is she?"

"In The Otherly, let's go," the woman said.

She felt more comfortable with the camera set back to rest against her chest, near her heart. "What's The Otherly?"

"Come with me and find out."

Luci laughed a sceptical one syllable. "I know better than to go anywhere with strangers."

The woman sighed, "That's why you should ask who I am."

Luci squinted hard into the fog, which showed nothing of the scarily stunning face. She didn't want to entertain this woman's request, but she also claimed to know her mother's whereabouts. And she couldn't risk passing up a lead.

"Is she hurt?" she asked.

"No," the woman replied.

Good. The girl relaxed. "Where is she?" she asked.

There was no response.

"You told me you knew where my mother is. Where is she?" Luci repeated.

"I've answered that question twice now. Your mother is in The Otherly. Besides, I thought we were starting with my name."

"Is this some type of game to you?" Luci asked.

Dead silence.

The girl caved. "Fine, what's your name?"

"My name is Grentsth, and I'm the gatekeeper of The Otherly."

"OK, Grentsth, can you please tell me what The Otherly is before I even consider following you?" Luci asked.

"A parallel world."

Luci furrowed her brow. "I don't like the sound of that."

"An alternate universe," she said.

"Not sure that sounds any better."

"I suppose not, but it's my job to deliver you. The sooner we go, the quicker the task is completed. That's the faster I can go back to floating peacefully in the dead forest."

"This is sounding worse by the second," Luci said. She tried to look around for an alternative route to following a flying woman with a cracked clay mask for a face, but the fog remained a mystical barrier to the world Luci knew so well. "How do I know you're not going to hurt me?" she asked.

Dumb question.

A snort. "How do I prove my sincerity to you?" Grentsth asked.

That's a legit question, thought Luci, *and I have no idea.*

Freezing droplets from the fog clung to her clothing, causing violent shivers.

"Get rid of this fog," Luci commanded.

An irritated sigh from the woman preceded a single clap. Then, as if a fan turned on, the fog blew swiftly out of the cave. The mist charged down the highway, collecting every inch before funnelling back into the clouds and disappearing. The sun tipped to the west, indicating evening would fall soon.

Luci blinked. She turned back to the flying woman and took in her appearance in the light.

She wore a *chong kben* pantsuit decorated with printed waxy lotus flowers. The cloth hung limply off the woman's body as if a mere skeleton held the broken porcelain head. In the light, she looked ancient. Her shattered palm turned upward to shield the sunlight from her eyes.

Luci took a long fresh breath, savouring the clean air. "That was something, thank you. Now I have to go call for help," she said, glancing to where the car sat deserted.

She stood to exit the shallow cave.

"Lucille, I'm not playing anymore," Grentsth said.

"Pardon?" she asked. "How do you know my name?"

"Everyone in The Otherly knows your name."

"I don't know what your—"

Grentsth twisted thin porcelain fingers tightly around Luci's wrist.

"What are you doing?" Luci shrieked.

Grentsth's superhero grip slid up Luci's arm. She shrank back from the pain the flying woman inflicted, hitting with her opposite hand.

"Let go," Luci demanded.

Grentsth's frozen lips didn't move with her words. "There's no time for this. I need to complete my task so I can get back to relaxing," Grentsth said.

The flying woman burst into the air, dragging Luci with unnatural strength. They darted straight to the opposite wall of the cave. The girl screamed in anticipation of smashing into stone, but suddenly they were through.

They soared above a miniature forest made of dollhouse-sized trees. Luci's feet dangled as Grentsth flew her through the air away from the cave. The trees became taller as they travelled, like a forest built on separated decades of replants.

"Stop!" Luci hollered.

The flying woman spun her head as if it were unattached to her body, and murmured. Then she attempted a smile, causing new splinters to spread from the corners of her mouth. "There's no going back."

The trees shifted into an ominous collection of heavy leafless branches that hung like dead men from nooses.

The venomous honey voice of Grentsth filled the air. She was singing, but Luci didn't understand the words. The song flowed like water, each syllable longer than the last, like waves crashing atop each other. The forest swayed as if basking in Grentsth's foreign music. Luci couldn't deny the melody was nice, as it faded the eeriness in the forest. She hoped she was indeed moving towards her mother.

Grentsth slowed, and Luci relaxed. Her muscles tense from being pulled through the air. The woman loosened her grip and lowered until Luci's feet nearly touched the ground, then swooped into a clearing and through a tunnel. It was pitch black for a second, then they emerged on a long flat stone.

That's where Grentsth let go of Luci's arm. She fell with a plop to the freakishly flat rock. Luci looked around. There was no one else there. Silence.

"Where's my mother?" she asked.

Grentsth pointed to the end of the flat rock. "That way."

Beyond the drop-off was a landscape devoid of high-rises and aeroplanes. Instead, it looked like a wildlife reserve with cartoonishly bright colours splattered on mountain ranges and rolling hills. Luci took a step, and Grentsth shot overhead to swim in the air.

Luci walked between scattered bristlecone pine trees. Thick green vines coloured the leafless trees, sprouting from the rock-bursting roots.

At the edge of the stone, lime-scented water spewed magically from the cliff lip. It crashed forty feet below into a steamy pool that trickled down into a river. Like millions of diamonds, the spray sparkled into one perfect cloud where Grentsth floated.

Wow, Luci thought, then said, "But why the dramatics of bringing me here? If my mother is down there, I mean."

Grentsth rolled to her back and shrugged. The cloud shifted

beneath her movement as if she were on a pool floaty. "This is as far as I can go."

"Where is she then?" Luci asked.

Grentsth rolled her eyes, which sounded like scratching marbles together. "In The Otherly. I don't know how many times I have to tell you this," she said.

The porcelain woman dropped through the cloud, breaking it into a halo. Then, beneath the cloud, she closed her eyes, pretending to sleep.

"I get that, but where exactly?" Luci asked.

Grentsth waved towards the landscape beyond the cliff. "Somewhere that way."

Luci's stomach dropped. The land stretched far. Too far. "How will I know which way to go?" she asked. Then, on second thought, she added, "You promised you would take me to my mother."

"I have. Welcome to The Otherly."

"But I don't see my mom. And saying 'that way' looks like a huge amount of land to cover. Can't you take me right to her?" Luci asked.

"No, as the gatekeeper, I am chained between Earth and the entrance to The Otherly."

Luci didn't see a door. "Where's the entrance?"

"You don't pay much attention at all, do you? I just brought you through the gate. It's abstract. It would help if you had a key to open it," Grentsth said.

Luci crossed her arms. "Let me guess, and you're the key."

Grentsth popped an eye open, smirked, and kicked off the cloud to shoot overhead towards the cave. Luci ran after her, yelling, "Hey! How did my mother get in this place if you're the key? Did you bring her here? I need more answers." The woman didn't stop. "And I was just starting to like you!"

That made Grentsth stop. Her head spun on a beanbag neck.

"No, I didn't bring her here. I don't know how she got here." She winked with a chalkboard scratching sound. "And I like you too," she beamed.

Luci sighed, resigned to the fact that she'd have to do this alone. "Please, can you tell me how I find my mom from here?"

"What will you give me for the information?"

Luci dug in her pocket and produced the pack of gum. She opened the package to find three pieces. She stuffed one back in her pocket and gave Grentsth two sticks of flat Juicy Fruit bubblegum.

Grentsth ran the foil under her nose, inhaling the sugary scent. Her strained breathing sounded easier for a moment. "Smells yum. Find the man with the yellow fields. He'll help." She used her ceramic fingers to pry her mouth open and stuffed both pieces of gum, foil included, into her mouth. The force of her chewing caused flakes of porcelain to rain down from her cheeks. She flew to the cave. Just before disappearing, she turned back. "I almost forgot. You can't return to Earth until you complete three trials to open a door."

"What?"

Grentsth disappeared into the cave.

A sound next to Luci made her jump. She turned and was face to face with a doe the colour of fresh caramel on ice cream. The deer dipped her head. "Is she always that helpful?" Luci asked, not expecting an answer.

The only way into the lands was down the waterfall.

The sound of thunder overhead, yet a glance up told her the sky was a smooth blue sky. Perfectly coloured, like a movie backdrop. She couldn't even see the sun to tell which direction she faced. *Strange*, Luci thought. She'd seen the sun before the fog, and it had seemed to be setting. Now it appeared to be midday with how bright the sky was.

She walked back to the edge of the waterfall and looked

down. The doe followed close beside her. At the bottom, next to the white-capped pool, was a mint-green grassy knoll, where something lay curled in a ball. Luci saw it was a fawn between the wafts of crashing water mist. His leg was haphazardly twisted, and he lay still in a pool of cartoon-red blood. His chest was hardly rising and falling.

The doe nosed Luci's elbow. She moved away from the doe because her skinned flesh stung viciously. The doe's caramel eyes were pleading with silent tears.

"That's your baby, isn't it?" Luci asked without expecting an answer.

The doe stared with sad glossy eyes at the growing red puddle beneath the fawn. A fall from this height, the baby deer was lucky to be alive.

With no plan, Luci examined the drop for what felt like forever. The rocks along the cliff face were jagged, unlike the unnaturally smooth lip she stood on. The cliff was the height of an Olympic diving board, and the mental image of diving into a pool made her gag.

The width of the waterfall was narrow, leaving half the cliff bare. She could climb down, but how would she get the fawn back up? There was no way she could climb with an injured deer on her back.

She needed to get down to find her mom. She'd hopefully be able to help the fawn too.

The doe disappeared for a moment and returned with a mouthful of vines ripped off a tree.

Eureka!

Luci thanked the wilds for the rock-scaling knowledge her father had always insisted on sharing.

Her father spoke in her mind, *Overestimate, never underestimate, the length of rope you need.*

A massive tree sat on the edge of the drop. Vines hung from

branches over the edge. Luci thought she saw one vine slither and reach. Impossible. She squinted at the greenery, which held sporadic banana plant-sized leaves.

Luci unwove vines from trees. Others she had to rip off. Some fell off in bundles as if wanting to be collected and part of the solution.

She coiled several piles of the building material, guesstimated how much she needed, then collected double the amount. Finally, Luci tied vines into rope under the crystalline blue sky with a furrow on her forehead. The sky never darkened or changed from blue.

After what felt like forever, but could have been as short as a couple of hours, she completed seventy feet, more or less, of the braided vine. Hopefully, not too much less. She stood over the piles and contemplated what to do next. Her father's advice came to her through the fog of uncertainty.

Don't step on your rope. The bends will cause weak points.

Luci looped one end over the forty-five-degree bend in the tree before dropping the length down the cliff, and then she tied the ends together. A firm tug. It should be strong enough.

It stopped several feet from the ground. Luci hoped it was fewer feet than bone-breaking distance.

Preview the route, Luci's father said in her mind.

Luci knelt and took mental snapshots of the path down. She noted where the small ledges were, anywhere she could rest if needed.

She made a harness by tying the larger-than-her-forearm leaves and vines together. She stepped into it. Snug. If she happened to lose her footing, it might save her life. It was no belay, but it would do.

Luci looped a smaller rope around the harness and attached it to the rope hanging over the cliff. The saddle would slide down along one vine, and she would control the descent speed while holding the other rope.

That was the plan. Now to just step off the cliff and put it to the test.

She sat down. The doe nudged her with that damp nose again.

"I know. Time is low for your baby," Luci said.

She turned and lowered her body over the edge. She stretched to the first foothold and stood against the cliff, forty feet in the air.

She faked courage as if her father watched. She'd never attempted this alone. She didn't even want to think about the fact she didn't have proper climbing equipment. But she had confidence in her rock-scaling abilities.

A pebble fell, and her foot slipped.

The unexpected action made her palms sweat.

"Don't be cocky," she said to herself.

She glanced at her pink flats, growled at her stupidity, and kicked them off. They plopped into the roaring pool below and disappeared.

She lowered to the next ledge. Her bare toes gripped the titan-sized rocks.

Keep your rope hanging free.

Luci glanced up at the tree. There were no obstacles to prevent the rope from gliding smoothly. Another stone came loose, and this time a cascade of rocks tumbled. She clung to the sheer rock. Spray from the pool below splashed up from the rocks, but she was too high for it even to reach her toes.

Heights didn't bother her, so looking down wasn't an issue, but she kept her eyes trained on the next step she wanted.

Look to where you want to go. If you don't want to fall to the bottom, don't look there.

Concentrating on her father's advice kept Luci moving down the cliff. She pressed her face into the unsympathetic rocks for breaks.

Watch for rotten rock. Like fool's gold, it's there to deceive you.

Luci slid her foot along a thin ledge, moving the loops down the vine to reposition them. Then took another reaching step down.

Stay away from cracks in the rock. They are not footholds. They are body droppers.

The vertical drop peppered with fake footholds seemed to mock her. She shuddered at the realization that the cracks mimicked Grentsth's face. She glanced up to the top of the cliff but saw only the mama doe's face watching.

Each climb is like a Rubik's cube, a riddle to solve on your way.

Luci's father reached out an invisible hand to show the way.

Distribute your weight to your feet. Don't rely on your hands.

Even in her mind, he spoke kind and confident.

Don't hug the cliff face. It doesn't love you. It wants you to fail.

Another manoeuvre and she was near halfway to the bottom. The rocks collected droplets from the splashing pool below now. Her confidence flatlined, and her descent slowed.

Don't trust your equipment. It's your body and brain that need to work.

Luci's hands stung, and her muscles cried from exhaustion. She wished Grentsth would have flown her to the bottom of the cliff.

Luci felt the warmth of her breath reflecting off the cliff. Her hands shook when she tried to reposition a weakening grip.

She stopped for a rest.

A memory of an old photograph of her father came to mind, with his bright blue eyes shining up at the invisible cameraman on a bridge. Her father hung in his mid-air harness. The drop worthy of a bungee cord without an ounce of fear. He'd been at least seventy feet in the air. Neon-green grass bordered the picture. It was a perfect reflection of the pride he took in his work as a rock blaster, even in the face of danger.

The image brought strength to Luci.

She descended the cliff, thankful for her father's long hours teaching her the butterfly knot, slip knot, and double fisherman's knot. Those simple loops in the vines right now were holding her life away from death.

The fall might not kill you, but a sudden stop will.

The cliff ominously smiled as Luci's breathing increased. She was tired. And thirsty.

The middle is no man's land, don't linger, push forward.

Grentsth's voice carried over the top of the cliff, "Look at you go."

Luci growled, "It would have been faster if you'd flown me to the bottom."

"That goes against the rules of the trial," Grentsth called.

Luci rolled her eyes and descended another step. "Of course."

"What was that?"

"I can't wait to find my mother," Luci yelled.

"Yes, your mother, Keres, will be happy when you find her," Grentsth called back.

Keres? Luci jerked her head up, but the sudden movement made her hand slip. Then the rope snapped. Her foot skidded, and she fell.

CHAPTER 3

L uci landed hard. Her head spun. Then she slipped into unconsciousness.

She's in the car. It's night-time. The lodge sitting in the headlights is Toad River, and her mother is bringing the suitcases into their number nine cabin. It sits in a row across from a ferocious river, high in the Northern Rocky Mountains. Icebergs crashing downstream create the bass, mixing with the late-night songbird's treble to make a northern melody. Tall evergreens, coloured teal, sage, and emerald, waving glistening snow under the moon whisper tenor for the north song. Frozen crystals cling to the shifting blades of long grass behind the cabins. Beyond the field sits a frozen manufactured lake that reflects the glorious moon above.

Now she's walking the circular track with her mother, keeping pace, step for step. Luci is snapping pictures of suspended air bubbles beneath the water's surface. The lake is brimming with enchanted jewels under the moonlight.

It's daytime. Luci's hiking the wooden pathway to the springs with her mother ahead. There is no railing to prevent them from stepping off, but there are signs asking people to respect the foliage. The electric green ferns are steaming, sprouting between clumps of melting snow.

They arrive at the change room. It's an open-concept wooden structure with an archway that acts as a peephole to the beauty of the natural springs, squared off with walkways and wooden structures. A winding bridge off to the side sits closed. A warning of "bear attacks" hangs over stunning hand-carved wooden planks and overgrown flora.

She changes in the electricity-free, vaulted-ceiling, rough-cut-lumber building, inhaling the woody smell before stepping down the broad steps into the steamy sulphur pool with her mother.

Evergreens hang over the edges with massive snow piles and spicy pine cones. Cloistering the water are wooden handrails, elegant benches, and artificial waterfalls. Luci wades to the super-hot water spilling out from between millions of tiny pebbles. Natural ice formations cling to every surface, melting winter's fortune back into the pool. Geometric patterns are etching into sheets of ice that cover the tree bark from root to crown.

Her mother bounces from one foot to the other to prevent her toes from freezing to the icy wooden planks. She mermaid dives into the pool and swims to where Luci is standing. They're both smiling.

Luci is swaying her hands through the water at the warmest

spot she can manage. Any closer to the natural hot spring, where the water boils and spits from between rocks, she would scorch some skin. Her mother is kicking up the silky bottom into plumes of dirt that float to the surface of the mulberry-green water.

Now they're investigating a manufactured wooden waterfall. It separates the warm pool from the cold pool. Her mother is sliding like a penguin over the slippery wood. Luci is calling for her mother to wait. She's clambering over the waist-high barrier to avoid dipping her face under water. Her mother is swimming to the pool's far end where a fallen tree lays, making a doorway. Luci doesn't notice the tree-root-made tunnel until her mother dives underneath.

The sapphire water smooths, wiping away the ripples from her mother's kicks. Luci sees her mother's head pop up far down the tunnel. There are rows of grottos, darkening into an abyss.

Luci ducks into the first chamber and swats at frosty branches, grabbing her hair. They scratch her skin in the cool water. The level is dropping lower.

She hears something distant.

Tree limbs are drawing malevolent silhouettes along the surface of the shallow water. Branches close into a wall behind her. The sound again. Vines cling to the roots of ancient trees. The same roots have grown out of the banks and drape over the dirt edges into the water. Wave after wave smashes into Luci's chest. She sees her mother ahead for an instant, on the other side of the assaulting trees. Then she sees her mouth open in a silent scream. Luci tries to reach out for her mother, but the tree branches push her back.

They pull her under the water and hold her to watch. Darkness pulls off the banks and enfolds her mother. More shadows stretch through the waves, driving straight at her mother. Luci is screaming, but the waves swallow the sound and her oxygen. Her mother is getting pulled away.

———

Luci woke with a start on a muddy bank. She rubbed the back of her head. The harness remained tied around her waist but had snapped off the vine rope, which was left dangling in the air.

The dream left her skin cold from the dried sweat. Correct that—it was a memory. A memory of a daymare from her last day in Liard Hot Springs. Where was she now? Halfway between Bear Lake and Prince George in an alternate dimensional world called The Otherly. Did the daymares follow her?

Luci furrowed her brow as she glared at the mute blue sky. The solo cloud had drifted down, so close she could almost reach up and touch it. She clambered back to her feet, determined the day at the springs wouldn't be the last time she saw her mother.

She palmed water from the falls into her mouth. It was fantastic and bit through the soreness of her throat. Nothing felt broken, but the adrenaline she'd been running off of after the car accident was gone. Luci wished for something she could put water in. Or food.

She looked up the cliff. The doe stared back.

"Grentsth?" She yelled.

No answer. Then Luci remembered why she'd fallen. Why did Grentsth say her mother's name was Keres? She hoped it didn't mean Grentsth brought her to The Otherly looking for the wrong woman. There was one way to find out.

"Grentsth!"

The broken-faced woman was gone. Luci peeled herself off the muddy bank. Her muscles ached, but she managed the distance to the fawn. He didn't even lift his head to acknowledge Luci, if it was a "he."

"Hey, little guy," she said.

She crouched to the ground to appear less intimidating. Wild animals, she knew, could be dangerous, especially injured ones. His eyes opened with strained effort and followed her movements. He whined when Luci reached out to him. He sniffed at her hand, then placed his head in her palm. The fawn even let Luci lift him without a fight. He stared into her eyes as she carried him to the base of the waterfall. Tying the fawn snug in the harness, she hoped the ropes would hold.

Luci looked up and met the doe's large eyes. She dug her toes into the mud. Then, like with a pulley system, she yanked down on the rope so the fawn would travel up. Her knuckles turned white with the effort. The fawn's life depended on this single viny lifeline. And as much as Luci needed to find her mother, this fawn would die without his.

The task of having the deer move smoothly up was daunting. As the fawn passed Luci's face, she thought the baby smiled. More rope pulled down, and the baby broke through the cloud on its way to his mother.

With control, Luci pulled no more than a handful of moss rope at a time. But one rock slid past her face. Then, numerous rocks cascaded around Luci. She ducked, but the rope slid some through her palm.

The vines jerked, and she saw the baby deer crash back down through the cloud. He was going to fall.

CHAPTER 4

Luci scrambled to grab hold of the ropes. She wrapped the vine around her waist and slammed her body weight down to get the fawn up over the brow of the cliff. The waterfall seemed to glare at Luci. But she succeeded.

One last twitch of the baby deer's tail as he disappeared over the cliff edge. A spray of water sailed from the pool like a celebration of Luci's achievement, causing water crystals to dance in the air.

Luci held the rope tight until she felt the weight disappear from the opposite end. That's when she knew the doe had collected her baby.

She was alone again.

The only way down the valley was a narrow grass strip next

to the river. There was no other way to go. But the idea of being close to water made Luci's stomach roll in sickness, so she popped the last piece of gum in her mouth and focused on each bite. The water flowed, unrelenting, with waves beating along the banks. Bulky chunks of sand crashed into the river, making her feel less assured.

Luci walked hunched over, weighed down by her thoughts of her mother. Her sore feet dug toe marks in the dirt as she pushed forward, and her gum was losing flavour.

She was comfortably warm, but that made her feel more off. It had been cold on the highway where she lost her mother. Here, there was no sign of snow. She glanced at the sky. Where was the sun? She searched the sky but to no avail.

The high ridged mountains forced Luci to stay in the valley. The boulders on the river banks shrank, making her feel optimistic she would be away from the water soon. Maybe even find help. Unfortunately, she hadn't seen another person yet, which sapped that faint thought of promise. The mountains shifted to rolling hills that sat like unbaked dinner buns. The air was fragranced by exotic flowers, which Luci saw growing in apparently tended patches. She touched the velvet petals on the purple galaxy-spiralled flowers and yellow spikey buds. There were pink and green tall grasses that bordered the flowers. A bird swooped in for nectar and startled Luci. She felt silly for getting spooked by a sweet little bird. Chipmunks stuffed their cheeks with flower buds with their eyes concentrated on her.

Woes distracted by the fairy tale landscape, she thought. At least here, the daymares didn't seem to reach her.

It was all too perfect, an unnervingly serene landscape with no electricity poles, houses, or roads. There wasn't a sign of other people anywhere. Of course, her mother would love it, but that was a reminder of how miserably alone she was.

Luci's footsteps were the sole marks of man in the valley, so when she found a game trail, she felt a thrill of hope. Her tense shoulders relaxed.

The ground shifted to a downhill slope. The raging water broke apart the river banks in front of Luci's eyes. Spray flew as pieces of rock crashed into each other, ripping chunks out of the bank. Ahead, the river poured into an enormous lake. A shudder of realization made her gasp: she had to cross the river here. There was no way to follow this moving water unless she were in it, but swimming meant drowning for Luci.

A fallen tree lay randomly across the river. There was no other way.

Luci crouched in front of the tree that created the bridge. She wasn't sure about this idea. She had rappelled down a cliff with no problem. But tiptoeing across a river on a half-rotten tree? That's a whole different picture, and one she didn't want to develop. She tested the stability of the tree bridge by chucking large rocks at the centre. The log didn't budge from the attack, which was a good sign. But secretly, she hoped the tree would crash into the water, forcing her to find a different way to cross. Yet, here she was. She had to cross. Luci pushed on the dirty roots trampled into a perfect foundation, inviting her first step. The crown sat on the opposite bank, waving branches full of leaves like a hand. The river raged and spat debris at the log bridge.

Luci tied her hair in a curly knot behind her one ear, told her stomach to stay still, and took her first step on the log. She felt dizzy and nearly fell straight away. Luci jumped back to solid ground and took an extra moment to collect herself. Then she decided she needed something to help her balance. Driftwood! The one thing she was good at finding. Luci looked around and spotted a sizeable petrified stick with a smooth top that fit nicely in her hand.

She stabbed the stick straight into the water, which increased her confidence. But she still hesitated before her first step up.

Luci looked again for an alternate route. There wasn't any. Over the river was the way to find her mother.

She took the first step over the water onto the fallen tree. She puffed up her chest and pretended to be brave. "For Mom," she said.

Luci's heart didn't slam in her chest this time. Instead, it stopped. Her knees shook, trying to prevent her from taking another step. Animal traffic had beaten the bark on the tree down to a smooth flat top. That made it slippery. She wiggled the stick deep in the river to ensure she was steady.

She watched each foot placement, almost burning a hole through the bridge with her stare. One step, then another. Slow. Luci looked up to the opposite bank. The end stretched far away.

"Oh, my wilds," she muttered.

The tree bridge moaned with each step, and the river smacked beneath the tree. Even Luci's breathing was scaring her. Luci demanded that her legs remain slow and steady even though they vibrated with nerves, wanting to run.

She was making progress.

A small bump against her balance stick made Luci wobble. Then another. She risked a glance down to see hundreds of tiny fish swim past.

"Really?" she grumbled. She lifted the stick and plunged it back in for her next step.

A large fish jumped out of the water and slammed his grotesque head into the bridge. It looked like he had a sword attached to his head. However, these weren't fish but small sharks with jagged teeth, snapping out of the water. The petite shark shook his head as if dazed, then dived under the tree and swam away. Luci tried to ignore the realization that the snapping predators grew larger with each step she took towards the bridge's centre. Eyes glared at her below the surface. Spiteful jaws scraped the underside of the log. Luci yelled at the sharks and used the stick to swat them.

Her breath caught in her throat when she recognized them as 125-million-year-old goblin sharks. *Of course*, Luci groaned. But she didn't want to be chum. She calmed her nerves by counting her steps.

Past the centre, close now. The assaulting sharks had heads so large they stuck out of the water. Their flesh was a pinkish purple and wrinkled, and there was a snout beneath the sword-like formation on their heads. Most piled upstream against the tree with mouths gaping out of the water. The ones that did make it under created an awful scraping sound with their teeth on the tree.

Suddenly, the sound of water sucked into a tornado caught Luci's attention. Her head snapped up, looking farther up the river. The sight was from a nightmare. A monstrous goblin shark displaced half the river and all the smaller sharks. They flapped helplessly on the banks, gasping for oxygen.

The raging water shot rocks into the air. Bloodstained teeth snapped as the shark swam straight for the bridge.

She ran.

Don't fall.

Don't.

Fall.

Luci was almost to the other side.

The shark was destroying the river on his approach, with crashes and bangs to the side of her.

Her toes touched the tree's crown. It was the end of the bridge!

Then the shark hit the tree.

The tree buckled, knocking Luci's legs out from under her. Her back struck the bridge when she fell.

The force of the river whipped the balancing stick out of her hand. Luci grasped for something, anything, to save her. The bridge shifted under her. The plunge into the cold river cut off her scream.

Luci gasped, and water rushed into her mouth. She breathed in water and choked on it. Her eyes stung. *It's a daymare,* she hoped. But with lungs burning from the lack of oxygen, she knew it wasn't a daymare. A massive wave pushed her up for a split second, where she gained half a mouth of oxygen before plummeting again.

Luci pushed water down with her arms. She tried to climb the ladder of life to get above the surface, but more waves appeared. Finally, the water swirled and slammed her into boulders.

The water stank of decaying fish and tasted of her failure.

A light broke through the water. Luci's arms felt like jelly. Something bright swam towards her in the river. She reached out to grab hold, but the undercurrent denied her the luxury.

The bioluminescent object charged at Luci. Her throat felt tight, but every breath rushed water into her lungs. The light flickered between the strong waves that swept her downstream. The current granted Luci a quick breath above, then dragged her away from sanctuary again. Suddenly, a dazzling burst of light announced the arrival of the object.

A dragonfly. Underwater? His wings were flapping in a separated sequence. He stopped two inches from her nose, pushing the water away, creating an air bubble.

Luci gasped in a mouthful of fresh air. She felt something like a bead slide down her throat, and she was breathing underwater. Her eyes locked on the submerged dragonfly. Enchanted by his unnatural size and location, Luci didn't notice the hand crashing through the water's surface.

A firm grip yanked her out of death's grasp. She collapsed to the grass with a hard thud.

Luci gasped, which hurt. She coughed and vomited, which also hurt. It was pain and relief that made her laugh and cry.

A hand touched her shoulder, melting away the burning pain stuck in her lungs. Air moved smoother in her chest, and she could breathe normally again.

Luci rolled over to thank her saviour but screamed instead.

An Easter Island statue stood over her. His face was so close that she could smell a sickening honey scent on his breath. He blinked, and she scrambled away, sliding around in the wet grass.

Red lips spread into a wide grin, exposing square teeth the size of Tic Tac boxes. "Are you alive?" His words on each syllable were hard, like slamming cupboard doors.

His black eye sockets camouflaged his black pupils and irises. A ferret was curled in a ball on his triangular head with its eyes closed. Black hair covered his unnaturally long arms and his giant hands hung on the ground from his three-foot stature.

She pushed herself to sit upright and struggled with each word through a strained throat. "Yes, I mean, I think so."

The sleeping ferret wrinkled his flat caramel nose and growled. Or was it a chirp? Either way, it was an angry warning. Luci tried to climb to her feet but slipped and fell on her back. The man moved to help her up. She waved him away. "No, no, I'm fine."

Luci's words caused the ferret to jerk awake. The ferret stood, frowned, then rewound his little body and resumed sleeping.

"Are you sure you're alright?" the man asked.

"No, actually, I'm not sure."

His watermelon-sized palms covered his ears, the size of peanuts, on either side of his head, then he yelled, "Can you ask questions quieter? Don't you know my ears are painfully sensitive?"

Luci frowned, "You're the one yelling questions."

"Am I?"

Luci stood on wobbly legs. His behaviour reminded her of copycat, a game Lane would play. "I'm too tired for games."

She wiped the Rebel with her shirt bottom, but the cotton was just as dirty as the camera. She sighed. The man took a step forward, put his face in her personal space, breathed on her camera, and then wiped the lens with his shirt sleeve, which was also wet with muddy water from saving Luci. Then he turned his face up and grinned with large square teeth.

Luci took a step back. "Thank you for saving me, but please, can you give me some elbow room? Back up a step or two?" she asked.

"Do you want one or two?"

Luci furrowed her brow, "One or two what?"

He didn't move. "How many steps?"

She grumbled, "Two, at least."

He grimaced and covered his ears again. "Do you remember that time I told you my ears are sensitive?"

"Are you OK? You know, up here?" she tapped the side of her forehead.

The man backed up a few steps. He tapped the side of his head. Then turned his head and pointed to his tiny ear. "Do you see how small these are?"

Luci chuckled. She considered him. He did save her and didn't appear threatening. Also, he didn't fly like Grentsth. That was something.

The ferret snored.

Luci yawned.

"Are you tired?"

"Yes, very. I've been through a lot," Luci said.

"Will you let me help you?" he asked.

"OK," she said hesitantly.

The man held his hand out, and she placed hers in his. His grip wasn't rough like Grentsth's had been. It was delicately strong. Warmth seeped into her hand, up her arm and rejuvenated her tired muscles.

Her weakness melted away like the smoothest sands on the edge of a river. Luci's fear dissipated as well.

She glared at the river where the massive goblin shark drew silver lines in the water. The destroyed tree bridge sat in the river like a sad troll.

"Do you want some tea?" he asked.

"No, thank you. I feel much better and must be going."

She walked past the man towards the hills in the distance.

"Where are you going?" he asked.

"I have to find the yellow fields—"

"Yellow? Do you mean like canola?" he asked.

Luci stopped and looked back, "Yes, it could be canola. There's a man there that knows where my mother went."

"Which mother?" he asked.

"Pardon?"

"Do I grow canola?"

Luci decided she must have misheard his question, and this new one sounded like an answer. But she was also getting irritated with the veiled information. "I don't know, do you grow canola?" she asked.

"Do I?" he nodded.

That was enough. Luci said, "Look, I don't know who you are or why you keep answering my questions with questions, but I need to find my mom and get out of here."

Luci turned to the hills and walked towards them. Footsteps behind her told her the man followed. She glanced back.

The man stared at her with his black eyes. Then the black Luci assumed was soot began to spin. The colour drained around his eye sockets like water down a tub. She nearly tripped. His eye sockets settled to a royal blue that sparkled with aqua crystals. Luci gasped. "What are you?"

"Have you heard of Memegwaan?"

"No, a what?" Luci asked.

"Who is Zavian?"

"What?"

"What is Memegwaan?" he asked, then added, "Who is Zavian?"

"Huh?"

He grinned, and his eyes paled to a yellow. "Did I stutter?"

"Wow, OK, you don't need to be rude. Memegwaan—"

He cut her off. "Who is Zavian?"

"Right, Zavian is your name. Got it. But look, you're the one following me. You can just turn around and go another way. I'll find the man with the canola fields alone," Luci said and turned back to the hills.

"Is that allowed, Miss Luci?"

She spun around, "How do you know my name?" she asked.

"Doesn't everyone in The Otherly know your name?"

"But why?" she asked.

Zavian shrugged. His eyes shifted yellow. Then he mimicked her tone. "Why not?"

"This is like everyone except me knows the punchline to the joke that is me." Luci sighed.

"Are you funny? Do you know a joke?" he asked.

Luci shook her head and moaned. "Can you only speak in questions or something?"

"Is that what I'm doing?"

Zavian's eyes blended back to black.

Luci rolled her eyes. "This is worse than dealing with Lane."

"Who is Lane?" he asked.

"My kid brother."

Zavian patted his chest. "Can I have a kid brother?"

"Look, I need help. But asking me questions is not helpful. I was in a car accident, and now my mother is missing. Grentsth brought me here saying my mother is in The Otherly, but then she said something else," Luci broke off. She remembered the name Keres. She didn't understand why that name and her mother ended up in the same sentence.

"What did Grentsth say?" Zavian asked.

"She said my mother's here."

"Which one?"

"Why do you keep saying that?" Luci asked.

"Don't you have two moms?" he asked.

"No. My mother's name is Ruth. She has shoulder-length blonde hair, glasses, and is shorter than me."

Zavian sped up to walk next to Luci. "Are you here looking for your mom?"

Luci glanced sideways at him, trying to decide if he was messing with her. "Yes, my mother, Ruth," she said.

He fell back in stride behind Luci. "Do I know Ruth?" he asked.

"She's lost, and I need to find her."

"How do you find what's lost?" Zavian asked.

Luci's mouth went dry. They crested the hill, and she felt relief when she saw a yellow field in the distance. Zavian stayed two steps behind her. He moved like an elk steps in a forest. Luci's feet made enough noise to scare all the wildlife away. The yellow field was in sight.

"Why do you only speak in questions," she asked after some time of silence.

"How do I know?"

"You should just try to make a statement. Be sure of what you're saying and state it. That would fix it." Luci said.

"Does fixing a quirk change the person?"

Luci crunched her nose. Zavian was a smart man for one that couldn't even put a statement together.

"I suppose it does. I wanted to say thank you. For, you know, saving me at the river," Luci said.

"Why would I leave you to be eaten by Deryn's shark?" Zavian asked. His eyes faded to royal blue once more.

"Who's Deryn?" Luci asked, then her jaw dropped. "Wait, did you mean you stood there long enough to recognize the shark before you jumped in to save me? I almost died!"

"Did you die, though?" Zavian asked, his eyes spinning yellow.

"You could have helped sooner if you saw that shark coming."

Blue eyes again. "Wouldn't I drown in water?"

"Wouldn't I?" Luci snapped. She felt sick. Her mother was missing. And some "Deryn" tried to feed her to a goblin shark? Luci slumped over. She badly wanted to sit down and pout. Exhaustion mixed with nerves was overwhelming.

Zavian grabbed Luci's hand, and she felt the same electric energy rush through her arm. Her sadness and worry eased. She pulled her hand away.

"Please don't touch me. I don't even know you."

Zavian's eyes sunk to black. "Don't you?" he asked.

"No, I just met you. This whole place is new to me." Luci said.

"Is it new? Didn't Keres—"

Luci threw her hands in the air, exasperated. "There's that name again," she said.

"Didn't Keres send me to keep you safe?" Zavian asked.

"You didn't do very well. A shark almost snapped me in half!"

Zavian sped up his march and passed her. Then he bent, plucking mushrooms from between burned grasses. "Are these morels? Don't they grow after a fire? Did you ever know such wonder produced after the near-death of a forest?"

Zavian stuffed the brain-shaped mushrooms into his pocket. "Is your situation the aftermath of a calamity? What beauty will this bring?"

Luci thought of the car accident. This other world. The

Otherly. "I suppose. But why did Keres send you to protect me?" she asked.

"Why did Keres send me to protect you?" Zavian retorted.

She replied curtly, "I've had a hard day." She crossed her arms but cringed at the shot of pain from her skinned elbows. She looked at the torn sleeves. They were blood-soaked and now had clumps of mud hanging from the cloth.

"Do you want my clothing?" he asked.

"Well, if I ever heard an awkward question before, it would be that," Luci replied.

Zavian ran ahead and crouched to the ground.

"Where do you live?" she asked.

He wasn't paying attention. Instead, he put his hand on the ground. As Luci approached his side, his other arm shot out and crossed her body. She looked to where his hand sat planted in the mud next to a muddy dog print. Deep claw marks warned of sharp claws. "Not dog, wolf," Luci corrected herself aloud.

"A wolf?" Zavian said, his eyes royal blue. "Are there wolves here?"

"Looks like it," Luci said.

Zavian's eyes snapped to neon pink. "Can we go now?" he asked.

Luci's fingers explored the deep ridges in the paw print.

She recalled her father's stories of blasting at Site C and finding large wolf prints near their camp. He'd said the size of the footprint estimated the animal's weight. This wolf would be possibly 200, maybe even 250 pounds. Luci cringed. "Yes, we should keep moving."

"Are wolves allowed in The Otherly?" Zavian asked.

"Wolves go where they please."

"Will it come back?" he asked.

A squirrel chittered. Zavian's eyes returned to black. Then he turned to face the critter. Luci watched the two stare at each other. Then the man nodded. Great, he's crazy. Maybe it wasn't such a good idea to allow him to follow.

She started walking again, faster this time. Zavian kept pace, two steps behind, down the hill and through the yellow field until she arrived in front of a cabin. Zavian was right behind her.

Two lumber pillars held up the awning over three wide stairs that led to a vine-weaved door. They looked like the same vines from the waterfall.

Luci wearily looked around. She expected the cabin's owner to appear and chase her away. With no sign of any angry huntsman, she stepped on the first stair. The vines peeled away from each other, uncreating the door, leaving her to see into the empty cabin. She jumped back from the vine's voluntary movement. "Are those snakes?" she exclaimed.

"Is that what you call Cattywampus vines on Earth?"

"Um, no," Luci said to the man behind her. Then she stepped onto the second stair and called into the cabin, "Hello?"

"Hello?" Zavian repeated from behind her. Then he walked past her up the steps, and the vines high-fived him.

Luci smirked, "You live here, don't you? So, you're the man Grentsth told me to find."

Zavian looked back at Luci, "Is it mother Ruth or Keres you're asking about?"

CHAPTER 5

The phone rang. Deryn Moreth's eyes shot to the old rotary telephone, and she recoiled. There was only one person in The Otherly with enough magic to call on that phone. And it hadn't rung in years.

A bird smacked into her window, causing Deryn to jump. Why did her sister make her jumpy? She ran her hand through her black hair, which had involuntarily spiked into porcupine quills. She glared at the phone, hoping it would stop ringing. It did not. She picked up the headset. "Hello?"

"Sister, I need your help."

"Keres, can't you at least say hello first?" Deryn asked.

"Useless pleasantries."

Deryn looked out the window to the bird fluttering on

the ground. His wing appeared broken. Dummy. "If you need something, the best approach is with some form of flattery. Even if it's a simple hello."

"The girl has arrived."

Deryn dropped the phone. She fumbled, trying to pick it up, and hoped her sister hadn't heard her klutzy movements. "What? Has she made it past the river?"

"Yes."

Deryn wondered how the first line of defence, Sprig, her goblin shark, had failed. "That's not good," she said.

"Why do you always think so negative? It's great news! Wonderful, spectacular!" Keres said.

"The last time you brought someone in, I had to rescue them from Obscura!" Deryn said.

There was a pause on the other end of the call. "That was unfortunate, and look, I know we haven't always seen eye to eye. But this time, it's different. This girl will make a change," Keres said.

"What if I want nothing to do with it this time?" Deryn asked.

Keres laughed.

The kettle screamed its readiness. Deryn tried to reach the red pot with the phone in her hand, but the cord stopped short. Keres rambled on about sisterly duty and whatnot. Deryn rolled her eyes and set the phone on the floor to remove the kettle from the heat. She could hear her sister's rant through the earpiece before she even picked up the phone again.

Deryn put the phone to her ear.

Keres's voice was snarling. "Don't you want rain this year? I bet sweet peas won't produce in a dry summer."

Deryn snorted. "What would Mother Nature think of that?"

"Oh, for five cents, I'm not scared of her," Keres said.

"Aren't you?"

"This isn't about me. I need this girl brought to me," Keres said.

She looked to the window again. She had to act fast. "Why can't you get someone else to help? My gate sits broken again because of you," Deryn said.

"Because you keep telling the animals horrible lies about me," Keres snarled. Then lightning snapped outside the farmhouse window and lit a tree on fire. The bird jumped up and hobbled away.

Deryn growled and dropped the phone for a second time. Then she ran to the door, swung it open, and screamed at the horses to put the fire out.

Into the phone, she yelled, "What was that for?"

Keres laughed. "At least I don't abuse animals."

Deryn considered slamming the phone down. Her hair slicked into buffalo horns. "I don't. I'm a strict keeper with firm rules."

"If that's what you call it."

Deryn considered Keres's threat. If she held back the rain, her crops would suffer. Then she would have no food to pay the mine animals, which would mean no stibnite to crush into kohl for her make-up. Deryn's hair smoothed back into long rabbit ears, laying straight down her back. She sighed, "OK, I'll help."

"She just got to Zavian's," Keres replied.

"Zavian? That dumb Memegwaan? Why would she go there?" Deryn asked.

"Just go collect the girl. He'll keep her until I can find a way down there," Keres said.

The line went dead.

"Yeah, like Mother Nature would allow that," Deryn said to the empty phone line. She set it back on the receiver. The tea leaves in the bottom of her mug remained starved for water. There was no longer time for tea today.

Deryn dashed out the front door. Zavian's cabin was a few days' travel from her farm, even if she used all her magic to fly.

Outside, the horses had made quick work of putting the tree fire out. Deryn marched with heavy boot stomps to inspect the broken front gate. She scowled at her beautiful iron gate hanging from the latches between perfect rows of bamboo fencing. Chipmunks. She was sure of this, and figured it was the same ones that ate her flower gardens along the river. She removed her apron and tied it around the gate to keep unwelcome guests out. The quick fix would have to do for now.

Deryn marched to her horses huddled around the burned tree. Buckets of water hung from their mouths. They had done an excellent job, but she knew better than to give praise. That would let their heads get big, which could cause less compliant help.

Toll smiled at Deryn, dropping his bucket of water. The fifteen-hand Quarter Horse sported a black and white puzzle-piece pattern all over his body.

Mother, he sent.

She scowled and sent back, *What have I told you about calling me "Mother?"*

Toll sadly huffed, *You can't be every animal's mother.*

George and Boll, the bay-coloured twin Clydesdales that stood at twenty hands, turned to collect more water.

Toll's not helping, George sent.

I am, Toll sent to George, then turned to Deryn. *He bit me!*

I don't have time for this, Deryn sent.

But, Madame, it hurt, Toll sent.

The whine in Deryn's mind sent her into a rage. She kicked the water bucket, which bounced off the tree and hit Toll on the leg. He whinnied and limped around.

Stop, you're acting a fool, Deryn sent.

My leg is broken.

Deryn dug her fingernails deep into her palm to stop her anger. *No, it's not. Everyone, line up!*

The horses lined up like soldiers.

George exposed his gums to Toll, who didn't notice, too busy swatting flies with his tail.

The flies come because you stink like cow dung, Boll sent.

No, the flies come because he's about as bright as cow dung, George sent.

Madame, please tell them to stop, Toll sent.

Madame's boy, Boll sent.

Boys, Deryn sent to all three, *give me your attention! Fortunately, there is no time for your shenanigans.*

The twins stopped, stood straight, but Toll hung his head, scolded.

Deryn turned to face George. *I need you today, my son*, she sent.

Why don't you take the dumb one, then us intelligent guys can get more work done, George sent.

Deryn glared at George then looked to Toll. *Maybe I will*, she sent.

Ha! I was kidding, Madame, he's useless, you know, George sent. *I'm your best choice. I'm the strongest.*

Deryn walked between George and Boll. She climbed on Toll's back.

Let's go, my son. We have essential matters, Deryn sent.

She turned to face the other two, George and Boll and sent, *We'll discuss your behaviour later.*

Toll bounced with excitement to the point where he couldn't walk a straight line. Deryn dug her knees into the soft flesh behind his belly to redirect his energy.

I chose you to punish the others, don't make me regret it, Deryn sent.

Toll walked with high knees towards the gate. Deryn opened the broken gate, and she instructed the other horses to repair it. Toll broke into a gallop across the fields.

Once they were some distance away, Toll slowed to a canter.

I do the most tilling. George and Boll only pretend to pull the equipment, Toll sent.

Please don't make this a day of ratting out your brothers.

Where are we going? Toll sent.

To the mines, Deryn sent. "I have to get rid of this girl before Keres finds her," she said.

What's that? You know I don't understand words, Toll sent.

Nothing, my son, can you run faster?

Pardon, Madame. A soft voice sent.

A dragonfly flew around Deryn's head with electric amethyst wings shocking the atmosphere with different colours on each charismatic flap.

To check-in, Madame, I found a girl, he sent.

Was it the girl? Deryn sent.

Yes, but the plan didn't go as expected, the dragonfly sent.

He landed on Toll's soft white mane.

Oh? Deryn sent.

Fingernails bent from the pressure she applied to her palm.

No, well, I had to give her the breath, the dragonfly sent.

Had to? Deryn sent. She dug her nails deeper.

Yes, well, you see, she would have drowned if I hadn't.

Deryn unclenched her fist. *That's unfortunate. I suppose I will have to demote you.*

The dragonfly lifted to fly away. *I am dreadfully sorry. It has been so long since a human has entered The Otherly. However, my compassion outweighed my judgement.*

Indeed, Deryn sent.

Her hair spiked into a kingfisher Mohawk. Toll staggered as Deryn pulled her energy and threw it at the bug. The dragonfly fell to the ground.

Deryn directed Toll to the side to avoid stepping on the nymph sobbing on the ground.

CHAPTER 6

Luci stepped onto the third wooden stair. The vines reached out like a welcoming hug. She swatted them away, unnerved by Zavian's remark.

"Why'd you say Keres is my mother? My mom's name is Ruth," Luci said.

"Is that what you think?"

Luci shook her head. She was done with games. "Where's my mother, Zavian?" she asked.

"Don't I wish I had the answer?"

She hesitated at the door. "You don't know?"

"Don't I know?" he asked.

Why did Grentsth direct her to Zavian? Luci felt misled. She entered the cabin behind Zavian in the hope of getting more information.

Vines pulled from all corners of the house and set the table for a feast.

"These vines, they're alive?" she redirected.

One vine formed a hand and held it out to Luci. She accepted the greeting with nature's child.

"Isn't everything alive?" Zavian asked.

The vines pulled a wooden chair out and waved for her to sit. "I suppose. But common shrubs aren't this helpful," Luci said.

Zavian turned and moved towards the kitchen. "Would they be accommodating if you were evil?"

Luci admired the glass sheet balanced on a tree-root ball that made a table. She could see each twist of the roots beneath the table. Around the cabin were open archways that exposed four rooms: a bedroom, a bathroom, a room with a silver pot that held hundreds of vines, plus the kitchen where Zavian busied himself. Green stocky vines spewed from the corner of every room up to the roof, then out into The Otherly. The last room was the strangest, with a staircase that led to nowhere.

A wall concealed by vines and leaves piqued Luci's curiosity. She noticed a bunch of rock-creature formations that sat in piles on the floor. *Great, I'm relying on someone who builds friends from rocks.* Another notch for crazy, and now lonely too.

A chandelier made of silver dandelion with hundreds of miniature candles lit up spontaneously and swung above her head. Luci stood and reached out to touch the chandelier. A vine curled around her wrist and waved a finger at her, a warning. She smirked.

Something crashed in the kitchen. Luci tipped back on the chair to see Zavian bustle around the kitchen. He accidentally knocked a jar off a shelf, which bounced then smashed on the compact dirt ground. The vines produced a dustpan and swept the broken glass and bits of dried meat from the broken jar off the floor. Zavian turned and caught her gaze. He held up a second jar. "You want some tea, Miss Luci?" he asked.

"Can you tell me now how you know my name?" Luci inquired.

"Would I be able to keep you safe if I wasn't told your name?"

"I get that, but who told my name? Who knew I was coming?" Luci asked.

"Wasn't I told by your mother?"

Luci jumped, banging her knees on the table. "You do know where my mom is!"

Vines slithered down from the chandelier to recentre the glass tabletop.

"Doesn't everyone?" he asked.

"Zavian, what is that supposed to mean?" Luci asked.

"What does anything mean?"

"Where's my mother?" Luci demanded.

"Isn't Keres the Keeper of Equilibrium? Doesn't that mean she's in Equilibrium?"

"Keres! There's that name again!"

Zavian appeared in the dining room with two steaming mugs. "Are you angry? Isn't your tea ready? Will tea soothe your rage?" he asked.

He pushed a mug to Luci. Then he took a massive gulp of his hot tea without flinching. Luci saw tiny wisps of steam dance into the air, holding shapes of stars, hearts, and moons, then dissipate.

"I just want to find my mother," Luci said.

"Do you want me to show you how to get to Keres?" Zavian asked.

"No!" Luci pushed the mug away. "I want to find my mother, Ruth, and get out of here," she said.

Zavian downed his tea in one gulp. The steam poured from his nose. "What makes you think Ruth is your mother?" he asked.

"She raised me. Of course, she's my mother."

"Do women of Earth always birth and raise their children?" Zavian asked.

The ground seemed to become quicksand, and she felt like she was sinking. Nothing made sense. She silently asked the wilds to assure her this was all a daymare.

"You're telling me I was adopted?"

"Do I know this word?" he asked.

His eyes dimmed to a bright mossy green. His emotions reflected in the colourful orbits as Luci's feelings pulsed painfully behind her eyes. As the only redhead in a family of blondes, she had always felt like the sapling outside the forest. She supposed it made sense. But she also didn't want to believe it.

"Did you not know? Isn't Keres trying to protect you?" Zavian asked.

She snapped, "I almost died. How is Keres protecting me?"

"Wasn't that Deryn's shark?" Zavian shrugged. "How was Keres involved?"

He pushed Luci's mug closer. "Won't you try your tea?"

Luci lashed out at the mug. "I don't want tea. I don't even want to be here!"

The cup spun, causing the tea to spill onto the glass table. The calamity echoed in the cabin for much longer than it should have. Zavian's eyes snapped royal blue, and he sunk back in his chair. The ferret's head popped up, twitching his nose. He jumped onto the table, where he lapped up the spilt tea and swayed his tail in the air.

Luci bowed her head. "I'm sorry. I didn't mean to do that. I just want to find my mother, my Ruth, and get back to normal life."

"Didn't your life become abnormal when you came to The Otherly?" he asked.

His eyes faded to steady black.

"I suppose, but this is a lot of information. How do I even know any of this is true? My mom never mentioned adoption. So, I could only have one mother. My Ruth," Luci argued.

"Aren't two mothers better than one?" Zavian asked.

Luci considered his comment, but her thought was of all the mean stepmothers from Disney movies she'd watched as a child. "Not always," she said.

She pulled the mug over as her apology. The ferret retreated to his place on the man's head to sleep.

Luci bent over the mug. The tea smelled of honey and lavender. She took a sip that burned her tongue. But it also brought a wave of epiphanies.

Zavian wasn't to blame. The car accident wasn't his fault, and neither was her mother wandering off. Wilds knew he didn't even have anything to do with her adoption. If Keres was her birth mother, why had Luci not heard about this until now? Why hadn't Keres tried to come to see her before?

Zavian pulled out a blue tin. When he opened it, Luci smelled black liquorice. He proceeded to roll a cigarette.

"Don't you know those are bad for your health?" Luci asked.

"Are they?"

Luci grabbed the tin from Zavian. "Yes. Smoking causes cancer and other terrible diseases."

She emptied the contents. Zavian's eyes dulled to grey. Luci dropped her eyes. "I'm sorry, I don't know why I did that," she said.

"What do I have now?" he asked.

Luci pulled a Kleenex from her pocket, which disintegrated in her palm. "I have nothing as well. My camera and some trivial pocket objects. But they're soaked and ruined now. I've lost my shoes, my mother, my whole world, it seems. I don't know what health rules are in The Otherly. Maybe you can't get sick. But that tobacco, you don't need."

"Why should I trust you about this?" he asked.

"I had to trust you pretty quick," Luci said.

Zavian sulked as he got off his chair and walked to the kitchen. Luci watched as he took jars of fruits and vegetables off the shelves.

His voice carried from the kitchen. "Do you want food?"

"No."

"Wouldn't a snack distract you?" Zavian asked.

Luci sighed. She watched from the table. The vines helped Zavian as he worked, but they also formed bunny ears behind his head and moved plates when he tried to reach for them. Luci chuckled.

Zavian poked his head out. "What's funny?" he asked. The vines flapped for her not to say.

She waved him away, smirking. Another sip of tea warmed her insides, making her feel comfortable for the first time in hours. Or was it days? She frowned, not sure how long it had been. The accident felt long ago already.

Zavian reappeared with a plate full of sliced fruit and charred vegetables. Luci popped a pale-yellow carrot in her mouth that burst with flavour. She ate two more before moving on to the charred bok choy.

"Do you want clean clothes?" Zavian asked.

Luci nodded with her mouth full of lemony vegetable juices. She felt full of energy, and figured clean clothing would make her feel that much better.

Zavian disappeared through the archway of the room with the vine pot. One step in, and the vines weaved closed behind him. He emerged a few minutes later with an armful of clothing. He handed the pile to the gaping girl.

Luci blinked at him. She wanted to ask so many questions about how the magic of this world worked. But, instead, something inside insisted she trust how it worked. It was magic, after all.

She walked to the bathroom and stepped through the doorway backwards to watch the magic of the vines weave the door closed. She turned to face the bathroom. An oval mirror met her dishevelled appearance. She looked like wolves had raised her, with curls twisted around sticks and clumps of mud dangling on the ends. She glanced at the shower and considered the luxury to wash away the evidence of nearly drowning, cliff scaling, and highway scrambling. But when she looked at the dried blood over her temple, she felt it was the last thing that proved this wasn't a dream. Or a daymare. Her mother was indeed missing, and Luci needed to continue.

Luci lifted the camera off her neck and tried the power. She pined deeply to see a photo of her mother right now. Tears welled in her eyes when the camera did nothing. She set it down, heartbroken.

She stripped her dirty, tattered clothing and tossed them in the hamper. She pulled on the clothes Zavian had supplied, which freakishly fit. The outfit was a black shirt, blue capris, black flats, and a baby pink knit hat. She wondered if Zavian shopped at Ardene as she dropped the baby-pink hat on the side of the bathtub next to her broken camera. A side glance in the mirror made her change her mind. She pulled the toque on and stuffed her hair inside to hide it.

Curiosity about a woman with the same fiery red hair made her feel guilty and want to hide the hair more. She locked the thoughts of Keres in a box in her head and left the bathroom. Keres could have found Luci if she cared to.

Luci stopped at the kitchen doorway. "Zavian?"

He pushed a large pan of food into a clay oven. "Yes, Miss Luci?"

"Do you know where my mother, Ruth, is?"

She'd asked the question already, she knew this, but the answer seemed to be just out of reach. But, on the other hand, she was sure the information was in Zavian's mind somewhere, buried under questions and uncertainties.

"Don't I know everyone in The Otherly?" he asked.

"Is my Ruth here?" Luci asked.

"What did Grentsth say?"

"She said you knew where my mom was," Luci said.

"Don't I know where Keres is?" Zavian asked.

Luci breathed through her frustration. "I'm not asking about Keres. I'm looking for my Ruth."

"Did she get summoned to The Otherly?" he asked.

Luci considered the question. "I don't know. Maybe?"

"Isn't that the only way to enter?"

Luci's chest felt tight. "Are you saying someone brought her here on purpose?"

"Who would do that?" Zavian asked.

Then the realization. "Who wanted me here the most?" Luci retorted.

"Do you mean Keres?" he asked.

"I'm afraid I might."

"But how could she from Equilibrium?"

"How do I get my mother and get out of here?" Luci asked.

"Didn't Grentsth tell you about the trials?"

"Yes. But I'm asking about my mother, Ruth, right now."

"Do I know something about your Ruth?"

"That's what I'm trying to figure out," Luci said. She rubbed her temples. "Maybe this is all just a drawn-out daymare."

"Do the daymares muddy your clothing and make your stomach growl?" he asked.

She touched her temple. Maybe she wanted this to be a daymare. Luci sighed. She ate a sugared strawberry which burst with delicious juices, creating a perfect distraction.

Zavian held three plums out for her. "Won't everything make sense in its own time?"

"I hope so, but I'd rather know right now," Luci said.

Zavian left the kitchen, went to the room with the pot and vines, and retrieved a purple knit sweater. He said, "On Earth, do you get all your combined knowledge at once?" and held the pullover out for her.

"No, but I'm scared my mother is hurt. I ask for information, and I keep hearing half stories," Luci said. She finished her tea. It had cooled to the perfect temperature and calmed the quaver in her voice.

"Can I tell you anything to ease your woes?" Zavian asked

"Tell me that my mother is safe. Tell me I'm stuck in a daymare," Luci said.

"What if you are?"

"Then, well, it means I've gone off the deep end," Luci said.

She thought of all the times Dr Premiate had speculated that the cause of the daymares was trauma. Luci recalled no such trauma. Now she wondered if being born in a place like The Otherly, with strange creatures around, and ripped from her biological mother would settle the issue.

"Didn't you say you can't swim?" Zavian asked.

Luci snapped the purple sweater out of his hand. "It's an expression." She rolled her eyes. "You know, like insane. Mentally losing grip with reality."

"Isn't that just a different way to live? Does everyone experience life the same?" Zavian asked.

"I guess not."

"What if these daymares are sightings into The Otherly? Wouldn't your true home want to call to you?" Zavian asked.

Luci walked to the cabin door. Her mind spun relentlessly. "How is this place my home when my family lives 700 miles away? Maybe I'm not the girl everyone is waiting for?" Luci said. "Maybe you all have me mistaken for Keres's daughter when I'm not. Which is all the more reason I need to find my mother,

Ruth, and if you don't know where she is, I need to go and keep looking."

Nausea bubbled in her stomach at the thought that she'd potentially travelled far away from where her mother wandered lost on Highway 97. The idea that she was looking in the wrong direction *and* the wrong universe was sickness in Luci's throat.

Zavian shook his head. His eyes spun to pink. "Do you think we are all wrong?"

Yes, but Luci didn't want to say that out loud. Instead, a strange feeling unravelled in her chest. A rope, tightly wrapped, that restrained something she'd sensed for a long time now. Like the truth behind the daymares was tied up in there somewhere with the strands of her real life.

"If I am this girl, why was everyone waiting for my return?" Luci asked.

"Doesn't what is made in The Otherly belong here? Doesn't the missing limb always give ghost pain?" Zavian asked.

Did she belong here? She wasn't sure she wanted to know the answer. "Where's Equilibrium?" she asked.

"Don't you know it's in the sky?" Zavian asked.

Luci threw her hands up, exasperated. "Keres is in the sky! Of course, she is. This is all too much for me."

She reached for the doorknob, which was missing.

"I want to go," she said. The vines didn't move.

"Where do you want to go?" Zavian asked.

"Into the sky. To find out if Keres took my mother."

"Can you walk into the sky?" he asked.

Luci hung her head and said, "I need to get out of here. I need air. Open the door, please."

The vines opened the door, but Luci didn't move. Her chest felt tight. That rope pulled, knotted, and held her in place.

The sky was uneventful—no visible signs of someone sitting up there watching. Still, Luci had yet to see the sun. A wall of trees cloistered the fields in front of Zavian's home on two sides, with hills on the third and raspberry bushes, towering like a drive-in movie screen, on the fourth side of his property.

Zavian spoke behind Luci. "Maybe Efra knows where your Ruth is?"

"If I find her, can I leave?" Luci asked.

"Will the gate open without three trials completed?"

Luci had her answer. She had to do these trials, find her mother, and get out. Keres would fit in that mix, or not.

Zavian placed his hand on her elbow. This time, Luci didn't pull away. Instead, his touch seeped reassuring warmth into her skin.

"Do you have a healing touch or something?" Luci asked.

"Don't humans have a healing touch too?"

"I suppose with love," Luci said.

CHAPTER 7

Luci left against Zavian's wishes. He said she had free will and allowed her to go, although Keres's instructions, as per Zavian, were to stay at the cabin. But then, how did Luci know to trust what Keres wanted?

Luci shook the thoughts away. She had to find out what had happened to her mother. And there was a pull in her chest that willed her out the door. Zavian stayed as instructed. Luci left.

The urge to keep moving, find her mother, complete her trials, and get home was overpowering. She cycled through Zavian's directions to Efra's house in her mind, which just involved deciphering questions.

Through the forest to the mines, where, Zavian warned, Luci had to be stealthy. After the sideway dune, a lake held Efra's home on the underwater-side of a log structure. Luci didn't like that idea, as it involved more water.

Help Efra complete a trial. Then she'd only have one more to get back to Earth. And she hoped he knew of her mother's whereabouts.

She secretly hoped she could meet Keres before she left. But given a choice, she would take her mother and go. She didn't want to think of the possibility of the gate opening without finding her mother first.

Luci walked through the forest. Even with the sky eerily lit, it was dark and gloomy in the woods. She remembered the wolf paw print and walked faster.

She weaved through a stinky marsh. Muddy water splashed up her legs, and each step threatened to swallow her foot. However, the flats Zavian had given her stayed on, even with heavy mud layered on them, and surprisingly kept her feet dry.

The forest shrunk, and the mountains ahead grew to frame a hickory-grey pond. The scent of nectar was kicked up by the tiny feet of bees as they slipped between flower petals. Luci quickened her pace. Wafting mist danced in the stale daylight off the pond's surface. Then movement made Luci duck to hide.

Lily pads ruffled, and cattails bowed as a tall figure rippled the pond's surface. It was a swan floating serenely across.

Instinctively, she went for her camera, but it wasn't there. It sat broken at Zavian's cabin. She sighed heavily. The swan looked up and stared at her until Luci broke the gaze and walked away. Strange.

Luci saw lines of bustling animals at a surface mine, dug deep into the ground like a giant shovel scooped the contents out. She'd made it. Luci ran, feeling time press against her temple. Every second she couldn't find her mother was a headache.

Ruth Catalina Flask—that name had been her whole life. She tried to recall her furthest memory: when her teacher sent a teddy bear home as a project, it was kindergarten. Young Luci was supposed to draw pictures of their sleepover adventures. But she'd been so caught up in tea parties with the bear, she'd forgotten until Monday morning. Her mother had skipped morning coffee to help Luci draw the comic strip. She'd got an A.

Luci reached the opening to the mines. Animals bustled around pushing, pulling, and carrying wooden crates full of silvery-black rock with crystal formations. It was like the animals of Noah's Ark had been put to work in a mine.

Luci recalled Zavian had said to be careful. She crouched and ran to a crate sitting alone. A barrel of monkeys drew near. Luci didn't feel hidden well behind the container. She scrambled inside. It was devoid of any smell. The stacks of palm-sized crystals she sat on were shaped like chapels and coloured like bejewelled coal.

The crate bumped into action. Animals were chittering outside as Luci rocked along a track hidden inside the crate. She hoped she was moving in the right direction to get through the mine.

The crate stopped, and Luci looked up to a sandy dune. The animal sounds grew further away, and Luci risked a peek out of the container. The animals had pushed the crate halfway up a dune. Luci scanned the busy mine until she found a wooden archway at the base of a dune that looked to have been sliced off the ground and tipped on its side. That had to be the exit. That's where she needed to go. At the bottom of a sideways hill, as Zavian had said. The lake where Efra lived would be on the other side.

The base of the mine was a solidified glass sheet. Mine trails were littered everywhere. They were sideways, slantways, and backways in and around the dirt mounds. They led down to the centre stretch of the massive glass floor. All the dunes funnelled towards this stretch, which led to the exit. Flamingos, hippopotamuses, giraffes, dairy cows, pelicans, and even polar bears huddled at the bottom near the exit, blocking her escape. They seemed to be on a break.

A flock of ostriches bustled past with wings full of the black crystal. One stopped. Luci ducked down, but the bird popped his head into the crate then jumped back, screeching.

A commotion broke out below, creating a perfect distraction for Luci to make her escape. She hauled herself out of the crate but remained hidden as she watched for a window to bolt for the sideways dune. An ostrich below flapped around erratically, hissing and knocking crates over. He rushed up the dune straight for Luci crouched behind the crate. He stopped long enough to make eye contact. Then he faked a charge causing Luci to scramble backwards. He lifted his head and bellowed a deep boom to the other animals. It gave Luci the chance to make her escape.

She bolted past him and slid on her feet down the dune. Surfing down the dune was the closest she'd ever come to actual surfing, on account of her aquaphobia, but she held her arms out for balance like a pro. The sand was amazingly compliant. If it weren't for all the mine animals funnelling towards her, she would have enjoyed the ride.

A hippopotamus sat on his bottom, waiting for a rhinoceros beetle that was carrying a water droplet to him, and watched Luci intently. Then, finally, she tumbled the last few feet to the bottom and smashed into the glass floor with a crash. She barely avoided colliding with the hippo. He scrutinized her clambering to her feet but remained sitting as she turned to run for the exit.

A loud bang sounded behind her, and the glass floor shook. She lost her footing and slipped. She accidentally bit her lip and tasted blood, but didn't fall at least.

Luci drew close to the exit of the mine. A commotion made her risk a glance backwards. The hippo was on his feet now and charging. An army behind him bellowed and hissed. Luci, not looking ahead, crashed hard into something. She fell backwards, dazed, and looked up to the side of the mine exit. There was such a short distance she needed to go for the exit archway. As the heavy steps grew closer, Luci rolled over and scrambled to get through the exit. Crackling sounded. She could see the sparkle of the lake on the other side through a tunnel.

Rocks fell from above as she ran through the darkness. The dune crumbled behind her as she made her escape.

A support beam wavered at the end of the short tunnel.

"Wilds, no," Luci pleaded.

She dashed for the exit. Boulders crashed from the ceiling, brushing just the edges of her curls from beneath her toque.

An explosion from behind threw her out the last few feet. Luci hit the ground and rolled. The mine exit sealed shut behind her.

Luci lay on her back. A fluffy white cloud appeared. It spun, lowered, then flipped over before pausing and starting again. It couldn't be an explosion mushroom cloud. There was no burned-lemon-peel smell. She stood, and the cloud jumped a foot higher. Dizzy, Luci fell back to her bottom. She looked up where the cloud had lowered to hover above her head.

Could it be?

"Keres?" she asked.

The woman did live in the sky. She supposed this cloud might be Keres's doing. There was no answer to her inquiry, but as she walked away, the haze followed.

Luci's stomach growled, reminding her of the plums in her pocket. She pulled one out and ate it gratefully. The sugar rush lessened the ache in her muscles.

When she reached the lake, she frowned at the murky brown water. Trees lined the edges of the water, with roots that shot straight down, leaving no beach of any type. Luci stood on the drop-off edge and looked down, but saw only her reflection. The pink toque made her look ridiculous. She tore it off her head and tossed it in the water. A grotesque one-eyed fish, the size of her palm, swam up and swallowed the toque in one gulp.

She wished she could jump in and dive to the bottom. Get this trial over and done. But if she drowned now, it would be the end of the search for her mother.

Stupid swim lessons, Luci thought. But, after failing every class since "Crocodile", her mother had still smiled with understanding in her eyes.

Luci wondered if she'd ever see those eyes again.

She still didn't want to jump into the lake to search for Efra's home. A glance around the lake showed no sign of any houses. And Zavian clearly stated *in* the lake, not *near* the lake. She let go of the hope this home sat in an empty lake. That was reaching too far.

Luci approached the edge, where rows of perfectly cut logs floated in the lake. The wood created a stunning geometric pattern on the surface. They looked sturdy enough, but they banged like approaching monster footsteps in a nightmare of being chased.

"It's the logs," Luci said to her shaky knees. She couldn't seem to command her feet to move her to step off the land onto the floating logs. "I did this at the river." She tried again to step onto the cold deck, but her feet stayed planted to the solid ground, glued by her subconscious.

A creak behind made Luci look back. A pine tree's branch swung straight for her head, forcing her to jump out of the way. She landed with a thump on the floating logs.

Water splashed over the logs onto her clothing. On hands and knees, Luci crawled. Worry crept into her mind. She didn't want to fall into the lake.

A pine cone flew past her face.

"What in the wilds?"

Luci glared at the tree, expecting to see a mischievous squirrel.

Instead, she saw all the trees nearby had bulked up their pine cones near the ends of the branches. They drew back, ready to fire the projectiles. She scrambled to the far end of the cold deck of logs. Pine cones whistled past her head. Luci frantically searched for a door to Efra's home.

"Stop!" she yelled at the trees. They continued and even added in sharp needles that pierced through the air. A pine cone clunked on the back of her head with a thud. The cold deck felt massive as she scoured for a hidden trapdoor. There had to be something, anything to tip off where an entrance would be. A hailstorm of pine needles rained down, making it difficult to see and dangerous to move.

Then Luci had enough. The lone cloud still hung overhead. "Keres, make them stop!" she pleaded, not expecting any type of response but also at the end of her wits. She covered her head as the onslaught increased. Then, strangely, a train sounded. Luci snapped her head up. What she saw made her scream instead.

A tornado raced straight towards her. She grasped the slippery logs as best she could. The screeching tornado jumped the logs altogether and spun ferociously through the trees. Every needle and pine cone blew off the trees along the bank. Then the tornado disappeared into the small white cloud above. Luci jumped up and cheered. The branches on the trees hung sad, drooping like the shoulders of an unhappy man. Then they sprung back up and slowly filled in with new green needles. For the trees, it was new ammo. Luci searched the sky for the little cloud, but it had vanished.

She heard a faint sound under the floating logs.

Like a child crying.

Luci ran to the edge of the logs, but the sound faded. She knelt to listen then crawled back along the cold deck. There was a smear of colour between the logs. The sound grew louder as she traced the underwater shades. Through the slivers, Luci saw square bases of furniture. The house was down there. There was even a ceiling fan that spun vigorously.

A house attached to the cold deck, upside down.

With the daunting task of finding a way inside, Luci followed the house's square boundary, looking for a door.

A glance at the trees showed Luci they were rapidly thickening up with ammo. Her only choice would be to climb in the water and feel around for the door. She didn't like the idea, but it was all she had.

She stood on the edge of the floating logs, felt that tug in her chest, and followed it by slowly lowering herself into the water. It was cold and dirty. It was water. Yuck. Luci held onto the floating timber with one hand and felt beneath the logs. The water suddenly spun up around her as if a whale had appeared and swallowed her whole. Darkness engulfed her, then faded, and she screamed underwater when she found herself standing upside down with her feet seemingly glued to the bottom of the logs. Air poured out of her in bubbles.

She pressed her eyes closed, waiting for the impending drowning she'd always feared in her life. But when she breathed air in through her nostrils, she opened her eyes. She breathed again. She opened her mouth and panted. Still, no water drowned her.

Upside down in the water, beneath the surface of the lake, Luci breathed as if she were standing on land. She remembered the dragonfly in the river that saved her from drowning. Had he done something?

A sparkle flickered through the murky water. Luci bent forward to see. It was a doorknob, miraculously clean plated gold as if not submerged.

It's Efra's upside-down house! Luci took a step forward, and her face came up against the door.

She knocked.

No answer.

It was such a strange feeling, knocking on a solid door underwater. Luci tried several times, the water pressure pushing back against her fist. Finally, with no answer, she turned the handle, which spun effortlessly in her palm, and the door swung open. Luci stood right side up, or upside round, to the opening of the downside house. She collapsed to the floorboards when she stepped over the threshold as if gravity remembered to do its job. Luci, drenched, laid in a crumpled heap on the arid floor.

The door creaked shut and somehow didn't allow a single drop of water to enter behind her. Luci tried to compose herself before the homeowner appeared, who she hoped would be Efra. She was thankful he hadn't witnessed her klutzy entrance.

She stood and was about to say hello when a child's voice squeaked.

"How did you get in?"

Luci wiped away the muck glued to her clothing. "I, um, knocked several times," she said.

She scanned the single-room, furniture-packed home for the voice. Cabinets with peeling paint, three-legged tables, splintered chairs, dilapidated couches, drawers with no dresser, and crooked bookshelves littered the house. "And besides, you didn't lock the door," she added.

The voice snapped with a tone that reminded Luci of her brother's hissy fits. "That is not what I meant!"

Luci took a cautious step around a sideways table.

She kept him talking to track the voice down. "Sorry, I don't quite follow?"

"I meant, how did *you*, a girl, get in my home?"

"Pardon?"

"Did I stutter?" the voice asked.

Luci squeezed between more furniture. She wanted to snap back, but she had to show patience like she would with her little brother. She purposely stomped for the hidden homeowner to know she was approaching.

"That was rude," Luci said.

The answer was a one-syllable laugh.

She stepped around two bookshelves that were stacked one atop the other. The drawers stood end to end next to the shelves. Peculiar. An orange couch sat in the centre of a large white shag rug. The pristine-looking sofa, one of the only objects sitting upright, looked as if it didn't live in a single-room house underwater. Along with the shag carpet, it was much too clean to be here.

"To be truthful, I'm not sure how I got here. First I was floating in the lake, looking for your door, then I was just upside down, but standing upright in the water," Luci said.

"That's how it works here. Everything is upside down in Wayward Lake. But you didn't answer my question," he said. "I want to know how *you*, as in a basic girl from Earth, got here breathing underwater? There is no way *you* could have walked through water. You're just a girl. A basic girl."

Luci's cheeks heated, evaporating the drops of lake water into steam. "I'm not basic."

"No, you couldn't be, could you. Otherwise you wouldn't have got in here," the child-like voice said.

"Well, there was this dragonfly …" Luci trailed off.

"Ha!" he laughed sarcastically, "That makes more sense."

She rounded the couch to see a Memegwaan like Zavian, but this man was ancient. Brown age spots splattered across his face like spilled paint. He appeared beyond the possibility of living, but Luci figured anything was conceivable in The Otherly. He sat cross-legged on the floor with nothing but a rhubarb-leaf diaper. His skin, the colour of burned bark, hung off his body as if it were trying to crawl off his body. Unlike Zavian, this Memegwaan sported a small mouse, squeaking with each snore, nestled within strands of silver wavy hair bunched into a literal rat's nest. Same triangular head; same wide red lips and box teeth.

Thick black eyebrows hung off the sides of his face, wavering when he frowned. Damp lines ran down his cheeks from tears, Luci guessed, and he chewed his fingernails ferociously.

They held each other's gaze for a moment. Luci wanted to yell at him for his comment, but his condition made her anger deflate. Instead, she felt empathy for the miserable-looking man. "Are you Efra?" she asked.

He rolled his eyes and huffed. "Why?"

Luci brushed a spot clean of chewed fingernails to sit across from him.

"I'm hoping you are," she said.

Puddles of muddy lake water spread onto the floor from her clothing, but the man didn't seem to notice anything except the fingernails he chewed incessantly.

"Why?" he asked again without even looking at her.

Luci pulled his arm down to remove the fingers from his mouth. He rocked faster and stuffed his fingers back into his mouth.

"Because I am looking for Efra, he might know where my mother is," Luci said.

The man spoke between his fingers. "Yeah, that's me, not like anyone cares."

"I care," Luci said genuinely.

She reached over, removed his hand, and gently held it.

Efra glanced at her, then stuffed his fingers back in his mouth. He looked terminally desperate.

"Do you really?" he asked, then shook his head, making a throaty sound. "No, you don't. Why would you care? You just got here."

"Yes," Luci said. She thought for a moment. "I do care because you're alive, and anything living deserves care and attention. I might not know you, but my heart breaks for the woes you go through. Whatever is ailing you that you sit here and cry?"

"Who said I was crying?"

Luci patted his arm as a friend would. She broke his line of sight into nothingness with her face. It was a trick her mother used to do when Luci was little and the daymares had started. Luci had been so scared that she couldn't make eye contact. Her mother would spend long minutes calming her down. Then the two together would catch the girl's soul, as her mother would say.

"Efra," Luci spoke gently, "what bothers you that you chew your nails down to the flesh?"

He removed his fingers from his mouth and looked at them as if realizing for the first time.

She carefully grasped his hands and held them, but Efra lifted his left foot to his mouth and continued to chew nails. Finally, he spoke muffled words between his toes. "I have no more room for my treasures."

"Oh?"

"I want to build my house bigger. Otherwise, I have to leave anything new behind. If I had more things, maybe I wouldn't be sad."

"I can help you, but I must tell you, objects won't make you happy," Luci said.

"Maybe." He considered this, then looked her in the eye and said, "Or maybe if my house were larger, I could set everything out nicely. That would make me happy."

"Yes, I suppose you're right. How do I help you build a bigger house?" Luci asked, worried about the tight rope in her chest that seemed to be winding up tighter with each passing moment. She needed to find her mother.

His face raised with anticipation. "Can you help me get more logs?"

"Yes, I can do that. But first, I need to ask you something," Luci said.

He nodded.

"Do you know where my mother is? Her name's Ruth. She has blonde hair and glasses the size of plums. She's quite shy, but once you speak to her, she lights up like an old friend."

"No. I haven't seen your mother or anyone for that fact. I don't know what a plum is. But I did hear there was a commotion at the labyrinth," Efra said. "What's your name? Since you know mine, I'd like to show care for you too."

Luci pulled a plum from her pocket and offered it to Efra. "My name's Lucille Flask. Most call me Luci or Luci-two." Repeating the nickname from her mother made a tear spring from her eye. "And now, I guess, Miss Luci. This is a plum."

Efra cocked an eyebrow at the plum. "Can you put things in it, Miss Luci Lou?" he asked.

"It's food. And most definitely tastes better than fingernails."

He sniffed the plum, said thank you, and licked the skin. "I don't know."

"Try," Luci insisted.

Efra took a bite, scrunched his nose, and stuffed his hand back into his mouth.

Luci waited a few minutes for him to move. Instead, his eyes bounced from one lopsided furniture piece to the next. Then, finally, she said, "Should we go get the wood now?"

His eyebrows lifted in surprise and met in the middle for a perfect black unibrow. "You still want to help me?"

"Of course," she said and stood, holding her hand out to him. "Let's get you more building materials." Luci smiled. At that moment, she felt he needed her the most.

Efra unravelled his legs and wavered, trying to stand with creaks and pops. Then, finally, he cautiously accepted her hand. She helped him up to his feet.

He hustled off towards a dresser that lived on its side. Luci stood awkwardly by the couch, unsure what to do next. She watched Efra pull on a straw hat, but looked away when he pulled weaved pants and a blue shirt out of a drawer.

"A dragonfly, you said?" Efra asked.

Luci shrugged. She heard his footsteps approach and looked back to see him catapult towards her and plant a dry kiss on her lips. Luci was so shocked she gasped, but it felt more like Efra was the one who gasped.

She scowled and was about to smack the misstepping Memegwaan, but he quickly darted back across the room to a porthole in the wall. Efra swung the metal window open. Water reached in like a giant's hand and grabbed them, tearing Luci from the safety of the underwater house.

Icy cold water slammed against her chest. Luci coughed and choked on the murky water, wondering what had happened to her dragonfly breath.

An object below Luci smacked into her and lifted her out of the water.

"Wilds, Efra! You could have warned me," she snapped.

Growling that she continued to end up in bodies of water, she wiped the muddy water from her eyes, which scratched like sand. Then, finally, she found herself seated on the back of a hefty one-eyed fish and moaned.

"I don't do well with aquatic life."

Efra sat happily on the fish in front of her. He patted the fish's head. "Don't worry. Jones here doesn't like the taste of basic girls, only bright-coloured furniture. Then he poops it out whole. That's how I get so many fun objects. Granted, it takes time for the fish smell to fade."

Luci grimaced. She didn't like Efra calling her basic. She didn't like sitting on a fish named Jones. "I'm not sure that information is reassuring," she said.

Efra requested Luci's sweater, which she gratefully gave up. The clothing was soaked anyway, and her tank top would probably dry faster without the heavy sweater holding water in. Efra tore it in half, then tied half to the end of a nearby cattail, creating bait resembling a bindle. He held the weed out in front of him and swung it near the fish's nose.

Jones managed one slow blink, then took off, trying to catch the sweater that dangled. Waves created by the overgrown flounder lapped the banks. Luci sprawled out on his greased back, clinging with all her strength so as not to fly off into water.

They jetted through the lake towards a second floating woodpile. Luci relaxed as the pace steadied, moving in a nice straight line. She sat up and held Efra's shoulders. She almost enjoyed the ride on the monster fish because at least he didn't seem to be trying to kill her.

Efra lifted the bindle high in the sky, making Jones follow his nose and stop a mere foot from the floating logs. He tossed the other half of the sweater into the fish's mouth. The giant fish graciously swallowed the cotton blend. Efra placed the bindle bait on Jones's back for safekeeping. Then he slid off the side of the fish into the water, swam over, and climbed onto the wooden planks. He motioned for Luci to follow.

She saw the expanse of water she had to clear and shook her head. "I can't swim," she said.

Efra mumbled something and coaxed the fish closer to the logs.

This amount of space she could manage. She jumped off onto the logs, which were pandemonium compared to Efra's home floor.

Efra pointed to the messy pile of fallen trees. "I need four good-sized logs. Jones will tow them, but he often gets distracted and ends up in the wrong place. Can you hold the logs together while I steer him? The last time I tried on my own, the logs floated away."

Efra pulled two butt-cuts off the pile himself. He tossed them effortlessly into the water. They sunk for a moment, then sprung up out of the water. The wave caused the cold deck to shift. Luci threw her arms out to the side for balance. More waves threatened to push the loot away.

"Catch those!" he yelled.

Luci was thankful for her height as she stretched her legs over the logs and pulled them back to the edge of the woodpile. She sat with her bum on the cold deck, her legs dangling in the water, holding the logs.

"Miss Luci Lou, can you grab moss rope?" Efra asked.

"From where exactly?" Luci asked.

"In the middle, over there."

"But if I let these go—"

"Never mind, they're fine now," Efra said.

Luci sighed. She clambered up and watched the logs for a moment, which seemed to have settled. Then, while peeking between cracks to look for an underside house, Luci set off to locate Cattywampus vines. Beneath this cold deck was vacant space, not even a beaver.

Efra tossed more logs into the lake. He seemed impossibly strong and appeared to be walking on the water's surface between Jones and the floating woodpile.

"Seems anything is possible here," Luci said.

"What's that?" Efra asked.

"Nothing," she grumbled.

An extensive collection of mossy plants offered plenty of vines. Luci collected some easily. When a bug squirmed free of a huge vine and jumped straight onto her knee, she lurched backwards in surprise.

The bug wasn't discouraged and clung to her capris. He

appeared to be doing some strange dance with his back legs kicking out.

"What are you doing?" she asked.

He stopped, blinked, and then jumped to the logs. He spun in a circle, wiggling his back legs in the air. Luci's eyebrows lifted in curiosity when the bug kicked up a plume of dirt that hung in space between his antennae. He was writing a word in the dirty air—*fear*.

Luci gasped. "'Fear'?" she read aloud.

Efra called her.

"What do you mean 'fear'?"

He kicked more dirt up and wrote, *Efra = fear*.

Luci scrambled up quickly but then tripped and fell with a crash.

Efra yelled, "You OK over there?"

Luci grabbed armfuls of the vines and stumbled back to the man. He had dozens of logs in the water now. They all lined up square behind the fish. He examined the pile of vines.

"Good," he said and climbed back onto the fish. "Now tie those to the four best logs and toss me the ends."

Luci didn't understand what the bug was trying to say. Should she fear Efra? He seemed like a distressed child.

She leaned over the logs and tied vines around them. In the end, there were four logs with constrictor knots tied to each rope in Efra's hands.

"How's that?" Luci asked.

"Perfect. Perfectly perfection. Soon, it's time for your trial," Efra said.

"I thought helping you was my trial?" Luci asked.

"Oh no, Miss Luci Lou, that was merely a pleasant side quest. I do appreciate the help, though. First you have to climb over Jones and stand on the two logs in the centre. Then use your feet to keep the logs together while I steer us home."

"Um, so essentially, I have to water ski," Luci said.

Efra smirked, "Yes, but here is an extra rope. Just hold on tight," he said.

Luci saw no way around this task. Even if a bug told her to fear Efra, she needed to complete this trial to open the door to Earth. She sighed and climbed off the woodpile onto the two logs tied to the fish. With one foot on the centre of each plank, she waved to Efra that she was ready, although she was far from ready. Her knees rattled, and she felt bile rise in her throat. The Memegwaan settled on Jones's back and tossed Luci one end of the braided vine. She faintly wondered when he had time to braid the ropes, but threw the thought away. She bent her knees and centred herself as Efra intently swung the remainder of the sweater in front of Jones. He started slow.

"I'm going to drown," Luci muttered. She wondered if the bug was watching. Jones started his movements slow and moved deliberately. Finally, she grew confident as they moved across the lake. She even stood straight and grinned.

Efra lifted his bindle bait, and the speed increased.

The logs shot out of the water, and sure enough, Luci was water skiing. Her legs wobbled from nerves and her fight for balance. She tried to tell her cramped hands to let up on their grip, but it didn't work. Either way, she was doing it. A slow grin spread on her face.

She pushed her legs gracefully to ski along the waves. "Woo-hoo!"

The adrenaline rush faded, and Luci held on to enjoy the ride. The fish swam happily with its sights set on the last half of his snack. Efra turned to sit sideways on the fish and grinned. Luci smiled as she waterskied across the murky lake.

Efra projected his voice over the splash of the water. "Are you having fun?" he asked.

Luci braved a thumbs up, holding the rope with one hand and called back, "A blast!"

"Good, now it's time," Efra said.

"Time for what?" Luci asked.

Efra grinned. "For your trial."

Luci turned the logs under her feet to create a bigger wave. "Is it about fun?" she asked.

"No, it is not. It is about fear."

And with that, Efra dropped the remaining half of the purple sweater straight into the water. The beastly fish screeched to a stop in the middle of the lake and plunged underwater.

Luci screamed. The logs drifted apart, forcing Luci into a split before she crashed into the water. The rope ripped from her hands, and the floating wood closed into a tomb above her head. The sudden stop caused a suction effect, pulling Luci deep into the dark olive-coloured water.

Luci thrashed her legs and arms, but they only smacked the bottom of the logs. She swallowed large gulps of water, trying to breathe. She kicked hard as the trepidation of drowning seeped into her veins. The muscles meant to save her sunk her like a rock. Her body was a burden. Luci shrieked underwater and watched in horror as the last of her air bubbles floated effortlessly to the surface.

The life-saving dragonfly's breath was gone. Luci could no longer breathe underwater, and she was drowning.

The tips of the vines found their way into the water and wrapped around one of her wrists. Efra directed them to pull her out of the water enough to see his face. She gasped air into her burning lungs as he spoke hotly on her face.

"Fear is important. It is more important, in fact, than fun," he said.

Luci coughed and tried to wiggle free from the vines. "Help me!"

"Fear of the dark, of being alone, of being judged. Fear of ultimately losing yourself in a nightmare or the end-all, that fear of death," Efra said.

"Efra," Luci squeaked out, "please."

His face fell from her plea, but he looked away. He waved his hands, and the vines disappeared. Luci plunged back into the dark water. She sunk as Efra impossibly stood on the water's surface above her. She realized she would drown with her eyes open.

Efra bent to put his face in the water and spoke with a deep sadness. "Falling, burning, choking, drowning. Fear is the sickness that causes death in a situation. But Miss Luci Lou, know that fear prevents us from running off a cliff when we cannot fly, from lighting a fire we cannot control, or attempting to float when we cannot swim."

Trapped in a death plunge to the lake bed, Luci kicked and flailed, trying to swim. But her body still settled in the grimy bottom.

The Cattywampus vines crashed through to revive her once more. Efra grimaced when Luci burst through the gravestone of water, crying for help with vines tied around her waist. She wanted to scream at Efra, but her throat felt swollen. Her trust ached as much as her lungs. She struggled to hold the slippery log with her weak muscles. She tried and failed to pull herself out of the water.

Efra stood over her and spoke words that sounded both scripted and painful. "To become grown, you evolve past infancy of emotions and beyond the basics of learning 'these are our fingers, and these are our toes.' Our hands can acquire the skill of writing sensible words, and our feet can master the art of running great distances. But our emotions try to prevent these actions, causing a stall in our growth. Fear is the strongest emotion. It will warp your words, halt your run, stunt your growth. Fear of failure. Fear of success. Fear of yourself."

Efra plucked Luci's fingers off the log as she cried, "Please, Efra, help me."

His tears matched hers.

She dropped below the surface with his words in her ear. "Let go of your fear," he said and pushed her further down.

As the light above the water dimmed to a memory, a thought crept into her mind. Maybe her mother didn't want Luci because she couldn't swim. Her mother, a natural mermaid, with a daughter who sinks like a rock. Her mother had always said people are naturally buoyant. Luci stopped thrashing. Maybe her mother left at the first chance she got. The sombre idea made her sink faster, with the murky water closing tightly.

Something slapped Luci on the shoulder, causing an underwater shriek that emptied the last of her oxygen. She sunk further. Then something hit her other shoulder. She flailed and spun around. Fish phantoms in the lake bumped and pushed her like a toy ball skittering across the concrete. Luci saw what looked like fish ghosts. See-through and the size of her palm, they were shaped like kittens wearing bedsheets and had sharp iridescent teeth. Her lungs filled with water when she gasped in horror as they played with her death.

CHAPTER 8

Luci's body wilted into the sands at the lake bottom, like a flower someone forgot to feed. She grasped handfuls of the water-bogged dirt and tried pulling herself along. Her chest tightened with each movement since she had no energy left. Her mind spun with pictures of her mom purposely running from the car while Luci was unconscious. Another handful of useless sand. The memory of her father wholeheartedly agreeing to the trip. Finally, her body settled into a deep indent on the lake floor.

Her head spun from the lack of oxygen and overabundance of worries.

An all-white fish with bones protruding smacked into Luci's leg. The hit broke the threat of unconsciousness. An undercurrent whipped past her face.

A dozen ghost fish pelted her side, causing Luci to painfully slither along the silty lake bottom towards the fast-moving funnel. Daylight shone through the surface far above. Luci grabbed a ghost fish as it swam past. He was slippery, but she held on. The fish swam ferociously, pulling her from the watery grave.

It wasn't Efra's fault she was drowning. It was hers. She had given up and succumbed to the weight of her emotions. She was worried and scared. She was full of fear. But there was no one to save her, it had to be her.

Luci let go of the ghost fish and grabbed another higher up. This one pulled her to the undertow, where she belted through the water. She kicked and pulled water towards herself with her arms.

Fear forces us into action. The idea blossomed in her mind along with her father's face when he had happily agreed to her northern trip. Did he want Luci gone too? Or did he want her to return stronger? But there was not an ounce of strength left in her soul.

Luci's muscles were soft, waving like seaweed in the current. Her arms and legs quivered from exhaustion. She grabbed onto a ghost fish, but he swam her back towards the bottom.

Fear is a virus that will spread if you let it. The idea released the weight that had settled in Luci's mind.

Her mother wouldn't have wanted this for Luci. Her heart told her that. Somewhere, she pulled the strength together to save herself. She had to continue her quest to find her mother.

Luci let go of the fish.

She kicked off one ghost fish to propel to another ghost fish, then another, until she broke the crust of the water.

Luci vomited water as she climbed onto the floating logs. She looked back, and a hundred ghost fish watched her below the surface.

She mouthed the words "thank you" and crawled until she got to solid ground.

Efra was gone. Jones was gone. And the logs she had waterskied on were tied securely to his underside house across the lake. She scowled, not sure if she had passed this trial or failed. He had the wood he required. But he'd stolen something from her, and that made her angry. The dragonfly breath could have prevented all that panic and near-drowning. Although, she wondered, would she have forced herself to learn to swim if she'd had the breath?

Luci lay for several long minutes with her face in the grass on the shore. She didn't even care if a spider crawled in her mouth. She was tired.

Luci rolled over and checked her pocket, but no more plums were left. She slowly peeled herself off the ground. "For Mom," she said.

Luci hiked back to the mines but stayed some distance back. The sideways dune continued to burn ferociously. The collapsed tunnel she had escaped through reminded her of the destruction she'd caused. She apologized, in her mind, to the animals in that mine. She hoped they had all escaped unscathed.

Luci searched for a route to the labyrinth Efra mentioned. It was her next best lead. She chose the path that seemed the least aggressive, away from the mountains and lake towards a forest.

The mint-green grass scratched where her legs were bare, adding to her emotional state. A moth flapped around her head as she walked. The colour of the landscape faded with each step. She wondered if she was walking into a daymare. Then, as if someone flicked the light switch off, everything drained to black and grey. So bland. The moth swooped past Luci's nose, bursting with an ashy glitter behind him.

A deep-rooted fear shivered down her spine. She had no camera to confirm if this was reality or a daymare. A hallucination. Crazy. She didn't want to be called crazy.

A different way of living, how could Zavian make it sound simple? Luci didn't want a different life, just an everyday life with her mother, father, and brother. School was fine as well.

She supposed classes could stay in the mix with the occasional movie night, and everyday life would be sufficient for her heart. But here she was.

Deeper into the grey world, Luci looked for the white cloud that she hoped was Keres sent to help. But, unfortunately, the only clouds above her head were black with silver streaks threatening rain. She kept her eyes down, trying to fight the idea she might be losing her mind.

A voice shattered her downward spiral of thoughts. "Such a pity when they're pretty and sad."

Luci swivelled her head around, looking for the owner. But, instead, she saw only that moth, velvet wings swooping among willow trees with gangly branches that stretched to the ground like bent over exhausted bodies. The moth steered up into the tree crowns, blotting the sky, and then disappeared.

"Hello?" Luci called.

A wind brushed the side of her face. Luci saw the moth again. His little face was centred with two pearl-like eyes, a smidge for a nose, and a circle for a mouth. He passed with grey bursts on every swift breeze.

"Suppose a little daft too," the voice said.

Luci spun angrily. "Pardon me?"

"I can see the simpleness glazing over your eyes. You have no clue what is happening here, do you?"

"Show yourself if you're to insult me," Luci demanded.

"Why would I give away the upper hand to a sad, simple girl?" the voice asked.

Luci frantically searched beneath curtains made of willow branches and under piles of leaves. There was no sign of anyone, yet the voice seemed to follow her. Finally, she frowned and said, "I am not simple."

The moth hoovered in front of her face. She flinched at angry eye markings that flashed with each downbeat of the moth's wings.

He landed on a tree branch, causing a light glitter-like substance to burst. The dust washed away the colour from his surroundings. His body followed the glitter down, and he grew into a Memegwaan.

But his eye sockets were a rotten fleshy grey, and he blinked one eye at a time.

"Sad," he said.

Luci wiped a hand over her face, pulling down on her cheeks and lips, trying to wipe away the emotion. She didn't want to speak to him. She didn't want to be near him, but she had to try at least.

"I've lost my mother, have you seen her? She talks about fairy garden homes a lot," Luci said.

"I have not," he said.

"Do you know where the labyrinth is?" Luci asked.

The Memegwaan lifted a hand and threw grey dust at the trees that surrounded them both. Luci took a cautious step back. A tree bent sideways, twisted to darkness from the grey dust, and pushed her towards the Memegwaan. Luci fought against the tree limbs that propelled her forward.

She was so close that when he peeled his lips back from gnarly teeth to answer, she could smell his rancid breath. "I do."

His triangular head swarmed with millions of tiny hookworms that suckled from his scalp. Luci gagged as the worms heatedly fell to the ground. He squashed the fugitives with his foot.

"Could you, uh, tell me, please?" Luci asked.

Willow trees were shaded dusty white, like chalk, and crowded in to block her. She found herself locked in a small space with the Memegwaan that gave her an ominous chill. But she needed to know the location of the labyrinth. She wished for Zavian.

"Sure," the mean-looking Memegwaan shrugged, "come closer."

Luci didn't want to move any closer.

The Memegwaan jerked a branch covered in cobwebs back and let go causing it to swing straight for Luci's face. She ducked.

"Why you—"

"Name is Ashier," the Memegwaan said. "Goodbye."

He threw his hands up, and more bland glitter flew over Luci. She sneezed. The tiny particles stretched through the air into black sheet-like forms that blanketed her. The material was ice-cold, like a winter wind stabbing her skin. She cried out. Then the blackout sheet slid from her face, and Luci realized she'd gone somewhere else.

She stood on a tall snow-covered mountain. Colours of the land around her mirrored an antique photo. The celestial sky, that should swim with stars and streaks of light, was solid drab of nothing. But the sun was there! A ghastly grey, like a memory of what the magnificent burning star had once been. It sat on the horizon with an evening kiss just before it would dip below the valley. She descended the mountain between mildew-shaded trees.

Withered grasses framed a dried-up riverbed weaving below, and the tight rope in her chest pulled her in that direction. The air grew deathly cold near the bottom. Tiny flakes of snow drifted to the ground but disappeared before landing. Luci felt confused. She felt more lost than before. This place was no longer The Otherly, and she was desperately far from help now. She could taste the raw panic rising in her throat.

An elk bugled in the distance, and she wondered if she was back on Earth, but then a freezing wind crashed through the dead trees with a sound like a banshee screaming, and Luci knew she was now even further from Earth. She jumped then ran the remainder of the way down the mountain.

At the bottom, she lowered herself into the dried riverbed to escape wind gusts. Luci ran towards the sunset and ignored the roar that grew in the distance. She couldn't handle any more setbacks. But the grey land decided otherwise as the sound increased, until she heard it as rushing water.

Luci searched the blackening landscape and found the source. It was water!

As if floodgates had opened, a massive wave rushed down the dry riverbed straight for her.

Luci bolted to the edge. The wave's roar drowned out the sound of her heart pounding. She risked a glance back that caused her to falter then fall.

Luci crashed hard. Sharp pebbles dug into the soft skin on her knees. She braced for impact from the enormous wave that chased her down the dry river bed.

But then nothing happened.

The water should have hit by now. But, instead, Luci gasped when she rolled over and saw the water sitting impossibly high in the sky as if stopped by an equally impossible invisible wall.

An ominous face stared at her through the wavering liquid partition. She took the opportunity and clambered out of the riverbed, breathless. The moment both her feet were on the land, the water crashed and smoothed out to flow gently.

Luci stood and brushed herself off. At least the run had warmed her blood for a moment. Her feet felt less numb from the cold. She looked up to see a large willow tree covered with long cobwebs that mirrored one she vaguely remembered from The Otherly. In the cobwebs, she saw the same livid face from the water wall open its mouth in a soundless scream.

Luci screamed. She ducked under the white billows hanging off the ghostly tree to move away from the face, but it shifted from one tree to the next to keep watch.

A branch heavier than her dread broke off, landing with a loud thump. The branch tore open a slit in the air as if the atmosphere were simply a cloth backdrop. Cobwebs spewed through the cut. Luci frantically clawed the mess away to see what was inside the tear.

It appeared to be an entryway to a dark place.

Her mouth went dry, and her inner voice silenced. This dark place felt like her daymares solidified. The rope in her chest jerked her forward. Luci tore at the small opening, making it large enough to climb through against her better judgement. It was the taught rope in her chest that insisted.

She pushed through swatches of thick webbing. The deeper she walked, the darker it became.

All she could see was darkness; the taste was dampness, and the only sound was a distant voice whispering. Then heels clicked on a tile floor—*tap, tap, tap*. The sound drew closer, but she saw nothing.

A woman's confident voice called, "Girl."

The darkness held Luci with sticky black cobwebs. She struggled for several long minutes before her arm finally burst free. When she caught sight of her hand out of the darkness, though, she shrieked.

The cobwebs ate the colour out of her flesh. They fed on the pigment until it was a grey ashy tone.

"Girl, this way," the reassuring voice said.

"Where?" Luci asked.

Her voice foreign, full of panic. The cobwebs crawled up her throat and into her mouth.

A polished seed of hysteria planted itself in Luci's mind. She pushed against the cocoon, making little progress, inch by inch.

"Come on, girl. Some distance further. I cannot see you," the voice said.

Luci flailed her hands until she hit something. A wall. She felt around for a door handle, but her hands pushed deeper into the dark material.

"Where are you?" Luci asked.

"That's it, rip the screen," the voice said.

Maybe this nothing she walked through was the by-product of her mind snapping.

Luci scared herself with the sound of her voice. "What screen? I can't see. I'm stuck."

She dug her fingers into the black sheet of webbing and pulled. It stretched and rebounded, too strong for her. Then a tearing sound. Luci pulled harder, pushing all her frustration of losing her mother into the rubber-like wall. She grabbed handfuls and tore.

The voice was encouraging. "That's it. You're almost through."

She smelled soot, the remnants of a coal fire. Then, finally, the sheet tore, echoing a rip of tinfoil, and she broke through, collapsing on a hard tile floor.

Luci laughed with relief as the peach hue returned to her skin. She was in a chamber where the air tasted stale, and all the noise in the coal-dusted space sounded muffled. Even her breathing was different.

A woman in a nurse's uniform, long ivory hair sweeping the floor as she walked a circle around Luci, heels clicking. *Tap, tap, tap.*

Luci's soft copper curls floated in the air around her face as if there were no gravity.

"Wh-what is this place?" Luci asked.

The woman answered by grabbing Luci's hands and yanking her to her feet. Luci pulled free with some effort, then asked, "Are you Keres?"

The woman's face came to life slowly. Every section lit up separately, like the gradual turning on of neon bulbs in a gymnasium. A strange smile spread along her lips. The movement exposed deep wrinkles packed with sooty dust, the only colour on her bone-white face.

Her black eyes twisted like kaleidoscopes with wisps shooting out occasionally. Her limp hair didn't move when she spoke with a bobbing head. The words spun from her mouth like cold silk against Luci's ears. "No, girl, but I could tell you something else entirely," the woman said.

"What's that?" Luci asked.

The woman shrugged, causing sharp cracks and pops. "It's not time to say."

Luci looked around for the exit. She didn't want to wait around for the right time to learn the information. "How did I get in here?"

"With your energy," she said.

"Huh?"

"It takes a special breed to enter. I've sensed you. Up there, walking around in The Otherly. I wanted to meet you," the woman said.

Luci swallowed. "What do you want to tell me?"

The woman smirked. "Well, aren't you a cut-to-the-chase type of lady?"

"I, uh, I'm trying to find my mom. Now, please, how do I get back? I need to go."

"My dear, there is no leaving," the woman said.

Luci swallowed hard, "I've heard this fact already. I only need to complete one more trial before the door out of The Otherly opens."

"You're not in The Otherly anymore."

Luci already knew this in her subconscious. "Where am I? I mean, where are we?" she asked.

Darkness hid everything behind the woman, yet her pasty skin eerily glowed.

The woman lifted the cardboard nurse's cap from her head like a greeting. "Can't you see where you are?"

"It's too dark. I can't see anything," Luci said.

The woman replaced the cap to her head, pinched something invisible in the air, and pulled. *Click.* A single bulb appeared, swinging from a chain, which gave a burst of moving light, revealing all that was hidden in the shadows.

Luci stood in a chamber with fire-scorched stone walls and piles of soot swept up to the corners. The room wasn't square or octagon but had thousands of walls, jutting in every possible direction. It was a myriagon. Rows of iron beds packed the single room. Each enclosed bed had a small opening where the occupant's head sat free on a table. The heavily chained lids creaked as balloons pulsed with artificial breath inside the iron lungs. The soft wheezing that filled the room made her feel nauseous.

Luci stepped towards the nearest bed. "Who are these people?" she asked.

"Food."

Luci jumped back. "What do you mean?"

"You're new here, aren't you?" The woman leaned towards Luci and inhaled deeply through her nose. "You smell new. How old are you?"

"That's none of your business," Luci snapped, stepping back from the woman. She backed into an iron lung where a frail woman tried to free her arm. The impact caused a pop, and Luci realized the ailing woman's shoulder had dislocated. Luci tasted bile in her throat. The woman in heels ignored Luci's distress and stepped closer again.

"My name's Chamier," she said.

Chamier lifted her hand to her chin as if posing for a fashion photo, then asked, "What's your name?"

Luci frantically looked around for an exit. Chamier tapped her toe incessantly, waiting for an answer.

"Luci."

"If you say so, girl."

"Well, it certainly isn't *girl*," Luci said.

She wanted to flee this place. But she couldn't tell where she'd entered or where she could leave. The chamber stretched further whenever she squinted into the distance. Maybe this was a trial?

A painful moan demanded Luci's attention. She noticed a man staring at her with thin hair clinging in patches on his scalp. Each breath drained the small fat deposits on his face. Chamier's word echoed in Luci's mind, *food*.

"Well, you certainly don't smell like a Luci," Chamier said.

She was intent on standing too close and waving her hand through the girl's floating hair.

Luci didn't like the way Chamier spoke. The word selection of "smell" and speaking of these people as "food". Luci tried to appear casual as she turned away and touched a set of chains on a nearby iron bed. The weight of the chains sent a shivering fear down her neck. Something felt very wrong.

"I don't know what that's supposed to mean," Luci said

"It means your mother is a dreadful liar," Chamier said.

"Pardon me?"

Chamier suddenly looked behind her as if called, but Luci hadn't heard a thing except for chains rattling.

"If your mother said your name is Luci, she lied. I can smell the deceit on you. You feel it too, sometimes, don't you? That tightness in your chest you don't understand. You try to prevent something from uncoiling since you don't want to know the truth. It scares you. The truth of what's hidden." Chamier paused, sniffed deeply, and then said, "Behind the reflection of the water. Between the waves of the flow of your life."

Luci's heart faltered. She forced her legs to walk to the next iron lung, mostly to get away from Chamier but also to escape what she felt was true. The Otherly had beckoned her, and the truth was unravelling in her chest too fast. Luci stared down at a deformed creature that looked vaguely like a brown bear. His fur was bleached white, and his ears appeared chewed or dissolved. Luci kept her face towards the iron lung but shot her eyes around, secretly looking for an exit. "Why are these ..." she hesitated, unsure she wanted to know the answer, "people here?" she asked.

The occupants of the iron lungs were mere outlines of people and animals holding on to the last tendril of life. Creatures of all types left to rot until all that was left were bony structures containing their tattered souls. Decrepit animals and withered people alike moaned throughout the chamber. A silent tear slid down Luci's cheek.

"They're ill," Chamier said.

Luci stepped between rows. "Ill?" she repeated.

Chamier hovered close behind Luci, and she felt cold fingers breeze through her hair, which made her pick up the pace.

Of all the iron-caged beds, not one appeared vacant. Some prisoners followed Luci's movements with glazed-over eyes, mouths creaking open, while others slept. Or perhaps they were dead. But all trapped in the same nightmare. A feeling of dread told Luci she should not be here. There was no trial to complete.

Chamier's fingers crawled along Luci's arm. "They are undergoing heal time."

"What do they need to be healed from?" Luci asked.

"It is not what. It is *why*," Chamier said.

The next bed held a woman with eyes sealed shut by crusty blood tears. Her eyeballs rolled behind the lids as if dreaming, but Luci felt they were more likely rolling in pain. Red tears trailed down her cheeks to pool in her hair.

Luci reached out to wipe a tear from the woman's cheek, but Chamier briskly pulled her hand away. "Why do they need to be healed?"

Luci knew she had taken the bait, but she didn't want to travel any further into this chamber. The faces became less human the deeper she went. Deeply pained cries rattled Luci down to her core. The directional rope turned against her and choked the air out of her chest. Before she realized what was happening, a wheeze escaped her lips that matched the sound made by the iron lungs. She covered her ears. She wanted to scream for them to stop.

Chamier suddenly clapped her hands, and the room full of painful screams muted as if a silencing blanket dropped. The faces twisted in pain when the wheezing stopped as if something invisible had snuffed out their breath.

Chamier's words slithered into Luci's ear like a worm. "Life is a virus. They need to be relieved of that curse."

Luci had to force words over her sandpaper-like tongue to say, "That's horrible." What she wanted to say was this made no sense. Chamier spoke like she was curing them, but it looked like she was killing them.

"Indeed, life is a horrible thing," Chamier said.

"That's not what I meant."

"Isn't it better to drain the virus of life? Eat it away to create powerful living energy rather than have it wasted?"

Luci turned and stared Chamier down. "Death. What you speak of is killing them."

"Not quite. A keeper's power drains when holding planes of existence together like this one or The Otherly. Even Equilibrium," Chamier pointed up, "requires an immense amount of magic. Up there takes energy from down here. So, where do I get energy? This place functions because of me, and I feed off it, or, well, the energy their lives give me."

"This isn't right," Luci said.

Chamier dug her fingers into Luci's bare arm. Again, the cold seeped in. Again, Luci tried to pull away, but this time, she failed.

"What is it you wanted to tell me?" Luci asked.

Chamier casually played with the strands of Luci's floating hair. The girl felt nauseous when she realized her hair danced, airborne, since she was full of the energy Chamier sought. The fresh scent of living power was what the woman had been smelling. Luci had to escape. Now.

"I can help you," Chamier said.

Luci didn't want this woman's help. "How?"

"Didn't you listen to anything I just told you?" Chamier said, her voice rising in anger. "I can cure you of this virus."

She grabbed Luci by both shoulders and shook her so hard that everything blurred. Then Chamier let go, and Luci slammed backwards into an iron lung. She wrenched her back by her hair, shook her again, then tossed her like a rag doll into the same iron lung. Luci's head hurt. A bolt above her head, covered in rust bites, snapped free from the impact.

A man half-rolled out of his iron confinement, but his legs remained trapped. He lifted his ghastly large head on a finger-width neck and opened his mouth. Leeches fell free. His coarse voice scared Luci into action when he said, "Flee, run, go!" He struggled to free himself. Luci grabbed him by the arms and tried to help. Instead, Chamier's body slammed Luci away.

She crashed into the next bed over and something cracked in her shoulder. A flash of pain made Luci fear she would pass out.

Chamier tackled the man. He screamed for Luci to escape as Chamier stuffed him back into the soul-eating bed. Luci wanted to help him, but Chamier was already slamming the lid back down on the iron bed. Luci wouldn't let his valiant attempt go to waste. Even in blinding pain, she jumped up and sprinted away. She ran to the nearest wall, searching for anything resembling an exit. There was nothing. She ran through a row of iron lungs to a second wall. Still no sign of a door or the seam she entered through.

Luci scanned the chamber. Every row of iron lungs looked identical. A perpendicular line appeared at the end of each, creating an endless loop of torture beds. She couldn't even see Chamier. Luci crouched to hide behind an iron bed, out of breath, scared, and very much in pain.

"You have to escape," a voice croaked.

Luci looked up at the creature who barely resembled a woman. Dark pits remained where her ears should have been, but there was still a small flap of skin to hold pearl earrings. Her eyes were sunk so far back they sat on either side of her head, just above her ears. Grotesque but desperate to get information across to Luci, she forced words between each breath.

"Leave. While you still can."

"What's happened here?" Luci asked. Her nerves made her want to scream the words. But, instead, she stuffed her fist against her mouth to stifle the need to cry out.

"Discarded by The Otherly. Tossed away. We were locked here. The nurse came. If we leave, she'll drag us back. If we stay, we'll become something evil. Help us. Please," the woman pleaded.

"How do I help?" Luci asked.

A pause, the lung shuddered with a breath. "You need to know."

Luci peeked around the edge of the iron bed but still didn't see any sign of Chamier. "What do I need to know?"

"The name of this place." Breath. "If you learn it," breath, "you can seal it."

"What's the name?" Luci asked.

"I do not know," the woman whispered. The iron lung stopped breathing for another long moment, then resumed. "Only keepers know."

"OK," Luci said, "OK, I will find out. I'll seal this place."

The woman closed her eyes. Luci put a hand on her hot forehead to comfort her. Blood gurgled between her teeth, and the wheeze of her iron lung stopped. Luci hit it to make the breathing start again.

The single bulb swung in the distance, washing light over the area. Luci saw the seam where she'd entered. In an instant, she was on her toes, ready to dash for the light. But she felt a strange tickle on the top of her head. Her hand went up instinctively. A stiff tuft of something was stuck, just there in her hair. She gripped the object, which made a sickening crunch sound. Bile rose in her throat. She pulled the thing from her hair and opened her palm. To her fright, it was a pasty white spider. She flung it to the ground, disgusted. The spider sprawled out on its back with its legs kicking in the air, making an awful squealing.

The spider found its centre of gravity and jumped back to its feet. Legs bent for a split second before it lunged at Luci's face. She swatted the spider away in mid-air with adrenaline-driven accuracy. It flew through the air and landed with a splat, then scurried under the closest iron bed.

Gross. Luci shuddered. She turned a corner, and Chamier's face was right there, staring straight into the girl's energized soul.

Luci fell to her butt and yelled, "Stay away from me!"

"Too late for that," Chamier said.

"What you're doing here is wrong. These people's lives are their own, not for you to drain for your powers. They should be released back to Earth," Luci yelled.

Fuelled by the sorrow of a pleading woman, Luci jumped up and stood toe to toe with Chamier. She hoped her tall frame would intimidate Chamier. But, instead, the woman tilted her head to the side, like a puppy misunderstanding a command, then pushed Luci to the ground with surprising strength. She was strong. But Luci was angry. "You can't keep me down. I will find a way to stop what you're doing here. I will find a way to free these captives."

Chamier laughed. The lids on the iron lungs banged. "No, you won't. I'm the keeper, girl," she snarled. "Every Otherian knows no one ever leaves here."

The spider crawled out from under the iron lung. Chamier plucked him off the floor with her long twisted nails. The spider kicked and squealed in the air as she held him up, examining the insect. Then she swallowed him whole with an exaggerated gulp. Chamier fell to the ground on her hands and knees. On contact, each appendage melted into the soot-covered floor. They stretched into long spikes, elbows snapping at alarming angles and stretching impossibly thin.

Chamier's sneer petrified Luci in place. The fear forced her to watch. The courage she had felt a moment ago dissipated.

Chamier kicked her legs out like a donkey, and they doubled into four. Then doubled again into eight. She slammed each new one down with a ground-shaking bang. She stood twice the size as before, now a giant white spider with hundreds of black kaleidoscope eyes.

"I love the darkness, and it loves me," Chamier declared. Then, far away, the single bulb burst into shards. Total darkness. "You fall in love with the solitude, the power, and the glare of a dark corner."

Luci crawled between the iron lungs unobserved, since Chamier was distracted by her monologue.

"This place is not for the faint of heart. At the core is a heart that wants to devour your soul." Chamier's words sounded further away.

Luci rolled through cobwebs under an iron bed. Then she felt a breeze roll along the ground on the other side. Luci turned to face the gust and smelled water. Never had she enjoyed the scent of water until now.

"Obscured from light, hidden in cracks and twisted shadows that you don't want to see. Obscure is the way of the wicked black heart in this place. And its beat matches mine," Chamier said, her colourful words strung through the air like aurora borealis.

Luci saw a sliver of light. Was that the seam she entered through? Luci crawled frantically. It seemed far away but occasionally sparkled, reminding Luci there was a chance.

Chamier hollered, "It's perfect for me, and I am perfect for it!" Her words caused a screaming uproar from the beings trapped in the iron lungs as if electric prods stabbed them at Chamier's will. She towered over the beds like a giant grown with vanity.

Luci caught a glimpse of Chamier. Her giant spider legs

pushed open piles of ash that burst into the air. Chamier was looking for her.

"This place is a centrefold for anywhere, a luminous ebony sheen between everything. A perfect parallel universe where you can hide to attack anyone," Chamier said.

She'd lost all her human features. Her back legs spun a black web that sparkled in the darkness as if electrified.

"Here should be claimed the place of miracles," Chamier said.

Luci jumped and ran the last distance to the seam in the far wall while Chamier was distracted. A crackling behind her warned Luci that Chamier had thrown the web; it was flying straight for her. Luci dropped and rolled. The trap missed.

Chamier shrieked while kicking several iron lungs away. Luci bolted. A second shadowy web revealed its approach with a whistle. Luci rolled under an iron bed to dodge the attack. She was close. She could see the pieces of glass on the floor from the broken bulb.

Luci refused to become another decrepit survivor fated to live until this demon drained her life energy away.

The ground shook as Chamier charged. Gone was the slight click of heels. Now it was eight crashing spider legs that echoed through the chamber. An iron lung burst open from the force of Chamier's footsteps. The casket spat out a corpse. Luci screamed as it seemed to jump at her. There was nothing left to the being except a fleshy hand that held a rose. Luci skidded to a stop to not crash into the skeleton.

"Take the rose," a voice whispered in her ear. The bone mouth didn't budge, but she felt the wind from the spoken words. She grabbed the rose without thinking, stuffed it in her pocket and lunged at the blank wall that held a sliver of hope.

CHAPTER 9

Luci slammed her eyes shut in anticipation of smashing into the black wall. The slit of light was tiny. Chamier wailed behind her, which told her she had aimed her lunge correctly. Thankfully, when she hit headfirst, it was like a wall made of soft rubber. It moulded around her body and pulled her deeper. Sanctuary. Silence.

She inhaled deeply with relief, but the material crawled in her mouth and slithered down her throat. She clawed, kicked, and fought the wall, and finally, her hand broke through. Something hit her leg. She struggled to look but saw nothing but blackness. She felt pressure wrap around her calf. Her panicked cry fell silent as Chamier pulled her back.

Luci fought to keep moving forward. She couldn't see

anything, but she did hear the crackling of Chamier's web grow closer. She used both hands and clawed at the rubber-like wall.

The tear stretched up to her forearm. *For Mom.* Luci's shoulder broke through. Then her collar bone, half her chest, and finally her head. She could no longer hear Chamier's electrical web. She gasped a lungful of fresh air and forced the rest of her body to freedom.

Then she was out. The blackness had let her go, and she slammed into the ground on her belly, winding herself. Luci quickly rolled over. She was under the willow tree, but there was no angry face in webs. The sky was a stagnant blue with no sight of the sun. The tree she lay under recoiled with a creaking sound and folded into the same black film from which she had emerged.

Luci lay frozen from fear or shock, half perched on her elbows. Her erratic breath wasn't even delivering oxygen.

She felt in her pocket. There were no more plums, only a plum seed. She was hungry and tired. Then she remembered Ashier and got moving. The mischievous Memegwaan could be lingering, or worse, helping Chamier catch up to Luci.

But what direction? She had to find this labyrinth Efra mentioned. There were hills to her right, mountains in front, and more willow trees to her left.

She stood and pointed in each direction.

She frowned. "No more willow trees." Then she turned. "Mountains, nope. I don't have the energy." And she turned again. "Hills ..." She saw a path, a flattened area where two hills merged.

It was about the best bet she had.

Luci trudged over the hills, weaved between short paths, and then stopped at a cave entrance dug into the dirt.

The cave smelled like rotten grass. Luci wrinkled her nose. She was about to back out of the cave entrance when she saw a light flicker ahead. The rope in her chest compelled her forward. She followed the mysterious light, her nose plugged with one hand, her other out in front to feel for obstacles. Finally, the light reflected off something on the ground. When she arrived at it, she was shocked to see the light coming from a diamond on the floor. She picked it up, then she saw another ahead. Mesmerized by the line of sparkling gems, Luci didn't realize she'd walked the length of the cave until it opened in a wide mouth that spilt her out atop a thin ledge. She set the diamond delicately on the ground since it didn't belong to her. She had bigger things ahead, like the high rock cliff. The bottom was not visible, but the rope in her chest insisted.

The ledge, dotted with tiny white flowers, ran the length of a school field. The flowers each had three identical green leaves with a spherical water droplet in the middle.

Luci stepped gingerly over the flowers. A bead of water dropped onto the edge of the cliff despite her careful movements. The ledge violently shook, causing her to plant her body against the cliff face. She'd never felt an earthquake before. Even living in the kill zone, waiting for the "big one" on Vancouver Island, this was the first tremor she'd experienced. Her foot slipped, causing her palms to burst into a stress sweat. Her heart banged against her rib cage. Her temples throbbed from worry. Then, after a long minute, the cliffside stopped shaking.

Luci heard a slam ahead but saw nothing except an endless cliff. Wonder made Luci kneel and reach for the nearest water droplet. The crystal ball reflected her face as she inched her hand towards it. She thought she looked aged but dismissed the idea and planted her feet as best she could.

Luci's steady fingers wrapped around the flower's wobbly stem as it swayed in the canyon wind. The bead of water didn't move from the edge of the flat-topped flower, but the leaves turned upward. A thousand more buds turned their faces to watch. She flicked the drop off, and it spurted into two smaller drops, then landed on the cliff edge. The whole mountain shook.

She snapped her eyes up in time to see a drawbridge lower two feet, then slam shut again.

Luci needed to drop the beads of water. All of them. Unfortunately, she imagined it would cause quite an earthquake.

She calculated her subsequent movements to be exact.

She looked back, and the dirt cave that had spilt her onto the cliff edge was gone.

The edge beneath her feet was not much broader than the spine of a thousand-page novel. The water would make the edge slippery, but the action of droplets falling was what made the drawbridge open.

Luci spent a long minute calming and readying, then yelled, "For Mom!" like a battle cry and sprinted along the crag. Rock climbing with her father put muscle memory in her legs that planted each step perfectly. She kicked off as many droplets as she could while she ran. The cliff angrily moaned and knocked her around, but she kept her forward momentum. A few boulders broke loose as the drawbridge creaked open. She was close. Water sprayed everywhere and splattered Luci's face, but she kept her eyes on the target.

A bird squawk broke her focus. She looked up to see a prehistoric-sized golden bird, with wings the length of a train car, creep out from a hidden nest. He flapped off his ledge with wing beats that echoed like an avalanche crashing down a valley. The bird's massive beak aimed to swallow Luci whole. She jumped to close the distance to the bridge, and her body slammed hard on the corner. The bridge was beginning to close, and she wasn't quite centred. The motion of it rising made her body slip to the edge. Her hands clawed, trying to grab something to pull her body up. She would soon get caught in the frame and crushed, or lose grip then fall to her death while the giant bird plucked her body to bits. The chains rattled on the draw bridge. It was vertical when her arms gave out.

She fell. The bird took the opportunity and swooped in for his attack. Luci grabbed the golden wing mid-air and swung her weight, making the bird fall towards the bridge. The bird snapped his beak at her and tried to throw her off. Luci used the momentum to ride up over the last opening of the bridge. She let go of the bird.

She crashed and rolled inside a second before the door sealed shut with a bang. Luci laughed like a lunatic. She'd made it.

Luci lay on her back, staring at the ceiling of the stone cave. No stalactites hung here. Instead, millions of bats unfolded their wings to glare. Their tiny hands held diamonds that swayed from their movement. *It's a good thing*, she thought, *bats are cute*. But the smell of guano burned the back of her throat.

Luci peeled her body off the poop-covered floor.

"Hello?" she called.

A few bats dropped their loot and flew off from the sound of her voice. Others closed their eyes to resume sleeping while gripping the diamonds.

The ground rumbled with heavy footsteps. *Stomp, stomp, stomp.* An immense shaking bounced Luci around with the diamonds on the earth.

Something massive, Luci thought. She looked around for somewhere to hide, but there was nothing in the open space. Then, suddenly, a fabulous light caused Luci to shield her eyes as if every diamond in the vicinity lit up.

When she peeked between her fingers, she saw a beautiful elephant stepping gingerly towards her. A single oval gemstone set between the animal's large brown eyes reflected the diamonds' light. The elephant had gold bangles that bounced and sang with each step. Glamour filled the damp cavern. The elegant animal made Luci gasp in awe.

Bats dropped from the ceiling and flew around, tossing diamonds to create a stunning archway above the elephant.

"Look how lucky I am. Finally, finally, there is company in my cave," the dazzling elephant said with a customer-service voice.

"How are you speaking?" Luci asked.

"Why, with my mouth silly," she giggled.

"Animals don't normally speak."

"Well, yes, but I'm a keeper, which gives me immense magical powers."

Her voice boomed on the last words. The bats dropped from their positions along the ceiling and threw diamonds around again. "No, no, no," she groaned, "not this again. Go on, back to sleep with you."

Luci noticed red tattoos of jewels and flowers dance across the wrinkled ridges of the elephant's body.

"Are you my beauty trial?" Luci asked.

"Beauty? Beauty, you say?" The elephant looked at her reflection in a large diamond on the cave floor. "Why yes, beauty is … wait, no. I'm a wisdom trial."

Luci chuckled. "I could always use more of that. I'm Luci, by the way."

"Yes, Lucille doll, I know who you are. But doesn't everyone?" She winked a heavy lashed eye. "I'm Gian Kaur," the elephant said.

"Lovely name, Gian. I'm sorry to intrude, but I'm looking for the labyrinth. A blonde woman may have travelled there?" Luci asked.

"I know the labyrinth. I never leave that place. Well, except to come here, to the bat cave. I haven't seen any blonde women, though," Gian said.

"Can you take me there?" Luci asked.

"We're in the bat cave."

"The labyrinth."

"Of course, I can. Why that's where we need to go anyway for your trial," Gian said. Her feet stomped excitedly causing the bangles to sing lovely melodies.

Gian turned around, her tiny tail swishing, and stomped further into the cave. Hundreds of diamonds vibrated into geometric patterns from her footsteps. Since everything behind her quickly faded to darkness, Luci followed Gian. Soon the shadowy grotto dissipated into a corn-created labyrinth. Luci gasped. What magic this place had.

At the beginning of the corn, hundreds of discarded diamonds littered the field. Those dwindled to just a few when Gian stopped at the entrance. It was as if the diamonds were rubbish that had stuck to the bottom of her feet.

The labyrinth was elephant-sized, with cornstalks weaving from one stem to the next to create walls that left no blank spaces.

Gian lifted her trunk, hesitated, and then lowered it. "I'm supposed to say something," she said. Gian turned around to look at Luci, who shrugged. Gian scratched her head with her trunk as if she were waiting for a prompt. Just as Luci opened her mouth, Gian Kaur straightened her posture and spoke. "Wisdom cannot be taught, not simply told or cheated to answer. It must be and can only be grown within you, Lucille doll. You cannot accept the wisdom of another. You must decide for yourself. Use experience to grow your wealth of wisdom. You sometimes, in fact, need to fail to learn. Travel the wrong direction, accept the dire results, to bask in the relief of your wisdom."

Gian motioned towards the labyrinth entrance. Luci saw three especially large cornstalks growing above the rest, equally distanced from one another and the gate. She could tell from the shapes attached to the stalks that each held an animal.

"You will have time to select the direction of only one animal. Then one will kill, one will die, and one will escape," Gian said.

"How will I know which one to choose?" Luci asked.

"That's where wisdom is applied."

Luci guessed there was only one exit but numerous pathways and many more dead ends. "How long do I have?" she asked.

"About the time it takes to get to one animal," Gian said.

"Wilds, Gian, I don't want anyone to die," Luci said.

"Then choose correctly."

The elephant lowered her trunk, and Luci lost her admiration for the animal. No matter how beautiful anyone seemed, she didn't think risking life for a trial was exemplary. Gian turned around and walked past Luci.

"Gian," she said.

Gian's response was a whisper. "One will die."

Luci thought she saw a sadness in the elephant's eyes before she faded back into the cave. Then the exit disappeared, and Luci stood alone.

She stepped into the opening of the labyrinth. "For Mom," she mumbled sadly. The corn immediately slammed the entrance closed. She felt deflated by the dead end to finding her mother.

Either way, she had to complete this trial to open the door to Earth.

Luci refocused her thoughts on the animals ahead. First, of course, the "one will escape" would be Luci's quickest exit, but then she would be dooming one to die. And one will kill? Is that how the one would die? Luci had to figure out what the animals were before she could decide.

At the end of the first hallway, a stalk of corn stood impossibly larger than the rest. It marked the three halls that lead to each animal. If Luci ended at the wrong location, it could prove disastrous, and not only to the one who would die—she might lose this trial and her mother forever.

The cornstalk stood as wide and tall as an ancient tree. Luci planned her route up to the top. But, first, she would have to step gingerly on the silky-smooth leaves and hope they didn't tear like paper. As she examined the stalk, corn husks opened and turned their ears to point at Luci like a threat. One even spat a kernel.

Luci grabbed the first grasshopper-green leaf and pulled down hard to test its durability. She shrugged. The foliage seemed strong enough. "Like climbing a rock wall," she said.

Luci hoisted her weight to the lowest leaf. The first step caused husks to peel back from their ears, forming spiky balls that lined the stalks like land mines. *Great,* Luci thought.

Nimbly, Luci reached for the next leaf. Her confidence grew as she ascended the stalk and didn't bend any foliage. She managed to dodge the spikes the whole way up. The angry corn ears were all empty threats, no follow-through. Some even closed up when she neared, unmasked again once she passed.

Near the top, one ear of corn had broken free of its husk. The little corn waited for Luci, standing like a man, smacking a baton made of husks against a splintered kernel arm. The corn man jumped at her nose, swinging the baton. Luci snapped back the end of a leaf above her and swatted him to the ground.

Above the labyrinth, Luci could see the grandness of the maze. It was perfection how the walls flowed from one corridor to the next. She tried to memorize the halls that slammed shut with dead ends to plan her route.

Luci examined the animal silhouettes.

The middle corn husk held a ferocious grizzly bear that roared and pulled on steel chains that shackled its vicious paws high in the air.

A kinkajou hung from a stalk with chains locked around his tail to the left. He swung miserably and made whimpering sounds that found Luci's ears even from a distance.

The animal on the right was a god-sized bald eagle. He flapped in the air with no chains to hold him back. He held his head high as, with massive wing beats, he smashed corn around him for fun. His ego kept him in place. Indeed, he knew he was the best choice.

If she ran to the eagle, he, of course, could fly to save the kinkajou from dying. Or would the eagle merely soar Luci away from the labyrinth altogether? She wanted out of here, but she didn't wish the kinkajou to die. And what if the eagle refused to help Luci? He wasn't trapped. He could cause her to fail this trial.

Luci felt there was only one honest answer. She descended the cornstalk, kicking away attacking ear spikes on the way. Then she chose the path in the direction she needed.

Luci wandered hallways for a long time, it seemed. The walkways stretched and bent into new galleries. She placed husks sideways to mark her path, and sure enough, she was walking in circles. She forced herself to run to cover more ground but came to a screeching stop when she reached a dead end. Luci hung her head and sulked as she turned to try another hall. The stalks swayed as she turned down a corn-way that felt darker, making Luci move cautiously. She felt something watching. Dark shadows crawled up the edges of the corn walls. A glance up told her the sky was still cloud-free and an unnervingly soft blue. Something felt uncanny.

She turned another corner, and the shadow followed. It was the dark place following her. Luci tried to squeeze between a few tall stalks. The wall was tightly packed, and she only got a few steps in before being pushed out. It was the cheater's way anyway. Her arms had got scratched up as if karma for trying the shortcut.

Luci ran. She turned each corner faster, trying to find the animal she'd chosen. The shadows crept along the ground. Long finger shapes reached for her. Luci's heart felt like it was skipping every other beat. She had to force her feet to continue. The shadow followed closely on her heels. She didn't know if it could easily pull her back to the dark place.

What was that place called?

A wall of shorter corn husks tempted Luci to climb over. She scaled the corn, and the shadowy hand followed. The husks seemed to grab at her as she frantically crawled along the top. The shadow grew solid. She scrambled away, but it caught her ankle.

She yelped. Claws dug into her skin. Luci threw herself off the wall, and the hand let go.

The darkness faded away.

Corn stalks snapped. A mighty growl vibrated the walls around her, and Luci rounded the corner to see the grizzly. The animal she'd chosen. He looked at her, snarled, and drooled. The chains pulled tight as his deadly paws flung towards her. The stalks cracked but held. Gian warned one would kill, and the corn seemed to be purposely letting the grizzly go free. His rage would take him straight for the easy target of the poor kinkajou.

Luci pulled the plum seed from her pocket. She cracked it in half between her teeth, sure she had broken a molar, but it was worthwhile now as she held an excellent sharp-edged tool. She sawed through the corn stalk that held the chain. It fell to the ground. Luci gasped when the chain dissolved back to a string of kernels. She ducked in time to miss the bear's free paw swing at her. She ran behind him and cut through the second corn shackle. The eagle screeched somewhere in the distance. Luci wondered if he was commanding her to stop and make her way to him. She ignored it. Then, success, the bear's second paw swung free, and it became too late to regret her decision anyway.

The grizzly claws slashed dangerously through the air. Luci ducked. The bear tripped and crashed his thousand-pound weight on top of her.

She curled in a ball. The bear sat back on his bottom and looked at her quizzically.

"It's OK," she said soothingly. The bear watched her movements as she crawled backwards and stood a decent distance away. Luci brushed the corn pieces off her clothing and risked meeting the grizzly's eyes. "I saw your agony, and I know the pain of not understanding," she said.

She'd felt it with her daymares. The blind rage against an unknown enemy charged the energy in her soul, and his eyes mirrored this feeling. The bear's chains, she was sure, would have held until his anger took control. Then they would have released him to charge at the innocent. For Luci, it was in her mind but equally uncontrollable.

The bear dropped his gaze to his paws. He wiggled his toes as if he hadn't seen them before.

"You may be powerful," Luci said, taking a step forward, "but don't let another's wickedness ruin you. Hate is a stain on your soul, and it only hurts you. Make the right choices now. Go and do not hurt the innocent. What you do now is called free will. Good choices strengthen your soul. And I choose you, dear grizzly because as much as I don't want the kinkajou to die, I feel in my heart that you do not wish to kill him."

The bear lifted his claws. But Luci knelt in front of him, her eyes even with his the whole time. "You are scared, as the kinkajou is. His life is intertwined with yours now, meaning your next move decides his fate. I release you, dear grizzly, from a life of endless misery. You don't have to kill anyone. You aren't forced to do anything you don't want to do. I set you free."

Luci recalled the bear attack signs at Liard Hot Springs. This bear had been scared as a prisoner. Now he was free. She touched his paws, and he looked up at her. Then he stood, towering above her.

Instead of turning towards the exit as Luci had hoped, he leaned forward. However, her confidence in the decision wavered.

The grizzly opened his mouth to expose a massive jaw that could take Luci's head clean off. She closed her eyes and grimaced with anticipation. Then a wet tongue greeted her instead of sharp teeth.

Her eyes popped open. The grizzly sat back with drool hanging from jowls.

The same dripped off her chin. "Yuck," she said and used a corn leaf to wipe the spit off her face.

Do you hear me now?

The words were unspoken but heard in Luci's mind.

Luci swivelled around. "What? Who was that?"

The bear stood again, swung his heavy arm out, and bowed with some effort. *It is I, Tabit, the Bear,* he sent.

"Why are you in my head?" she asked.

Tabit's voice sounded scruffy but kind in Luci's mind. *It's the mind language of The Otherly. Feel the words in your mind, and send them to me.*

Mom. She felt the word but didn't want to let it go. Instead, she looked to the bear, cocking an eyebrow. She thought the sentence, then focused on the bear's broad face and sent. *I want to find my mother, she's lost.*

Nice, that was excellent. And after all those bear fights by the springs, they think we have no sense of helping others, Tabit sent. *Also, I'm sorry you lost your mom.*

Luci smiled sadly. *Bear fights?* she sent.

Yeah, we get bored too. Never hurt anyone. Harmless tussles. Guess humans don't like seeing limping bears either. He shrugged. *I tell you, those bears were all sad losers,* Tabit sent.

Why are we talking in our minds? Luci sent.

I gifted you with the ability to understand all animals. We all have separate monikers, dispositions, and dialect, but we can all send the same in The Otherly. I believe you are entitled to share this space with us, an area where we can all communicate without cross-language barriers. He landed on all fours and shuffled away.

Thank you! Luci sent.

No, thank you, Tabit sent. He ploughed straight through the labyrinth wall. The giant bird screamed its irritation and pounded mighty wings as he flew away overhead. Luci knew in her heart that the kinkajou was safe. Maybe not free, but safe was better than dead.

When Luci stepped out of the labyrinth, she bumped into Ashier. He grinned mischievously.

CHAPTER 10

Deryn was angry, livid actually, about the broken gate. She fumed at her sister's control over her animals and the land. She planned a meeting with the animals when she returned, to remind them who's the boss. Deryn kicked Toll into a gallop. She needed to stop this girl before Keres got to her. Sprig failed, the dragonfly failed, now she had no lines of defence left, which meant the girl was wandering The Otherly free. She would not allow another catastrophe to occur, not during her time as Keeper of Animals.

What's wrong? Toll sent.

Deryn ignored the question. She followed a train of dark thoughts down a hole in her mind. Toll whirled his head back to see Deryn, which ended up with him tripping over his hooves.

He stumbled. Deryn used her magic to stop them from crashing headfirst into a swamp.

Toll! Deryn sent. She put pain into his name.

Yeah? He sent with genuine curiosity.

Deryn's palm twitched. Her palm wanted her nails to dig in and relieve the anger. She fought the urge. *Keep your attention on the path*, she sent to Toll. *I must hold an audience with an animal in the mines, and I can't afford unnecessary misfortunes.*

The ground turned from gritty dirt to dark mud. Toll's clumsy hooves slipped like he was a duck sliding on ice. Deryn grumbled and kicked him harder.

Who taught you to run? she sent.

You, Madame, Toll sent.

Never mind that just make haste, Deryn sent.

A night sky rolled in with dark clouds that Deryn hadn't seen in years. With it, a mugginess shifted the air to a sticky cool. Deryn glared at the sky. She wondered if Keres was watching her at this moment. Her sister, who always had the last say. Sister, who wanted this girl. Deryn had to move fast.

She directed Toll past a burn pile, one that had been smouldering since The Otherly began. Something looked different as they raced past. Deryn stewed on what was out of place.

Turn around, Deryn sent.

But you want me to hurry, Toll sent.

Deryn crudely grasped a handful of his white mane. *I allowed you to come this day, do not make me regret it. Listen to every instruction and obey,* she sent.

Toll turned a wide circle. Deryn slowed him as they approached a bundle of shivering leaves that sat suspiciously in front of the burn pile.

Here we are, Toll sent.

He stomped his hooves happily and glanced to Deryn to

receive praise. Instead, he received a sharp glare. She jumped down and kicked at the leaves.

A platypus stuck his nose out. *Please don't kick me,* he sent.

Leaves revolved around the top of the pile as he shivered.

Deryn dug her nails into her palm. *You should have more respect than this,* she sent. She felt the pulse of rage under her fingertips. The platypus should have given her the proper acknowledgement of Madame.

Is he injured? Toll sent.

Toll, mind your own business, Deryn sent. She used magic to push all the leaves off the creature. *Why are you hiding?*

The platypus hunkered further from Deryn.

Are you injured? Deryn sent.

No, he sent.

Why do you hide like this? It's not very dignified for an Otherian, Deryn sent.

They should have referred a hawk to deliver the message, the platypus sent.

Deryn stood. Dampness in her palm made her see red. He was wasting so much of her time. *Can you tell me the message?*

The furry platypus meticulously collected leaves to cover himself again. Once the creature was insulated comfortably, a sniffling nose popped out. After that, the shivering stopped, but the platypus still kept the message secret.

Deryn kicked the ground impatiently.

He's got nothing, Madame, let's go, Toll sent.

It wasn't my fault, the platypus sent.

Deryn knelt and controlled her words to sound kind, which was unfamiliar. *What was not your fault, my young son?* she sent.

Deryn didn't want to scare off the truth and bury facts under fear. Her palm was damp from plasma spilling where her nails dug. She tried to let up the pressure before it became true blood.

I told them we needed to stop her. I told them we had to ensure she stayed until you arrived! the platypus sent.

Did you stop the girl? Deryn sent.

She came through the mines, the platypus sent.

And?

And it was break time, so Potamus ignored her.

What? Deryn sent with a fierceness that sent sleeping birds bursting from the trees and to take flight.

Potamus was thirsty. I was thirsty too. It was almost lunchtime, you know? Then this girl arrived. She walked around like she owned the place, and I didn't know what to do. A human doesn't often appear in The Otherly. It's been so long that I honestly never thought it would happen again. I was slightly shocked and didn't move at all. Besides, I'm too small to do much of anything. But Potamus, he's the boss, and he brushed it off. What was I to do? But then, on her way out, she destroyed the sideways hill with some explosion, the platypus sent.

Destroyed? How did a human girl manage to destroy it? Deryn sent. She crossed her arms and tunnelled her nails into the soft underarm skin. The hurt drained her boiling rage.

The stibnite exploded! Madame, did you know these crystals were dangerous? The conclusion is we might be short for your make-up request. And now all the workers have fled. The mines burn freely, and no one will return, the platypus sent.

Deryn shrieked. Her hair flew up like a cobra's hood, readying to bite. The platypus jerked his nose back under the flimsy protection of the leaves. Deryn bellowed with such force that she blew off the leaves from the shivering creature's body, and the flame fizzled out on the burn pile.

Where's the girl now? Deryn sent.

I don't know.

Which way did she go from the mines?

I don't know, the platypus sent, snivelling.

What kind of useless help are you? Deryn sent. Ants scurried away, looking for sanctuary before she burst.

It wasn't my fault, Madame, the platypus sent, folding his tiny form diminutively. *Please forgive me.*

Toll stomped the ground. *Dark clouds come, Madame. Does this girl bring the strange weather?*

It's not the girl, Deryn sent and glanced at the sky.

I'm sorry, the platypus continued.

When was she in the mines? Deryn sent.

Yesterday.

A whole day! Why did it take you a full day to report this?

I'm sorry.

Sorry is not good enough, Deryn sent.

No one else wanted to come. You should—

I should what? Deryn floated into the air. *Be appreciative? Maybe you will pay for the negligence of all the mine animals!* she sent, inhaling sharply. The hair shaped like a cobra hood rattled and shook.

A sudden snap of wind knocked Deryn to the ground.

Madame! Toll sent, instantly rushing to her side. He helped her climb on his back.

Through clenched teeth, Deryn sent, *Take me to the mines.*

Deryn kicked a burned log off the pile as Toll ran past.

CHAPTER 11

Luci felt the hairs on her arms prickle like an electrical storm made of anger was coming. She lunged at Ashier, "You! I could have died down there, or worse, trapped by Chamier."

Ashier sidestepped, causing Luci to crash on the ground. "It's unfortunate that you escaped. The iron lung would have looked good on you," he said.

Luci lifted herself off the dirt and glared at him.

His mouth twisted up at the corners. "I can help you get back there."

She snarled, "Get away from me."

Ashier picked a worm off his head and popped it in his mouth. As he chewed, his jaw muscles rippled. Luci cringed, remembering Chamier crunching the spider. "I know where your mother is," he said.

"I don't believe you," she said.

"You don't need to because your mother will keep on her way anyway, regardless of what you think of me," Ashier said.

He leaned against a willow. He plucked another worm off his head, examined it closely, then bit its head off dramatically.

"Where is she then?"

He shrugged. "In the labyrinth," he said, then spat the worm at Luci.

That was enough. First, Ashier lied to her, and now he spat? She kicked at his knees, knocking him to the ground. In one swift movement, he rolled, then jumped back up. Luci charged at him, colliding hard into his chest. She tackled him. Ashier wiggled his hand out from under Luci and blew grey material off his palm. She quickly moved to dodge the attack of unknown dust blown into her face. Luci felt disorientated. She choked on the smell of that dark place. Then she had an idea.

She fell back, blinking through the dusty stuff in her eyes and demanded, "Why are you trying to send me back to that place?"

Ashier crossed his arms. "Don't matter to me much."

"Then why are you fighting me?" Luci asked, rubbing her sore elbow.

"It's fun."

"Maybe I'll just run away, and you won't have any more fun."

His face fell. Luci had hoped for that reaction. She added, "I guess I could stay, as long as you don't push me back into that place. You know, the dark place. What's it called?"

Ashier laughed. The worms wiggled from the movement. "I'm not that dumb."

He ran around Luci and smacked her back. Hard.

"Ooof," escaped from Luci's lips. She swung around, but Ashier was faster. He booked it around and bashed her other shoulder. Luci swung both arms, trying to deflect future hits, but Ashier's size made him perfect for dodging each swing. Luci tried to kick when the Memegwaan ran. Luci was too angry to let him get away. She chased after him into a field of tall white flowers.

Luci lost him in the flower forest. She slowed and stepped around the flowers cautiously. She expected him to appear at any moment.

Bugs crawled along the flower stalks sending warnings to her to leave this place.

Don't touch the flowers or be tempted to smell the buds, the bugs sent.

Luci could hear the popping of worms in Ashier's mouth. He chewed and walked. The sound carried.

Luci stood still for a few heartbeats to close her eyes and listen. The chewing grew louder. She readied herself, opening her eyes the second Ashier appeared. She attacked.

She threw a heavy fist towards his face. Ashier ducked and jabbed her arm painfully backward against a flower stalk. The moment her skin touched the silky hair-covered stem, her skin bubbled up into painful blisters. Her flesh screamed with pain. She cried out and pulled away.

"Ashier," she growled and spun around.

He punched her in the stomach, causing her to stumble back into the towering flower. This time he didn't run away.

Luci shook her head, then looked at the small man. She furrowed her brow. Who was he? She couldn't remember. It seemed a memory that was just right there, but as a blister on her hand popped, the knowing bled through her fingers.

His mouth twisted into a cruel smile. He wasn't a friend, she decided. Luci peeled off the flower, her skin swelling with watery blisters. Each new pop wet her shirt with drained memories.

"What are you doing?" she shrieked.

He folded his arms. "Hmm, not quite," he said.

He shot both fists forward and smashed them against Luci's chest. The hit knocked the air out of her lungs. She tripped, body-slammed the stem, which reverberated, and a single petal fell into her lap.

Luci stared at the white floret in horror. She knew it meant something. A wicked meaning that she had, but then it slipped away.

She glanced back at the flower. Why was she scared of this flower?

She looked at the man and snarled. But then she couldn't remember why she was mad. He was doing this. She knew that much. "Go away!"

"Nope, that won't do," the man grumbled.

He jump-kicked both legs into her chest, causing her body to snap the giant flower in half. She choked on the bile creeping up her throat.

A large flower bud landed in her lap. She picked it up, and blisters formed where it touched her skin.

She crumpled into a ball as the pain encapsulated her. Why did everything hurt so much? What was causing the pain?

"Hey, girl," a voice said.

She peeled her eyes up to see a man standing there, but he wasn't an ordinary man. He looked strange. Or maybe he was a normal-looking man. She didn't know anymore. What was a man? A blister popped. She rolled over to look at the thing looking at her.

"I'm a girl?" she asked. What did he mean? Was that her name? Girl?

More blisters appeared on her arms, grew, and then popped. Then she couldn't remember what he'd said.

"Who are you?" she asked.

He grinned.

"What are these?"

The girl held her arm up. Blisters appeared and popped. The blisters hurt. Her skin hurt. A quiver rippled her bottom lip. A sickness spread from the blisters to her chest and settled in her mind. The eruptions on her skin seemed to burst all her knowledge out. She gingerly touched her cheeks, where she felt new blisters emerge. Each volcanic eruption of clarity broke away. Then, suddenly, the thing turned to leave. The girl snivelled, "Wait, can you help me?" she implored.

"That will do just fine," he said. The thing swung in a frantic circle then turned into a soft grey moth. The moth thing flew away.

CHAPTER 12

Keres smoothed her hair behind her ear. Annoying how that one strand always fell in her face. She swiped away a space of cloud, which spun up her fingers like whipped cream pulling up from a spoon. She remembered whipped cream, but she never got the opportunity to taste it anymore. The cloud swirl parted like a broken necklace, rolling down her palm like pearls. Keres watched Luci fall in the giant hogweed field. Memory loss was OK. It would make the transition easier for her daughter.

A trumpet sounded, pulling Keres's attention away. She scrolled through the cloud view until she found Gian Kaur stampeding across Zavian's fields to the cabin door.

Keres swallowed her jealousy for the easily roaming elephant. She faintly remembered when she could walk those fields before

Mother Nature locked her in the clouds. It wasn't fair that Deryn was allowed to roam free as well. Deryn was the cruel sister, not her.

All Keres could do was watch. And command the weather. And call Deryn on the phone. But the conversations had long dried up. Just like the rains over The Otherly. Too much work on both accounts. Besides, what do you speak about when forced to sit around all day?

The clouds beside Keres sculpted into a painful memory of influenza ravaged bodies in the streets of 1930s' England. A dirty trick of Equilibrium, one that she couldn't control, was the entirely uncalled for nostalgias.

Keres lived everywhere and nowhere.

She ran her hands through her hair and tugged slightly. She tried to pull the emotion from her skull.

She swatted the memory clouds apart. She was clearing her view to see Gian again, but the clouds continued to pour in, teasing her weak state. Keres pined to know what the elephant was saying. She hadn't seen Gian leave the safety of her cave in many years, but Keres appreciated the elephant's concern since she, too, seemed to want the girl to arrive safely to Equilibrium.

Keres hadn't seen a human choose the bear in the past. They always went for the eagle, swooped in, rescued the kinkajou and held on tight as the giant bird attacked the bear to his last breath. Then Gian's magic would heal the animals from near-death, or even complete death, and reset the labyrinth to wait for the next recruit. Her daughter had chosen the bear, which was odd, and Keres had worried about the consequences. But the girl was still on her way across the lands. In the end, Keres didn't care how the trial played out. The endpoint had to be the girl with her. She felt a strange flutter of nerves in her stomach. Would her daughter like her?

Keres pulled energy from chains buried in the clouds, then forced the clouds to part for a view.

She scowled when Gian lifted Zavian with her trunk and choked him. How was the Memegwaan to keep her daughter safe if the stupid elephant killed him?

She read Zavian's lips. "Who are you to question Keres Moreth?"

Keres grinned. *Good man.*

The clouds closed over the view. Keres frantically swiped them away. She never had enough energy anymore, being stuck in Equilibrium. Finally, the clouds parted and showed Zavian on his back on the second step leading to his door, rubbing his neck.

Gian's mouth moved. "You will help me stop the girl before she gets to."

Keres tipped the scales that sat behind her with a hand, rushing rain clouds at the giant beast. Keres needed Zavian.

The red paintings washed from Gian's grey skin, diluting the elephant's magic. Then, finally, she fell to a knee.

Zavian's lips, "Isn't Keres only trying to meet her daughter?"

Gian's trunk smashed through Zavian's front steps, too close to the Memegwaan for Keres's comfort. Her lips formed, "How can you be so gullible?"

Keres tipped her hand and brought in a strong wind. She laughed as tiny pelts of rain stung the elephant's side. Gian eventually dropped to both knees.

Zavian stood. "Can I not stay loyal and help Keres?"

Gian Kaur turned and strolled away, her significant head low.

Victory. Keres pulled up a fluffy recliner from the clouds and sat back to allow her energy to recoup. She needed sleep.

But instead, she stared at the ceiling. She thought of all the things she could teach her daughter. Why would Gian try to stop this?

Keres got antsy sitting still. She swung the cloud view where she found her daughter lying among the giant flowers, playing delicately with a bud. At least she was no longer full of fear. Or worry for that Ruth.

CHAPTER 13

The girl stared at her foreign-looking hand. There were nails embedded in fingers. The fingers attached to hands which she could bend in all directions. The connection ran up to her shoulder but didn't seem to be hers. Something didn't feel right. The girl glanced up at the towering flowers. Was it normal to be a small girl among giant blooms? She wasn't sure. She didn't know her name, where she was, or why she was here. All she knew at that moment was that she was warm and comfortable. Laying among these flowers kept her safe. She supposed.

Footsteps approached. The girl searched for a weapon to protect herself if this thing meant her harm. A large flower bud was the only option. She didn't want any more pain. Her hands burned as she held the flower bud, but she wasn't sure why.

A voice said, "If she ended up in there …"

"Don't I know what that would mean?" another voice replied.

The girl scuttled behind a basket-like weaving of green-lace leaves around the tall flower stem. They intertwined with monstrous plants and offered her some coverage.

She saw her company first.

An elephant walked beside a thing, straight towards her hiding spot. The girl thought she had seen a thing like this thing before. Similar but different. In her hands was a flower bud. She dropped it, unsure why she held the flower bud if it burned her hands. Or was the bud stopping the burn?

"Zavian," the elephant spoke.

Do those animals usually speak? The girl couldn't remember. She forgot to be cautious and said, "Hello," with a smile.

The elephant stuck its trunk out to stop the thing before the beginning of the giant flowers.

The thing jumped up and waved its arms. "Are you OK?" the thing asked.

Then it pushed the elephant's trunk away and hastened towards the first wall of flowers. The girl stood on the other side. The enormous animal said, "Be careful. The effects of hogweed are unpredictable. She could see us as a threat."

"Isn't it better than staring into space until she takes her last breath?" the thing asked.

"Oh, yes. Like the previous daughter of Keres. That was unfortunate," the elephant said.

A petal pirouetted through the air towards the girl's shoulder. She wanted to touch the white silk, but a blister burst on her hand when she reached out. It smelled awful and was excruciatingly painful.

She looked at the thing. When did it get here?

"Can you please stop touching the flowers?" it asked.

The girl saw an elephant standing behind the thing. They both watched her.

"Why?" she asked.

"Doesn't it hurt when you hold them?" the thing asked. It stepped wide around the flower stalks and drew closer. The girl scooted backwards. Was this a friend?

But her hands did hurt a lot. She looked to the flower bud in her hands. "Yes, I suppose it does," she said.

"Can you put it down?" the thing asked.

The girl couldn't remember why she was holding it in the first place. She dropped the flower.

"Won't you come over here?" it asked.

The thing didn't come any closer. Instead, it allowed the girl space to move on her own. A flower wilted overhead. Soft white petals spilt to the ground between her and the thing. "Why?"

"Can we talk over here?" it asked.

She didn't remember a conversation with this thing. Was there something they were discussing? "Why can't I talk from here?"

The girl looked at her hands. They felt better. Maybe this thing had a valid point. She brushed the flower petals off her shoulder and stood.

"Couldn't we talk better if you were closer?" the thing asked.

The girl's face twisted, "What if it's a trap?" She realized she'd meant to think that sentence. Maybe there was something not right here. She looked at the elephant and the thing. They both had wide eyes as if watching an animal get swept downstream to a waterfall.

"It's not a trap," the elephant said. "We want to help you, Lucille doll. Please, just listen and get away from the flowers."

"I don't think I need help," she said.

"Aren't those blisters painful?" the thing asked.

He smiled, but the odd look of his wide red lips made her feel unsettled. She glanced behind her and realized the giant flowers went on as far as she could see. She looked at her hands. "They do hurt. What are these blisters from?"

"Aren't they burned from the giant hogweed?" the thing asked.

"Was that the answer or a question?" she asked.

The girl took a step forward. The thing seemed kind enough. She took another step, and a feeling of loss overwhelmed her. What had she lost? "What's going on?" Her voice cracked from the stress of not knowing.

"Aren't many things happening at this moment?" the thing asked.

She wanted to shake the feeling of not understanding.

"Be careful not to touch the flowers," the elephant said.

The girl stepped around carefully. "You're a man!" she exclaimed as she remembered the word she'd been seeking.

She pinned her arms to her body and tiptoed around the flowers.

The elephant waved her trunk. "That's it. Stay away from any blooms on the ground as well."

The man exhaled as if satisfied that she was listening. She liked the relief that came with understanding as she moved away from the flowers. They smelled toxic. Chemicals disguised with perfume.

A punch of agony hit the girl when she stepped away from the last row of white flowers. The overwhelming pain made her feel faint. Her steps wavered, and her body threatened to collapse. The man caught her before she hit the ground. He dragged her further from the flowers.

"Isn't it better now?" he asked. His black-ringed eyes stared without blinking.

Her body was free of the treacherous field, but her mind felt like a bag of water with a hole draining everything she wanted to retain. Her limbs were flimsy with pain.

The man sat down with his legs crossed. He gently laid her head in his lap. The elephant stood with her ears draped over the two.

"Yes, it is better," the girl said.

The man ran his hands over her hair, and she felt calm and reassured. Very unsure of everything but at ease somehow. The pain slowly dissolved under his warm touch.

"Would you like to see what we brought for you, Miss Luci?" he asked.

"Am I Miss Luci?"

"Yes," the elephant said.

The girl felt she knew the elephant. She had a name as well. If her name was Miss Luci, then the elephant's name was—

The man interrupted her thought. "Did I bring your camera?" he asked.

No new blisters formed on her hands or arms, for which she was grateful. She wasn't sure what a camera was, but she certainly felt better. Nevertheless, her throat stung when she whispered, "Who are you?"

"Am I Zavian?"

"I—" the girl began, "I don't know. I should know."

The discomfort increased as salty wounds burst on her neck and face. Miss Luci concluded that the toxins from the plants kept the worst of the pain away by pumping more poison into her system. She figured she was grateful for this man. But, no, she knew it.

"His name is Zavian. I'm Gian Kaur. We're friends," the elephant said.

"Do you want to see the camera?" Zavian asked.

"Do you always ask questions? Do you never answer the questions?" Miss Luci asked.

"What is a question other than the answer itself?"

He placed the camera on her belly for them both to view.

"Is this mine?" Miss Luci asked.

She picked the camera up. The weight in her palms was heavy and familiar. She rolled over, repositioning to her elbows, allowing her hair to fall into a curtain of red locks that made a private space to view the camera. To recall who she was. A name was nothing without the memories behind it.

Miss Luci fumbled with the camera several times until one button she pushed made the object hum then brighten. Miniature people appeared on the viewing screen. *They are my people*, her silent tears whispered.

Zavian leaned forward. "May I help you?"

"Yes, I mean, you are my friend," she said.

"Was that a question?" he asked.

"No, I know this."

Zavian clicked past the photos of the hot springs steaming through snowbanks, mountains layered like novels, and Grentsth floating like a ghost. Each image simultaneously pulled the memory through the poison.

"Who are we, really, if not the simple action of our heart beating?" Zavian asked.

The viewing screen danced past photos of Luci as a young girl. Then she remembered the camera was only a recent gift.

"How are these pictures possibly here?" she asked.

"Would your heart forget the love of your soul?"

Luci smiled at him through her curtain of hair. Zavian clicked buttons until he found a picture of a young girl holding a baby boy in an off-pink painted room.

"That's me. My mother painted the room pink thinking she would have a girl." Luci said.

"Who's the baby?" Zavian asked.

"That's my kid brother, Lane. I came here looking for my mother, didn't I? And now I'm told she might not be my mother after all."

Zavian backed out of her space. Luci lay on her stomach for several long minutes, looking at the impossible pictures. Then, strangely, there was a picture of her rock climbing while Lane was still in diapers. Her father stood at the base of the short climb with a wide smile.

Luci stopped on a picture of her mother collecting trinkets on the beach. That was when a daymare had chased her from the beach. She had felt embarrassed, but her mother still wrapped an arm around her shoulders the whole walk home. She swallowed the emotion that welled up her throat. "Mom," she said.

"Who is your mother but one who automatically loves you?" Zavian asked.

Luci touched her cheeks and felt the last blister disappear. Memories rushed back like birds to a nest.

Gian's red tattoos swam in a frenzy of hearts and stick figures hugging. "I'm happy you've come back to us," she said.

"How did you find me?" Luci asked.

"Would you believe it was Gian who instigated the search?" Zavian asked.

Luci chuckled. "But Gian, I thought you never left the labyrinth?"

The elephant's eyes brightened. "Yes, mostly. But I'd never seen the trial go as it had for you. You're something special, Lucille doll. Maybe you will finally break the cycle?"

"Cycle of what?" Luci asked.

"Of the corrupt keepers," Gian said.

"Oh, you mean Deryn. Yes, I heard," Luci said.

Gian kicked at the dirt silently.

"Did we fight before we rescued you?" Zavian asked.

Luci's eyes widened, "You fought? But why?"

"A tale for another time," Gian said.

Luci placed the camera strap around her neck. "How did you fix my camera? I thought it was broken for good!"

"Didn't I say morel mushrooms were good?" Zavian asked, winking as his eye socket faded to a dandelion yellow. "Is it time?" he added.

Luci stood. She forced the hair behind her ear. That rebellious strand sprung in front of her left eye again. She patted Gian's trunk and turned to Zavian. "Time for what?"

"Isn't it time to meet your real mother, Keres?"

"But I haven't found my mother, my Ruth, yet."

"Can't Keres see everything over The Otherly? Maybe she would know?" Zavian asked.

Luci glared into his face. Her teeth clenched, "Then why didn't you mention that before?"

"Did you complete three trials before now?"

"I've completed them! How do you know? I thought I failed with Efra," she asked.

"Did the Cattywampus vines tell me the door has opened?" Zavian asked.

"Yes, OK, let's find Keres and ask if she knows where my mother is. I'm more than ready to go home."

Hope swelled in her chest. Zavian held Luci's hand as they followed Gian through the willow forest. They didn't make it far before they heard voices, familiar and evil.

CHAPTER 14

The weight of Deryn's anger made her feel heavy. Her head, her shoulders, everything was too heavy to hold up. She slumped against Toll's neck as he galloped towards the mines. The wind carried drizzles of rain that cut like daggers through the air. Toll splashed through a mud puddle.

You're getting my new boots dirty, Deryn sent with venom.

Toll slowed to a trot.

Hurry, we're losing time! Deryn sent.

I don't understand your request. You want me to slow down but hurry? Toll sent.

That was the last drop in Deryn's bucket of fury that caused it to spill over.

"Toll!" she screamed and flew up off the horse.

Madame, sorry, come back, he sent.

Deryn flew the last distance to the mines with Toll directly below. She wasn't as fast as she used to be. So heavy. Deryn lost steam before she reached the entrance. She dropped to the ground from the weight of the anger she carried. Her face was wet. She felt confused. Tears? What was going on with her? A swipe on her cheek came away with smeared black make-up. Toll appeared beside her. Deryn quickly hid her face and wiped away the evidence of emotion.

What is it? Toll sent.

It's just. I think maybe I—

A crash ahead of them stole Deryn's confession. A mudslide tore half the dune away. Crates of stibnite slid down with overburden and made a mess on the ground. The rain increased, and Deryn glared at the sky. She was sure now that her sister was toying with her.

All the animals had deserted the place, abandoning the crates to sit ruined in the rain. But at least the rain doused the last few scattered flames.

Deryn heard movement behind a pile of boulders. Toll stood at her side with his ears back and his nose hidden in the side of her jacket. She flew up to scout around the mine and saw someone she wasn't happy to see.

Potamus. He sat pouting among broken beams. The fire burned new patches of sand into shining glass. Deryn frowned. Her hair snapped up to a rhino horn, and her nostrils flared. She dug her nails into her palm. It should only ever be her that created chaos in this mine. Potamus stood and took heavy steps that cracked spiderweb prints into the glass floor.

Deryn lowered down next to her old friend. He looked at her, then collapsed to his belly and gave a reverberating wail.

My work ruined, he sent.

Tears dropped to the glass floor. Deryn wanted to apologize, knowing his level of commitment to his work. But the feeling was overruled by the fury of him sitting back as the girl had walked past.

I could ruin you, Deryn sent.

Not like you haven't before.

That's not a fair statement. I never set this place on fire with workers here! Deryn sent.

My bad, those were just your hissy fits. That shut us down for a week at a time! Potamus sent.

And how about this? It was a simple request to stop the girl.

It wasn't my fault, Potamus sent.

Of course, it was!

Deryn's hair slicked into a viper's diamond head, ready to snap.

Now I have to get a tracker to find her, Deryn sent. *That cost will come out of your food pay.*

Potamus scrambled on fat toes and tried to run but slid clumsily. A sliver of glass cut deep into his foot, and blood spread out on the ground. Deryn lowered her hand to the red pool.

"Baaahooooo," the cry was of a dying animal.

The sound was some distance away.

Madame, someone needs us, Toll sent.

Yes, in a minute, Deryn sent.

But Toll ran off in the direction of the cry. Deryn scowled and followed the horse into the willow forest, out of the dunes.

Another desperate cry brought Deryn to a wolf cub, too young to know the mind language of The Otherly. Toll knelt beside the cub.

What can you do? He sent.

Deryn dug her nails into her palm, and the diamond-viper hair slicked into elephant ears. Toll stood silent. The torso of the young wolf was torn open. He wouldn't make it.

Deryn knelt in front of the cub. Then, behind a bush, a twig snapped. She imagined it was more mine animals coming to complain.

Deryn stood outside the growing pool of blood. It stained the dirt to a rusty black.

Blood and earth do mix nicely, Deryn thought, nails to palm.

"Baaahooooo," the wolf cried, pleading for help.

"You're beyond saving," Deryn whispered. She lifted her hand and waved it over his neck in a smooth motion. His neck bones snapped with a single click of her fingers.

CHAPTER 15

Luci scrambled backwards when the woman killed the wolf cub. "Who is that?" Luci whispered. She could hardly see with her tear-brimmed eyes.

"Isn't that Deryn?" Zavian asked.

"We need to get out of here," Gian said.

Tears rolled down Luci's cheeks. "Why would she do that?"

"She's Keeper of Animals," the elephant said. She tried to creep backwards but was too clumsy. There was no way to hide the sound of an elephant walking in the woods.

Fear crept up Luci's spine like a spider. "She's going to see us."

"You're right. We need to hide better," Gian said. She rolled her trunk over her legs, causing the red paintings to transfer like dough to a rolling pin. She swung her trunk and threw the magic at Luci and Zavian.

Luci tried to yelp when she saw Zavian melt into a dandelion, but the magic had shifted Luci's body to a wrinkly morel mushroom. Gian didn't change since there weren't any red tattoos left. The camera sat neglected in front of Luci the mushroom.

Deryn casually appeared from under a willow tree canopy just as Gian tiptoed behind a bush.

The woman rolled her eyes. "Hello, Gian Kaur."

A horse with his head low followed. Luci tried to attack Deryn. She couldn't even move a wrinkle.

Gian stepped out from behind the tree.

"Have you seen a girl travelling these lands?" Deryn asked.

"No," Gian said.

"Did she make it to your labyrinth yet?" Deryn asked, strolling to the camera. Somewhere in the distance, Luci thought she heard a phone ringing. She figured it was her imagination, but Deryn's head popped up as if she'd heard it as well.

"Nope, no one at my labyrinth for some time now." Gian turned to leave. Deryn smacked her hands, and the elephant's legs changed to skinny giraffe legs, which sprawled out in every direction, landing Gian on her belly.

"I suppose it wouldn't matter if you stayed right here then," Deryn said. She picked up the camera, and again Luci tried to lash out at the evil woman. Deryn turned the camera on and clicked through the pictures.

"Now, I know your face, girl," she said.

Deryn placed the camera strap around her neck and clambered on the horse. They took a couple of steps away. Then she looked back at the dandelion. "Don't find those often in The Otherly. It will work well for new hair colour." She flew off the horse, plucked Zavian the dandelion out of the ground, and kicked the puzzle-piece adorned horse to a full sprint.

The willow forest settled into silence. Gian lay so still on her belly that Luci worried she would stay forever a fungus. Her wrinkled eyes watched red paintings blossom on Gian's flesh. Finally, the elephant pulled three tattoos off and threw them at Luci.

Unlike shifting into a mushroom, changing back was a painful experience. First, Luci felt electrocuted, like she was in a pool of eels. Then she felt swallowed and chewed by a blue whale. Next, her legs sprouted free from bloody crocodile jaws, and pain snapped her spine into her regular height.

Luci jumped up. "She sent a shark to kill me."

"Sounds about right. Deryn does control with a firm hand," Gian said.

"I have to stop her," Luci said.

"You know, I should have been Keeper of Animals."

Luci wiped away tears that poured for the wolf pup. "I agree."

"The labyrinth is boring. I sit and wait. It's no fun. If I were Keeper of Animals, I would get to go many places."

"Yes, going places is nice. But so is being at home. That's a place rooted in you," Luci said.

Gian was on her feet. She wobbled but found her centre of gravity. The flowing red paintings appeared on her body, and her legs popped back to the grey wrinkled flesh.

"I have to stay in the cave with the bats all the time. The magic doesn't allow me to cross the labyrinth until a trial arrives. And those bats aren't much fun. They toss those diamonds as if trying to cut my delicate skin," Gian said.

"What are we going to do, Gian?"

"We need to get back to Zavian's cabin. The door to Earth will be open now. You can return home, Lucille doll." Gian lifted the heavy willow branches for Luci.

"No, I need to get to Keres. She might know where my Ruth went by having a look from the sky," Luci said.

"That's the problem. How do you get into the sky? Usually the eagle would fly the chosen up to Equilibrium to meet Keres after my labyrinth trial," Gian said.

Luci hesitated. "I can't leave without my mom."

Gian walked ahead. Her tail swung slowly.

"What if we go find Deryn?" Luci asked.

"She'll fight us if we go after her," Gian said.

In her being, Luci wanted to leave. But her heart sang a different tune. The idea of Deryn holding Zavian captive made her sick to her stomach. But she still needed to find her mother. Her best plan was to see Keres to ask if she knew where her mother, Ruth, went. Keres would have seen where Deryn went with Zavian the dandelion too. Hopefully.

The walk to the cabin was silent—on Luci's part, anyway. Gian chatted as if everything was right in The Otherly. Then, at the door, Gian waved goodbye and wished Luci luck. Luci thought it strange the elephant wasn't fazed by Zavian's absence.

The way of the keepers, Luci thought as she watched the elephant lumber away.

She didn't like it. A keeper should be all good with their power.

Luci sat on a chair and stared at the empty table. The vines seemed lost without Zavian. They peeled away from the walls and flopped on the table sadly.

Luci looked to the room with the staircase. Sure enough, a trapdoor in the ceiling had appeared.

"Mom," she said to the house.

The vines danced chaotically in the air. They were even going so far as hitting the ceiling to grab her attention. She knew what they were saying. She couldn't leave without her mother.

Luci had to find a way to Equilibrium. She had to speak to Keres. But how does one get into the sky? She walked to the kitchen. Instead of Zavian's kitchen, Luci saw her kitchen at home in Parksville.

Beside the fridge was a door that led to a storage room with another door. On the other side of that was a deserted hair salon. The empty cabinets and sinks had been a perfect location for Luci and Lane to play. Luci would sit in the styling chair as Lane brushed her hair. He braided intricate designs. Sometimes Lane would put balms in her curls and twist each one separately. He'd wanted to be a stylist. Luci wondered if he would ever do hair again with both women missing from the family.

She leaned against the archway in Zavian's kitchen and slid her back down the wall to the floor. Then the tears came. She'd held them back for so long. A vine reached over and touched her shoulder. Another appeared with a mug of steamy tea.

"Thanks," she said.

Leaving to go home without her mother would never happen. But there was a new nagging thought that she couldn't leave Zavian as a captive of Deryn's. Her head pounded. What was she to do?

The vines tapped her shoulder. She swatted them away.

The movement caused something to stab her through her pocket. She stuck her hand in and pulled out the crumpled rose from the dark place.

"I don't even understand why I have this. I just want to get into the sky to ask Keres if she knows where my mother is," Luci said.

The vines took the rose from her hand. Luci jumped up to grab it back but more vines piled into the small space. They pulled and stretched the petals into long sheets. A paper-thin sail. A second vine peeled the thorns down the rose stem, creating riggings and posts.

Luci jumped up and dragged the new rose hand glider outside. She grabbed the centre bar just in time as a strong gust of wind pumped into the sail. Luci lifted off the ground, aiming for the clouds.

CHAPTER 16

Deryn clung to Toll's back like a leech to a fresh leg. He seemed faster. She smiled, thinking her son was growing stronger even if she was growing weaker. Toll crashed through the willow forest without hesitation. She steered him wide around the hogweed fields.

Deryn could hear the phone continuing to ring, but she had her priority. Her sister would have to wait.

Toll slowed, then stopped to drink from a puddle.

We don't have time for a snack, Deryn sent.

It's not a snack. There's no nutritional value. And when was the last time we had fresh rain? Toll sent.

Let's go. Time is wasting, Deryn sent.

I don't know if I want to take you any ... further, Toll sent. He flinched as if anticipating a sharp smack.

Deryn sighed and sent, *I don't have the magic left in me to fly there.*

I don't want to walk you into danger, Toll sent, *and besides, you're heavier now.*

What? Deryn sent. She looked down at her body.

Is it the weight of your anger? he sent.

Deryn was about to give a rude reply, but then his question sunk in. She wasn't angry. Was she angry?

She noticed animals watched from a distance then hid when she approached.

Maybe, Deryn sent.

The den came into view, making Toll buck. *I won't go in there.*

He turned to leave, but Deryn yanked his mane to force him forward. The horse inched a few steps then stopped twenty feet back. He bucked.

Steady now, Deryn sent.

Deadfall lay overtop of a dugout. Deryn could smell the animals hunkered inside their den.

Why did you let those animals in here? Toll sent.

Quiet now, Deryn sent. Then, *Mighty Dragor, please lend me your assistance.*

A dirty paw with razor-edged nails smacked out and dug into the side of the dirt mound. A nose followed, centred atop an angry snarling mouth. Toll skittered backwards.

And why should I do that? A send from the den.

The animal howled, then leaped out of the den across twenty feet right at Toll.

The horse whinnied, kicked up in the air, lost balance, and fell backwards. Deryn tumbled off his back. The wolf circled and held his dripping snout over her throat.

Deryn kept her face blank. *Dragor, I need your help,* she sent.

Tell me why I shouldn't rip your throat out? Dragor sent. His eyes pinched together, and his hackles lifted. Toll scrambled away, leaving Deryn vulnerable under the wolf's open jaw.

You killed a pup today, Madame, the wolf sent.

Malice from Dragor's send stung Deryn in her mind.

It was a mercy kill, Deryn sent.

You promised us refuge from the Earthly cull, but you lied! He sent.

Her body tensed. *I require your help, mighty Dragor,* Deryn sent.

I'm thinking of murder, and your send is for help?

I'm sorry for your loss. The pup would have died anyway, Deryn sent.

Her hair swirled into small hamster ears.

He stepped back. Deryn knew he was a good wolf deep down. She'd seen it when he approached her on Earth many harvest moons ago.

She swallowed, then tried to appeal to the snarling wolf. *I humbly request your assistance in tracking a girl.*

A human girl? The wolf sent.

Yes, a human girl. She has come to The Otherly by invitation of Keres. I need her stopped. I can offer you a seed of magic to build an enormous den, Deryn sent.

She lifted the camera and held it out to the wolf. Dragor stalked circles around Deryn, making her hair spin into rabbit ears laying on her back. *This camera belonged to the girl. Her scent will be on this,* she sent.

The wolf exposed his teeth with a low rumble. *What good is a big den with a smaller family? I will not help you, and if you return to interrupt our peace another time, I will slit your throat, your horse's throat, and every animal that aids you in those treacherous mines you call solace.*

The wolf lunged with a razor-sharp claw at Toll. Deryn took advantage of the moment and sent a burst of funnelled energy at Dragor, knocking him back. She jumped on Toll's back, and they turned to run. Dragor swiped and cut the horse's tail in half.

With a second thought, Deryn turned Toll and made him circle back. *I would never ask for help from you after the loss you suffered, but I will have to send you back to Earth if you do not help me track this girl. Then you will indeed be on your own*, Deryn sent.

You could have used your magic to save my pup, Dragor sent.

I can't heal. It was a pity, an unfortunate loss for your den, Deryn sent. Toll kicked up, trying to run off, but Deryn pushed him to stay.

Dragor went silent.

Please, Deryn thought without sending.

Toll shivered violently.

It would be against my morals to help someone that has slain another, Dragor sent. With that, he slunk back into his den.

Toll turned to leave, but Deryn insisted he go closer to the den. The horse snorted and fought every step.

If you bring this girl to me, I will give you a seed of Otherly.

Silence.

OK, Toll, let's go, Deryn sent.

Toll galloped with Deryn on his back for some time before he asked her what the plan was.

Deryn didn't respond. The phone rang in the distance.

Madame, Toll sent.

Let's go home, Deryn sent.

When they arrived at the farmhouse, the phone continued to ring. The gate hung open, broken again, and the horses were gone. Fingernails deep in Deryn's palm calmed the storm inside.

Deryn snapped an icicle off the frozen vines and examined its perfect symmetry.

"This is not good," she said.

What happened, Madame? Toll sent.

It looks like Keres is getting impatient, Deryn sent. *Time is running out. We have to stop this girl before she meets Keres, and apparently, no one can do this except me.* The send reverberated and shattered all the ice crystals hanging off her gate.

She instructed Toll to fix the gate and ran for the ringing phone. She was nearly out of breath and energy by the time she picked up the phone. Keres's voice was malice through the receiver. "Where's the girl?"

"Hi, sister, nice to hear from you. You know, considering you never call me, this day is extra special. Two calls in one." Deryn said. Her enthusiasm was, naturally, fake.

There was a rumble outside the house. Deryn glanced out the window and saw Keres understood her sarcasm. The mounting weather was worrisome to Deryn. And it was irritating that when she asked for weather, Keres denied her, claiming she hadn't the power to pull together rain; yet she had enough energy to show her anger through the weather. Deryn's pocket wiggled. She glanced down at her long jacket, but Keres spoke again.

"She disappeared," Keres said.

"Who?"

"Don't play coy with me. You were supposed to bring the girl to me. And you can't even find her, can you? All your animals have failed," Keres said.

"How is that my fault?" Deryn asked.

"Because you were right over them!"

"What? When?"

"In the willow forest. You could have had the girl, but she slipped past you," Keres said.

"No, only Gian …"

Keres hissed her words which sounded like a file scratching along bone. "You know the magic that elephant holds. How stupid could you be? You're tampering with my plans, sister."

"I'm afraid I have to disagree with you. I'm not tampering. I'm outright destroying your plans. I don't want this girl to meet you anyway," Deryn said.

The receiver went silent for so long that Deryn thought her sister had hung up.

Keres laughed. "It's a moot point anyway. My daughter is on her way to me."

"That's impossible. No one can get into Equilibrium," Deryn said.

"Shows how much you know about her. That's why she's important to me. She's much more powerful than the rest ever were," Keres said.

"What about her real mother?" Deryn asked. The question surprised both women.

Silence.

Deryn persisted. "Where is the girl's mother? What have you done to her?"

In a low, reluctant voice, Keres said, "She sits at home, awaiting word on her missing daughter."

"You didn't take her mother?" Deryn asked.

"Oh, for five cents, Deryn, you think the worst of me. Don't you?" Keres asked.

"You only want to meet this girl, nothing else?"

"Why is it any concern of yours?" Keres asked.

"Because the girl disrupted my animals and ruined the mines. Now my workhorses are missing because your tantrum ruined my gate."

"That's a small price to pay. I had to give Grentsth a power-up from my magic to convince her to collect my daughter. She would never work otherwise," Keres said.

"That's not my problem," Deryn said.

Her pocket wiggled again.

"Make it your problem," Keres snapped.

"Why should I?" Deryn asked.

"Because soon it will be just you and I."

"What do you mean, it will only be us?" Deryn asked.

She glanced at the window, which was closed. Her pocket moved again, but there was no breeze from outside. Keres demanded her attention through the phone.

"I mean, once I get out of here, I'm going to drain all the magic from The Otherly. Then we can return to Earth. That is if you're with me," Keres said.

"But to take the energy from The Otherly, why, you'd have to kill every creature."

Keres made a passive sound like "meh".

Deryn stood frozen. "You can't kill everyone."

"Why not?"

"What is it you need that girl for?" Deryn asked.

Keres ended the call.

Deryn's pocket wiggled again. She remembered the dandelion she had stuffed in her pocket. She opened the fold and found herself looking in the face of a miniature Memegwaan with flower petals encircling his face.

She gasped and tipped the pocket inside out. The creature was only a few inches tall but ran fast as a cheetah, growing with each step. The Memegwaan slid under the door to make his escape. Deryn bolted for the door and whipped it open. Toll's face filled in the door frame, a daft smile on his face.

Hello, Madame, he sent.

"Toll!"

Madame, please, use the send. You know I don't understand words. Move!

Did you want that creature? I can stomp on him for you, Toll sent.

The horse turned slowly. Deryn squeezed past him, cursing his stupidity, but the Memegwaan was already gone.

Deryn sent angrily, *Wilds save you, Toll, for my wrath will be absolute for you!*

CHAPTER 17

Luci directed the hand glider as best she could as it rushed along the ground. It lifted, she felt the rush of wind, but it crashed back to the ground. This cycle went on several times. Luci ran, holding the glider high in the air. The trees grew closer, threatening to impale her if she failed.

Luci imagined it was a cliff she had to conquer. She ran and leaped into the air. A swift gust lifted her over the treetops, and she yelled excitedly. The hand glider went higher and higher.

Fear of heights was never an issue with a father like hers. Efra had forced her to conquer her fear of drowning. Now she was flying!

Luci soared high into the solid blue sky. There were still no clouds or an indication of the entrance to Equilibrium, and she wasn't sure where to look. A trapdoor, a seam in the sky. Or the door could be an upside-down waterfall for all she knew.

Her arms burned from the effort of holding on. In a desperate attempt to quickly find Equilibrium, she leaned back, making the hand glider climb higher. The wind picked up and whipped against her face. Her cheeks stung as if sunburnt, but there was still no sun.

A heavy black cloud flew past her face. It swung around her with a buzz. She realized it was a swarm of bumblebees. They flew up and stung the hand glider's sail.

The glider dipped from the insect's attack. Luci tried to outmanoeuvre the angry bees, but they seemed attached to her now. Every dip or turn she made, the swarm of bees pursued. They wanted her to crash into the ground. Luci was sure the buzzing swarm was Deryn's doing.

A single floating white cloud ahead held promise. Luci aimed for it. The buzzing anger pushed her towards treetops. She leaned back to fly higher and burst through a layer of white that wasn't there a moment before.

The stunned swarm of bees broke apart behind her. They weren't able to break through the layer of white cloud. Luci was free of their assault.

Then the hand glider bumped along the clouds, like a kayak running aground on a beach. Luci grabbed at the poles to slow her crash. They snapped. One splintered and morphed back into a rose thorn before falling through the cloud floor. Then another cut a large hole through the sail. Luci clenched her eyes shut. She felt the flying lifesaver break apart. The sounds were telling her she would fall to her death.

Then she was holding nothing. She readied for impact.

But it didn't come.

She wasn't even falling.

Luci opened her eyes to find herself sprawled on the ground surrounded by bright white. She squealed with excitement. This had to be Equilibrium. As the dark place held darkness in every corner, this was all consuming brightness.

The clouds were tight around her as if she were tucked into tight bedsheets. Luci crawled through the duvet. She wriggled through, like a caterpillar breaking free of his cocoon. Her feet pushed behind her. Her left foot accidentally cut through the clouds, dropping her leg dangerously.

Luci slid forward, away from the hole. She moved carefully to avoid her torso making the same mistake.

"Oh, wilds know I'll die today," Luci muttered.

The clouds seemed resistant, like the soft rubber walls of the dark place. Luci couldn't give up, not now. The crawl to get here felt safer than the dark place anyway.

Finally, she pushed clouds apart and slithered into a tiny opening. She pulled her body out and found herself on solidified clouds. Luci stood, her legs shaky and her palms sweaty.

She was suddenly nervous, like on her first day of high school. The nerves took over, and suddenly she regretted coming here. Luci stepped gingerly along the misty floor. For Mom.

Clouds of every shape floated around. It was a nimbus, lenticular, and stratus storage room shaded celestial-blue, powdery-pink, mustard-yellow, and ashy-grey. She squeezed between the weather stacks.

A crumpled form sat ahead among tall shapeless clouds.

Her feet felt heavy. She forced one in front of the other.

"Keres?" Luci asked.

A head full of curly auburn hair lifted. The woman's face turned, revealing a slim jawline. She looked worn out, beaten to a dusty image of a woman.

"Yes," the woman said.

Keres stood. Her hair fell in sweeping curls to the cloud floor. A crown of gems flattened wisps of bangs around her emerald eyes.

Her jewel-sparkled lips parted when she said, "Hello, daughter."

CHAPTER 18

Luci tripped. Keres bolted forward to stop the girl's fall, but she crashed to the cloud floor. They both landed a short distance apart on their hands and knees. Luci awkwardly looked up to her supposed biological mother.

The tension was too much. The tightly wound rope in Luci's chest finally let go, causing her to burst out laughing, and Keres chuckled too. This close, Luci noticed her white gown made of glistening jewels. Keres stood, jerkily wavering as if adjusted by puppet strings.

"I'm sorry for my sad state. I'm weary this day," the woman said. "I'm Keres Moreth, your real mother."

All the words Luci had planned to say fizzled out of her head. She said hello again and managed an awkward wave.

"You've had a long journey."

"I have," Luci said.

Keres lifted her hand from between folds of her silk dress and held it out. "I've waited so long for this moment."

Luci forced a smile. But she didn't take the hand. Instead, she stood of her own accord. Tiny wisps of cloud floated up between the two. The woman standing in front of Luci was as beautiful as she had hoped. But Luci solely fixed her mind on finding her Ruth.

Luci rubbed the back of her neck. "I, er, have been waiting too."

It felt out of place to ask Keres right away. She settled with small talk. The woman's face slowly came back to life. A breath of energy pulsed into her cheekbones. Luci quickly checked to make sure her hair wasn't floating in Equilibrium. The curly strands lay elegantly, same as Keres.

Small clouds crawled up Keres's dress, like kittens asking for a petting. Keres lifted her hand, and the sun showed its face, calming the clouds back to settle on the floor. Luci stood awkwardly with her hands folded behind her back. She didn't know what to do with them.

"I never saw the sun in The Otherly," Luci said.

"It's a lot of energy to direct a star," Keres said. She put her hand back into the folds of her dress.

The moon hid behind a cloud, like a scorned child in a time out. Then a rainbow crept up to them, bending and arching as it walked.

"Do you, uh, control them?" Luci asked.

"Yes, and all the weather in The Otherly."

"What about Earth?"

"Mother Nature keeps tabs on Earth," Keres said. She pulled up a fainting couch, shaded grey at the edges. She sat and patted the cushion next to her. "My child, please. Would you come to sit?"

Luci sat on the opposite end. She noticed dazzling crystal bracelets on Keres's wrists and large gem rings on every finger. The woman smiled, but Luci had a funny thought that there might be clouds stuffed in Keres's cheeks to hold them up.

The question of her mother's whereabouts sat on the tip of her tongue. But manners told her it wasn't appropriate yet.

"This place is amazing," Luci said.

Keres laughed. It brought some light to the space they shared. "Not sure about amazing. It's a lot of work. And often lonely. We have much to talk about," she said.

Luci sighed. There was no more small talk to be had, so she asked it. "I was hoping you knew where my other mother went? Her name is Ruth, you see and, well, I've been searching …"

Silence for a long moment, then Keres said, "Of course."

The woman bent to the cloud floor and twirled a finger. The clouds spun like old-style film on a spool, and a clearing opened. Luci leaned forward to see but moved away from Keres when she ran a cold finger down the girl's cheek. It was a foreign touch, not like her mother's warm hugs.

Luci pulled Keres's hand down into an awkward handshake. "Can we start like this?"

Keres laughed. Butterfly-shaped clouds flew around. She clasped both Luci's hands and caught the girl's gaze. "We can start however you'd like. I am happy to see you in person finally." She let go of Luci's hands and motioned to the cloud viewer. "Now, look. See, your Ruth is safe."

The image distorted, but Luci could see buildings, roads, and cars after a few seconds. A sight meant for a skyscraper. Luci knelt on the clouds to look closer.

"I don't see her," she said.

"That's strange."

Keres knelt across from Luci. She waved her hand. Inside the view, an ocean swam by, then the beachside Luci knew so well.

The picture zoomed in and landed on the oceanfront family home. Her mother stood on the balcony with a cup of coffee and her hair pulled into an elegant bun as if she were ready for work. She looked over the ocean. Not a crinkle of worry on her face.

Luci gasped.

She watched as her mother downed the last of her coffee and turned back into the home. The camera followed her expertly. She strolled to the table and opened the bag they'd used to gather trinkets. Her mother examined the shells, rocks, and driftwood they had collected only two days before the Liard trip that changed the girl's life. How long ago was that?

Luci's voice was no more than a breath. "She's fine?"

"Safe, unscathed," Keres added and brushed that lone hair out of Luci's face.

Her mother arranged the trinkets on the table, undoubtedly planning how to build the tiny fairy homes after work that night. Then she would sell them at the farmer's market. As if nothing had happened? She appeared utterly unharmed by her daughter's disappearance! Luci's eyes flushed with tears. She didn't want to cry, but oh, it hurt.

Luci stumbled backwards. Her foot ripped a hole in the clouds, and her leg crashed through. She didn't care anymore if she fell through, but Keres grabbed her hand and pulled her upright.

"You have to be careful. Only certain people can walk in Equilibrium," Keres said. She directed Luci back to the fainting couch. "You were born with magic, but it's young and unfounded due to your years on Earth. Now that you've returned, I can teach you how to pull up more energy. To use your magic."

Luci swallowed over and over again, trying to force away the tears that threatened to spill. Finally, she choked on the sob that crawled up her throat. Luci couldn't breathe for several long seconds. She desperately wanted to hide her face in the clouds to bawl. Her mother was at home safe, which was excellent, but she didn't seem to care Luci wasn't there, which was horrible. Gut-wrenching badness.

"Of course, it will take time," Keres said.

She didn't seem to notice Luci's burden.

Luci looked at the woman. "Does she know where I am?"

"Who? Ruth? No."

"Why is she not looking for me?"

Keres sat on the couch. She adjusted her silks over her legs and sat like a queen with perfect posture, perfect hair, perfect smile. "Only she could answer that," she said.

"How can she look happy?" The words fell from her mouth, which pulled the sobs free. Luci cried. She no longer cared. Her mother at home, not searching with posters and police, bruised her heart profoundly. Keres wrapped her arms around Luci. Still cold, her flesh was what Luci would imagine a dead man's embrace would be. Yet, she cried heavily on Keres's shoulder.

She pulled her head back and wiped her bubbly snot with both hands. Keres handed her slivers of cloud-made Kleenex. "Thanks," Luci mumbled. Then she composed herself, inhaling a long, jerky breath.

Luci thought about how she was supposedly adopted. Maybe Ruth regretted the decision. "Does she not care that I'm gone?" Luci asked.

Keres face shifted. "She did look for you," she said as if she had to force the words out.

"She did?"

"Yes, but, you see, you've been gone for many months."

Luci's jaw dropped. Time poured from her like a pulsing artery spilling out. "Months?"

"Time in The Otherly is far different than Earth. We live in separated esotericism."

"Eso, what?" Luci asked.

"Esotericism. A different plane of existence from what you've known. The planes contain humans, animals, monsters and plants; the magic we use in The Otherly is pulled simply from our beings. You're lucky to be one of us. To witness what is the ultimate plane of existence," Keres said.

"Do you mean I'm not human?" Luci asked.

"My child, you're shaped and created in the form of a human as I was once human. But not in the same sense you were used to on Earth. As I mentioned, there is much to learn. Your Ruth is your past now. Ahead of you is a whole world opening up. You just need to be taught," Keres said.

"If I'm not human, what am I?"

"You're an Otherian. Mother Nature brought my sister and me here to sustain The Otherly so that one day our plane of existence could aid others," Keres said.

"Who do you need to help?" Luci asked.

"People, animals, plants, life in every form. Even the ones invisible to the human eye."

"People can come here?" Luci asked.

She imagined her mother watching with pride as Luci swam in Efra's Lake.

"Not yet. There isn't enough magic to allow humans into The Otherly. One day, maybe," Keres said.

Luci wanted to ask Keres what the name of the dark place was. But her mind rushed fast with thoughts, worries, and ideas that the question pushed out just as quickly.

"Why didn't my mom ever tell me I was adopted?" Luci asked.

"She was put under a spell, of sorts."

"Does she know about The Otherly?"

"No. It was a normal pregnancy for Ruth. I simply imbued the infant with your being. You became Luci." Keres said.

"Then I am her daughter."

Keres frowned. "In a sense."

Luci stood. "Keres, am I Ruth's daughter or not? You're hiding something. I can feel it." She paced. "Why is no one giving me straight answers?" Luci asked.

"It's a lot for anyone to take in. Please, sit and take your time processing this and ask me anything," Keres said.

Luci remained standing. "What does this all mean?"

"I can fix everything now for you," Keres said.

"You can send me home?" Luci asked.

"This is your home. Destiny brought you here."

"No, Grentsth brought me here."

"If not then and there, it would have been somewhere else. Your sixteenth birth year beckons you back to The Otherly. It's all part of the balance," Keres said.

Luci huffed. "What kind of balance is that?"

"You felt it, though, didn't you? A tightening in your chest, pulling you to where you belong?"

"What if I don't want to stay here?" Luci asked.

Keres shrugged, "You know where the door is."

That wasn't the answer Luci wanted to hear. In some deep part of her being, she wanted Keres to want her to stay as much as she thought her mother wanted her home. And the tightness in her chest was still there. She kicked at the clouds. She couldn't think of a good answer. Finally, she said, "Oh."

"Are you ready to return the missing daughter to Ruth?" Keres asked.

Luci's head rattled involuntarily, trying to remove the smear of confusion. The remarks from Keres felt like a wet-towel slap on her face. But she supposed her mother, Ruth, should have closure as to her disappearance. And Luci still desperately wanted to return to her everyday life. She wanted to go back to school. She wanted to show pictures of Liard Hot Springs to her friends. And her father. And brag to Lane about the adventurous trip.

Lane. Oh, how badly she wanted her little brother to braid her hair with a wide grin again.

Keres stood and raised her arms. The dress parted to reveal a solid suit of gems with a heavily jewelled belt. She fisted her hands, and the clouds parted. The couch shook apart until small tufts of cloud fell to the cloud floor.

A giant silver beam broke free of the floor. It grew ten, twenty feet in the air, then split in the middle and crashed into two scales. The tambourine discs clanged loudly, ferociously tipping back and forth before settling into balance.

"What is that?" Luci asked.

Chains snapped out of the clouds. One chain attached from the sun to a scale through a steel loop then Keres clasped in her left hand. The moon connected to the right. Keres clapped her hands, and the scales banged.

"Are you ready?" she asked. Her eyes glowed, and her hair lifted into the air with energy.

Luci wanted to run, but she froze in place. "Ready for what? Keres, I don't like this."

"You'll like the result," Keres said.

She formed a triangle with her hands and pushed it towards Luci. It hit her in the chest, and she collapsed against the fainting couch.

Heat. On Luci's skin, under her skin, tearing through her skin.

The world tipped, breaking the clouds open. Luci broke away from her body.

The girl sitting on the couch screamed as she splintered into two people.

She felt her body slip. She felt the rope in her chest uncoil.

Then she was falling, but remained sitting on the couch. The rope tethered the two together. She watched in horror as her body dropped to the ground below, discarded like an empty crab shell. Was this an out-of-body experience? Then suddenly, the connection snapped, and her body down below stood, unscathed from the fall. The girl glanced up at the clouds with her now blonde hair and blue eyes, then walked through a doorway that suddenly appeared. She was gone.

But the girl still sat on the couch in the clouds. And she felt like a dream jolted her awake.

"Who is that?" she asked.

"That's Luci. She's gone home now. Ruth will be very pleased," Keres said.

"Is this a daymare?"

Keres swiped her hand through the clouds and pulled up a glass bubble that spun to a mirror.

The girl looked at the face in the mirror and screamed. It wasn't her face.

"No, my child, it is not a daymare. Those are over now that you've returned home. Your name is Justyce Moreth, and this is your real face," Keres said.

Justyce screamed at the auburn curls and freckle-free face. Keres pressed her cheek against the girl's rosy cheek.

"Near identical, daughter."

CHAPTER 19

Justyce waved her hand in front of her face. The fingers followed her commands. Her hair was the dark brown she'd envied on supermodels, but it wasn't her. She missed her red curls immediately. Her facial structure was broader, eyebrows bushy. The two moles that had been on her cheek were gone. Only one remained, and now it sat beside her left eyebrow.

"Your name is Justyce. My child, you were merely stored in the shell of Luci. You've returned," Keres said.

"I think I'm hallucinating."

"No, you're not. Didn't you always want a mother that looked like you?" Keres asked.

Justyce pinched and pulled at her new face. She moved the flesh along her cheekbones, trying to find herself underneath.

Then, drawing a line down her nose, she noticed it was smaller. This wasn't her nose. But an exact duplicate of Keres's nose. She dropped her eyes, no longer able to look in the mirror.

"My daymares were from being trapped in another's body?"

"I suppose. I saw you react, but whatever it was, was invisible to me. I always wondered, though, how deeply The Otherly connected with you. I guess it pulled visions from your true self, hidden in the shell of Luci." Keres said. She smiled, which unnerved Justyce. "That just proves how much you belong here."

Justyce couldn't have mustered a smile even if she'd wanted to. And she didn't want to. Instead, evil thoughts crept into her mind.

Justyce thought of the dark place. Suddenly she wanted to hurt Keres, "What's the dark place called?"

"We don't talk about that."

"Why not?" Justyce asked.

"Because I said so."

Maybe she would have been better off staying with Chamier.

"I watched you ever since you were born. Waiting for you to turn sixteen so you could return to me," Keres said.

Justyce felt heavy as the information sunk in. Raised by a mother that wasn't her own, having taken over another's body to suffocate their soul? "Why did I have to go to Earth until I turned sixteen?" Justyce asked. "Did you not want me? Why would you keep this from me until now? In those sixteen years, you never tried to find me to set everything right? What of that blonde girl? Is she a characterless soul now?"

"Babies aren't allowed in The Otherly. They have to be raised on Earth to learn how to be human. Compassion, love, humility. To know their roots of humanity." Keres looked away, "As I mentioned, I was never allowed to leave Equilibrium, which meant I had to watch you grow from afar. And I cannot speak of the other girl. Her body was a shell to protect you. The others seemed to have fared well enough."

"Others? There are others? Did you have more children?" Justyce asked.

"Yes, four boys and six girls."

"Where are they? In The Otherly?"

Keres patted Justyce's hand. "They grew and left this place."

"So, I can leave?" Justyce asked.

Keres shrugged. "I already said yes."

But Justyce didn't know where she would go. Her mother, Ruth, would no longer recognize her. The mirror sat against the fainting couch. Justyce purposely kept her eyes away from her reflection. Instead, she walked circles around Equilibrium. "I don't know how to comprehend all this."

Keres sat on the couch and smoothed her dress. "It's a lot to absorb. I understand you must be overwhelmed," she said.

Justyce felt more than overwhelmed. She stared at the moon as it hopped around, wanting time to shine in the sky. "Why did you not let the sun show in The Otherly?"

"Being Keeper of Equilibrium is a blessing, but also a curse. Rain is good for fields but disastrous if too much falls. Wind can help seeds fly around and destroy a robin's nest. I have to pick and choose the weather I allow to affect The Otherly. Sometimes it is easier for the sun never to rise and never show its face. The clouds can stay fluffy and risk-free. It's easier for The Otherly and me." Keres shrugged. "Everything requires balance. If I shine the sun too long, the grasses need rain to cool down. If too much rain, then they need more sun. Then the moon closes flowers for evening sleep, which causes bees to go hungry and die. It's easier to maintain a steady hum of nothing," Keres said.

Justyce considered all the animals that prefer night. She thought of how food would be scarce if there were no rain. Is that why she didn't encounter many animals? The most she'd seen were working at the mines. "That's cruel," she said.

"Did you know, every minute, one billion tons of rain falls to

Earth? That's a lot of power. I like to keep it simple. For example, for a cubic mile, that fog I created was less than a gallon of water. Much easier than a torrential downpour, don't you think? Compare that to, say, the air around a lightning bolt at 30,000 degrees Celsius. I don't have that much energy anymore, you know?" Keres said.

Justyce's jaw hung open. "The fog you ... created?" She sputtered. "The fog that caused the car accident where I lost my mother?"

"No, I'm your mother."

"You're a monster!"

"I'm not offended that easily, daughter. I shouldn't even be shocked by your confidence. I mean, you did choose the angry bear over the eagle," Keres said.

"You watched me the whole time?" Justyce asked.

The unanswered question hung above them. Justyce dug her toes in a cloud, but when a solo piece of hair fell into her eye again, she felt an impulse to pull her hair out and shriek. But that wouldn't change the truth. She felt it now, the relief in her chest, in her soul. There was nothing she could do about the past. She was who she was—Justyce, daughter of Keres. But to hear that that woman had sat up here watching made her disgusted.

"None of that matters anymore because now you're here with me," Keres said.

Justyce clenched her teeth. "I almost died. Several times."

"I cannot affect The Otherly or the beings on it, just move weather. I've known your face since you were born. And I'm sorry you almost fell during your trials, but I watched you grow stronger when you survived and overcame your fear," Keres said.

Justyce wasn't sure if it was agony or arrogance in Keres's voice. She dug her toes deeper into the clouds and tore a hole. This time she stepped over the hole like it was second nature.

"Careful, my child."

Justyce examined Keres's face. She didn't like how perfect her face appeared. How precise all her answers were. Did Justyce have a father? Assuming Brent wasn't her father, and that meant Lane wasn't her brother. She sighed. Was it even appropriate to ask?

Justyce threw away manners. She wanted all the answers. "Do I have a father?"

"Yes, your father is the king of the Memegwaans."

"Where is he?" Justyce asked.

"In The Otherly, somewhere deep. I can't always see everyone from Equilibrium, not if they want to stay hidden," Keres said.

"Why does he want to stay hidden?" Justyce asked.

"Maybe you can tell me if you find him one day."

"What exactly is Equilibrium?"

"A place meant to hold a balance between The Otherly and the dark place. The scales behind me bring energy that I use to create balance in our world," Keres said.

The scales banged in response to being mentioned. Their music was like an Inuit throat song.

"What's the dark place called?"

Keres rose from the couch, a harsh tone in her voice. "We don't speak its name."

"Why?"

"The better question might be, why did Deryn send you there?" Keres said.

"Pardon?"

"She's friends with Ashier, you know. Deryn sent you to Chamier's iron room, hoping you would end up chained there."

Keres pulled clouds up and spun them into two glasses of milk. She held one out to offer Justyce. The girl hesitated, then accepted it but stared at the drink.

"That woman is evil," Justyce said. Then took a sip of the milk.

"She is your aunt. My little sister, left on the streets with me. That was Deryn Moreth."

Justyce spat the liquid out and dropped the glass. It shattered, then reabsorbed back into the cloud floor and left no mess.

"That woman is your sister?"

"Unfortunately."

"Keres—"

"Please, call me Mother," Keres said.

Justyce lightened her tone but refused to repeat the word. "I want to go back to Earth. My family might not recognize me, but I still want to be with them. My brother needs to practice his hairstyles on me. I have much I want to accomplish still. I'm not sure I can call this place home," Justyce said.

Keres made her voice sickly sweet. "And you will return to Earth, but don't you want to stay with me for a little bit longer? Learn more?"

Justyce felt uneasy. A crinkle showed in Keres's perfect face as if it were just a mask.

Keres pulled a plate of cookies from the clouds, but Justyce waved the offer away. She stared at the view of her home. They sat and listened to the notes of the scales.

"Do you want to know more about the scales?" Keres asked.

Justyce could tell that Keres wanted to continue talking, but the girl wanted to wallow in her new woes. Her family would never know her again as their daughter.

"Yes." Justyce tried to keep the bite out of her voice.

"It is the most intricate piece of machinery you would ever encounter in The Otherly. The scales move depending on who is affected. I have to watch and balance every movement below. I don't get the freedom to leave, or at least not anymore. It's not just the sun and moon. It's everything from The Otherly gate to the ends of our world. Any animal death affects the scales, tipping slightly, pulling energy from me. I can use it to create and move weather. And I can use it to pull energy from other places," Keres said. The last word seemed forced.

"Neat," Justyce said.

"Look, I apologize for my wrongdoing. I shouldn't have caused that fog. But it was inevitable for you to arrive, one way or another. I am graciously happy you're here with me now," Keres said.

She crossed her arms and fumbled with her sleeve.

"When did you become jaded as a keeper?" Justyce asked.

"Part of the reason humans can't come to The Otherly is their emotions."

"What's the other reason?" Justyce asked.

Keres removed her hands from her sleeves to pull clouds into piles. They formed miniature people that walked in lines like soldiers. "Humans have only raw energy in them. They need help converting this to magic."

"Did you make the billboard?" Justyce asked.

"Yes."

findjustyce.ca. Keres walked over and placed a hand on the girl's shoulder.

"You need to rest," she said.

Justyce felt dizzy suddenly. Too much information? Awareness hurt, but Keres's hand on her shoulder seemed to do the opposite of Zavian's healing touch. "Yeah," she said with a yawn.

Justyce followed Keres silently as she led her down a cloud-made hallway. Every wall, ceiling, and floor had a slight bounce. Justyce had a fun thought that she could bounce around the room like the walls were all trampolines. But Keres's grip tightened. She felt both emotionally and physically tired.

Keres opened a pink-hued cloud door that exposed an equally pink cloud room with a pink cloud bed. Like a padded room. At least now Justyce knew she wasn't crazy. The daymares were her birth home beckoning. But the sight of a pink room was like a kick to her confidence. Keres offered the information that she slept only every few years. For a couple of days, she would snore. Justyce hardly listened.

Keres said goodnight with a motherly smile and closed the door without waiting for a response from Justyce. The clouds dimmed to grey around the room.

Justyce lay on the bed, suddenly very antsy. Ruth had always tucked her in, even once she became a teen. She sighed and pulled the cloud blanket over her tired body; it was like the top layer in a bubble bath but with no comfort. Instead, she stared at the ceiling as her mind raced.

Thoughts crashed over Justyce, threatening to drown her as she tried to sleep, but she couldn't even bring herself to close her eyes.

She climbed out of bed and tried to swipe clouds away. It didn't work. She frowned at the clouds. Wasn't she supposed to have this power too?

Justyce flopped back on the bed, but it was as if the bed sunk into the clouds beneath her. The grey of the surrounding room slipped to darkness that stunk of ash. She slammed her eyes closed. And the dark place pulled her in.

CHAPTER 20

Justyce crawled through the black sheen like it was a chore. She was happy for the distraction and, at this point, didn't care what Chamier wanted to do to her. This body didn't feel like her own anyway. She smelled the ashy coal, and it stung her throat. She crawled for what felt like forever.

Justyce crashed through a weak spot that tore open and dropped her onto the hard tile. Her knees stung from the impact. But the real shock was when she realized she had landed in a metal cage. She gulped hard. At least it wasn't an iron bed, but nearly as bad.

Chamier, in human form, stood on the opposite side of the bars with her arms crossed, tapping her toe.

"What's with the cage?" Justyce asked.

"It's to be sure you don't release any more of my food," Chamier said.

"These are people," Justyce growled.

She grabbed onto the bars and tested the strength she already knew they had.

Chamier laughed. "You're right, but also wrong. Point out how many still resemble people."

"Are you going to lock me up in a bed now too? Keres might have something to say about that." Justyce said.

"I'm not strong enough for that. Besides, you already know how to escape," Chamier said.

Justyce looked behind her to the black wall. A slight sparkle winked at her.

"This cage is for both our protection."

Chamier smirked.

"Then why did you bring me back here?"

"I told you, I have information for you. But you left so quickly last time," Chamier said. She strolled around to the other side of the small cage, running her fingers along the bars—*ting, ting, ting*. Moans grew from the iron beds. The single bulb that had shattered was now fixed, and it swayed in the distance, giving Justyce a glimpse through the soggy darkness.

"You tried to kill me last time," Justyce said.

"I didn't realize who you were. I knew you smelled different. You have two mothers, aren't you lucky," Chamier said.

"I don't know if I would call it lucky," Justyce said.

"Then let's just call that attempted killing a little game. How else am I supposed to bond with my sister?"

Justyce gasped, "Sister?"

Chamier winked, then stuck her tongue out like a child. Her tongue had lumps along the edges that looked like fleshy teeth. Justyce jolted back and collided into the bars on the opposite side of the cage.

Justyce shook her head. She was sure the comment was a trick. "Your mind trap won't work on me."

Chamier shrugged. "I passed all my trials, like you. But I refused to control Equilibrium the way Mommy dearest wanted me to."

Justyce felt dizzy again. "This can't be true."

"Why not?" Chamier asked.

"You're lying to me."

Chamier slammed her face against the bars. The impact caused her eyes to protrude, and Justyce thought she saw spider legs emerge from the edges like black blood veins. "Has Keres asked you to take the chains yet?"

Justyce shook her head. "No, why? She only wants to get to know me."

Chamier walked the other way around the cage. This time she aggressively ran her elbow along the bars, which caused the moans to louden. "Is that what she told you?"

"Did she do this to you? Is that why you carry such hate?" Justyce asked.

"More than that, she shackled me down here with the seal of O—" Chamier tripped over her word, "this place. That woman steals my energy. Don't get me wrong, this place has grown on me, but still, it's like Stockholm syndrome," Chamier said. She looked Justyce straight in the eyes. "I remember learning about that at school, falling in love with your captor. Now, whether my captor is this place or Mother dearest, I don't know. One thing I do know is that you're a prisoner too."

The statement was a punch to her guts.

"I assure you, I'm not a prisoner," she said to both Chamier and herself, but hardly believed it. "Why do I need this information? I already decided Keres is nasty. She admitted that she caused the car accident where I lost my mother," Justyce said. Her voice fell. "My Ruth."

Chamier continued dramatically as if the girl hadn't spoken at all. "She drags on the chains of our tie whenever she needs more magic. But it's never enough."

"Free these people, and I'll help you, Chamier," Justyce said.

"But I want your head on a tray."

Justyce stepped back.

Chamier laughed, throwing her arms in the air dramatically. "How scared you are of me! I love it! Not yet, don't worry, girl."

Justyce grabbed the bars, triggered. "I told you, my name isn't 'girl.'"

"Sorry, yes, dear Luci. I apologize," she said sarcastically.

"That's not right either. It's Justyce."

That stopped Chamier's flashy show.

"Is that all you wanted to tell me?" Justyce asked.

"Mother won't let you leave."

Justyce clawed at the blackness through the cage, trying to open a seam. "Chamier, I need to get back to Earth."

"That's a wonderful idea. I support that decision."

"Besides, Keres already told me I could leave, what makes you think differently?"

Chamier avoided the question. "Deryn keeps magic seeds in her home. There are only a few remaining after the creation of The Otherly. Keres used one to change me, then to chain me. You will need one to stop Keres," she said.

Chamier stepped back from the cage. Her pale face dissolved slowly into the dark gloom with each step.

"Why do I need to stop Keres? She's only trying to get to know me."

"Just one seed. Then I will release everyone. Like you asked."

Justyce hung her head and spoke to herself. "I never wanted any of this. I have this urge to go home still. But now it's not my home."

It's Luci's home, she thought.

"No, because home doesn't truly live where your heart is. It's where your responsibility lies." Chamier said through the darkness.

"Why did you try to kill me?" Justyce demanded.

From the darkness, Chamier's voice carried to Justyce. "I was just playing, but then you almost let my food escape. Which means I'll have to feel Keres's wrath. Get me the seed, or I'll take your head."

"Chamier!" Justyce yelled. "Chamier, I can help you, but I need to know the name of this place."

Her voice was a croak. "Obscura."

CHAPTER 21

Justyce crawled out of Obscura, after the cage and Chamier dissipated into darkness. She pulled herself towards the cloudy light. Chamier had irritated her, talking about killing her and then flaunting that she could trap her. How was she supposed to trust any of her words? Justyce felt a small win now that she knew the name of the dark place. But what was she supposed to do with the name? How would she stop more people from being trapped in there? How were humans pulled in if they couldn't come to The Otherly?

Justyce emerged in Equilibrium beside the pink bed. She lay down, wondering if she could navigate those Obscura squeezeways at will and not end up trapped by Chamier.

When she had counted three hundred sheep and traced her

eyes along each cloud outline, she turned her attention to her arms. They had the same slim muscular curve, but they felt different. Electric. They looked olive-coloured. She leaned over the bed and tried to open a cloud view again. This time, the clouds swirled and obeyed for a moment, then flattened. She rubbed her palms together as she'd seen Keres do, hoping for a mirror. As much as her new face and her new life scared her, she was curious. Either way, it didn't work. No mirror appeared.

She got up. Outside her room, Equilibrium was bright as day. Was it even night-time? The moon sat as a sliver on one bank of cloud, and the sun sat on the other. She turned down the hall and found herself standing nose to nose with Keres. *Was she standing there the whole time?* Luci wondered.

"Can't sleep?" Keres asked.

"No," Justyce said.

Keres rocked on her heels. "Sorry, I'm fresh out of sleeping potions."

Justyce blinked.

Then Keres added, "I'm joking. I can get warm milk. Or more cookies? Those are the choices."

Justyce smirked. She could go for a crabcake like Ruth would cook. "Could I, um, check on my mom?"

A bird chirped through the clouds.

"If that's not too much," Justyce persisted.

"Of course."

Keres turned and walked to the fainting couch. A nightstand had appeared next to it with a chessboard. "I thought maybe we could play a game as well. Before you go back to Earth," Keres said.

"Right," Justyce said.

What would it look like appearing on her mother's front step? Justyce wondered. Simply stating, "No, Mom, I am your daughter," even though she looked nothing like Luci.

Keres opened a cloud view on Justyce's home. *Luci's home*, she corrected her mind, and a lump formed in her throat.

The house was dark. They were all sleeping. Justyce sighed, and the clouds puffed up like dandelion seeds floating in a breeze.

"It's a lot," Keres said, "I get that."

"It's just. I don't know. How would I be able to hug my mother again? She won't ever look at me the same," Justyce said.

Keres put her arm around Justyce's shoulders. Her touch was less cold as if Justyce were warming up to her. Justyce wanted to ask for a mirror. She was sure that, somewhere in there, was the shy red-headed girl.

"How do you get food?" Justyce asked.

Keres chuckled, leaned back, smoothed her dress, and nestled in the clouds next to Justyce.

"The clouds give me everything I need. Birds used to visit more before Deryn poisoned their minds against me."

"And you could never find a way out? To come to see me? I mean, while I was growing up?" Justyce asked.

"I can't leave Equilibrium, not anymore. Mother Nature made it impossible. She used to give me passes, but she's grown cruel in her old age. Even if I found a way, tsunamis, earthquakes, and tornadoes are horrible scenes," Keres said.

"Where were you born?"

"Wolverhampton, England. August twenty-second, nineteen thirty-three."

"Wow, so you're," she paused for math, "eighty-eight years old?" Justyce asked. "But you look so perfect."

It was like Keres wore a mask of perfection.

"Eighty-nine in August."

Justyce tried to count on her fingers the difference. "How long in Earth time have I been here?"

"Eight years," Keres said nonchalantly.

"You said months!" Justyce snapped.

Keres shrugged. "I meant months in Otherly time. Four months to be precise. But if you were counting in Earth time, it's been eight years. Didn't want to scare you off right away. And besides, time passes no matter what or where you are. One way or another. You know, I still remember playing jacks with my little sister when we were kids. Then our whole family got sick, very sick. I got better, my sister got better, but our parents died from influenza. They left me in the streets with my little sister. I would have died too if Mother Nature hadn't arrived. She brought us here. She gave us jobs, made us keepers. But I still remember the jacks like it was yesterday," Keres said.

"I'm sorry you had a hard childhood. I had a good one, and I guess I should thank you for that in a way. But I do need to return. I've thought it over. There's no place in The Otherly for me," Justyce said.

"Very well."

"So, if you could just show me how to get out of here?" Justyce asked.

"Can I tell you a little bit of our history before we part ways?"

Justyce nodded and sat on the couch next to the woman, on the cushion farthest away.

Keres made hand symbols: hearts, circles, twirls, and bobs.

The clouds around Justyce's feet pulled up into magical white mountain peaks, ridges, and valleys. Between them dashed miniature cloud people. The girl reached out to touch one, but it skirted away like a scared rabbit. They were the height of her pinkie finger, if that. But their faces were detailed with smiles, moustaches, and bowler hats.

They pulled horses and chopped down trees, then seemingly changed their minds and left the trees to rot. The cloud people rounded up animals, butchered them, then took only a tiny amount of meat, leaving the rest to decompose and waste.

"Humans, on Earth, were greedy. A select few wanted refuge.

Those that wanted to escape the greed and wastefulness used ancient magic to split the world in half. And was it ever a show of magic."

The cloud people rushed into what looked like giant tree roots, a spinning ball of darkness above them.

"The ground quaked, and trees splintered as The Otherly split from Earth. One entrance, one exit. They soon realized they needed a gatekeeper to keep the unwanted, careless humans out. Grentsth was a beautiful geisha. They bought her with riches at the watering hole where she worked. But, instead of the promised jewels, they locked her in chains.

"The key to The Otherly was a seed of magic. They imbued it in Grentsth, the force of the magic, making her immortal but also broken forever. Her will to do anything was gone, and her memories shattered into a mirror-like cage. But they had their new world, and they were free from the greed of Earth's humans. They built colonies and grew strong. They began manufacturing their materials in The Otherly. But that took supplies that only came from wildlife. By wiping out forests and slaughtering whole herds of animals, the early humans of The Otherly duplicated everything they had tried to escape. Damning lakes to make hydropower ended with death, destruction, and greed. It was the cycle of Earth repeating itself. Finally, one particular man found a way to harness his inner energy as a magic source. He stole away in the middle of the night and practiced this magic deep in the woods. He hid and studied alchemy.

"In his cabin, he placed cuts of tree bark and animal fur into beakers. He added magic seeds and boiled the creations until he made a miniature man. So weak, this creature died inside the beaker, so he moved to pots and pans to create the wholesome and kind Memegwaans. Each new experiment made them larger and able to live longer. He became their king, and enjoyed many harvest moons with his new people. Then he dabbled with old magic. The type of magic that created The Otherly. He transferred his soul into a Memegwaan. Then he became immortal and the largest of the Memegwaans. Those people split and divided across the lands as per his instruction. To prevent any conflict, they live alone, mostly."

"What was his name?" Justyce asked.

She realized she'd turned to Keres and was intently listening now.

"When he was a man, it was Joshua Tabaiton. Then, as Memegwaan King, he became Baiton. He's your father," Keres said.

"Baiton," Justyce repeated.

"Each child that returns from Earth brings natural magic. For sixteen years, you collected energy from everything around you. The humans won't miss it. They don't even know how to harvest it."

"How do you harvest it?"

"In time, dear daughter, in time."

"When was Obscura created?" Justyce asked.

Keres's eyebrows lifted in surprise. The perfect mask twisted for a moment, and Justyce saw something she compared to Chamier. "You've learned the name of the dark place?"

"Yes," Justyce said. She bit her lip to stop saying more. Keres might be her biological mother, but Justyce still felt uncertain about her. "Can you tell me about Obscura?"

"That's a story all in its own, one that I don't like to touch on. But it was created for evil to be removed and stored. It's like Earth's gallows." Keres shrugged as if all those people meant nothing. "It grew on its own, filling the dark corners between our plane and Earth. That dark place became a blanket world that can pull evil from The Otherly or Earth, but that takes immense magic," she said.

"OK, so if Obscura is touching Earth and The Otherly, what

was the in-between place? The sun was there. It was the first time I saw the sun in months. So, what was that in-between place called?" Justyce asked.

"I know not of an in-between world," Keres said.

"Then I don't even know where I went," Justyce said.

"You are very powerful, although you may not feel it yet."

"Hmm."

"The Otherly is meant to be a safe place. You can say anything here."

Justyce snorted and said with a thick layer of sarcasm, "It's not very safe at all. I nearly died several times."

"I'm sorry for those situations. They were difficult for me to watch."

"Can I see Zavian? Last I saw, he was a flower stuffed into Deryn's pocket."

Keres chuckled but stopped when Justyce glared. She spun her finger to create a cloud view filled with Zavian's face.

Justyce felt relieved. "He's a Memegwaan again!"

Zavian's eye sockets were neon pink. The cloud view zoomed out to show the ferret on his head protected by a green army helmet. His ears poked out and wiggled, listening to someone speaking. Keres twisted her hand, pulling the camera out further. A group of animals stood with similar helmets. A pile of crooked spears sat among them.

"Oh, for five cents, why are the mine animals with Zavian?" Keres growled.

"At least he's safe. I was worried," Justyce said.

The hippopotamus from the mine was there with a concerned look and a frantically swishing tail. Flies buzzed around with rose thorns in their mouths like little weapons.

Keres frowned. Black lines burst from the corners of her eyes and bled down her cheeks. They weren't tears but threads of evil breaking free from underneath the mask of perfection she wore. Justyce was scared. She scrambled to her feet.

"I guess the time has come sooner than I expected," Keres said.

"Time for what?" Justyce asked.

"For a hug with your mother," Keres said.

Justyce backed away, but Keres leaned over and wrapped her arms around Justyce. The girl struggled to get out of the instant tightness around her chest. The words whispered in her ear were indiscernible. She wasn't even sure if they were a language.

An invisible force violently pushed the air out of her lungs. She breathed a syllable and shot forward from the pain. She tried to cry out, but her chest squeezed tighter.

Millions of gems lifted off Keres and smashed into Justyce's body.

The chains shot from Keres's sleeves and clasped shut on Justyce's wrists. Keres stretched as if cramped for too long, and more gems melted off her body and slithered to Justyce. Every jewel was a secret shackle.

Justyce's eyes were blind with terror. Immensely powerful restraints sealed over every inch of her body, chains disguised as jewels.

She gasped, forcing air into her lungs. "What is this?" she asked.

"My child, you're a perfect choice. The others, why, they were always weak," Keres said. She twirled around, ecstatic with the new freedom from the chains.

"Keres! What's happening?"

"They failed or got stolen from me. But by the good grace of you, I'm free!"

"Keres!" Justyce shrieked.

Heavy shackles dropped from Keres's dress and snapped around Justyce's throat and waist. They yanked her upright, forcing her to watch Keres's joyful dance. Once the chains were in place, they transformed back to sparkling crystals.

Keres placed a hand on the girl's chest and pulled a misty thread from between her ribs.

"And thank you for this."

Justyce collapsed. The weight of the chains was suddenly excruciatingly heavy.

Keres turned to leave. She held up her hands and laughed. "Finally."

"Keres," Justyce whispered, "help me."

Keres waved her off and said, "Now you control the weather."

"Don't do this."

Keres kicked away the cloud, looking for something. "You'll figure it out pretty quick."

Keres bent over and slithered into the clouds like a snake.

Justyce heard an animalistic wail. It took long minutes to recognize the tortured cry had come from her own throat.

CHAPTER 22

Hours passed. Or days. Justyce lay on the ground. She wore an elegant gown of entrapment. She was doomed to hold the balance, here in the clouds of Equilibrium—Justyce and eternity.

The chains were heavy on her limbs, but she didn't need to move. The chains would only allow her to move so far anyway. Was this her reward?

Diamonds of deceit reflected the moon that sat on the cloud horizon. The rock in the sky watched her sorrow. Justyce rolled away. The scales tipped, causing the sun to spring up and burn her face. She didn't care. She stared at the sun, asking the wilds for the star to take her sight, just like her mother always said it would if she stared long enough. Would this be more bearable if she were blind?

She swiped clouds away, trying to open a view. Instead, they lifted, then filled the small hole, like mashed potatoes with too much milk.

Justyce thought she heard shouts below and wondered if animals were burning up from the heat. She rolled back over and let both arms rest on the cloud floor at equal levels. The sun bowed out and left the sky as bland as she was used to seeing it.

Justyce felt more than fooled. She felt devastated, but she still couldn't let anything happen to the animals on the surface of The Otherly. Her entrapment wasn't their fault.

The sun slowly perked up again, too hot.

Justyce collected herself to stand and glared at the scales. They continued to tip to the left. She pulled her right hand high, and the scales balanced. The sun dipped back into the clouds. The moon jumped up, happily smiling. She lowered her hand only once all the blood drained. The sun shot back, hotter this time, forcing Justyce to resign herself to work and lift her right hand to balance. Again, the moon shone completely and spectacularly. The girl dropped both arms to her sides, and the wind gusted below.

"How am I supposed to make it balance?" Justyce asked.

No one answered.

She lifted both hands slowly and meticulously. Both stones disappeared back to their beds. The wind died down, and it was silent beneath the clouds. She plopped down on her bum, and a train sounded below.

There are no trains in The Otherly! She jumped up, and the sun pulled blisters from her cheeks.

Resigned to Keres's decision, Justyce adjusted her positioning between lifting an arm, bending a knee, raising a pinkie finger, and turning her nose until she found a strange posture that at least held the scales balanced, and she heard no extreme weather below.

With her left foot, she kicked the clouds until a view appeared. It showed a bright blueberry night sky with several thousand twinkling stars.

The moon smiled at Justyce. She forced a smile back. Birds burst into song, and she heard an elk bugle into the night, telling all the animals this land was his home.

Home.

Justyce wasn't going home. She dropped her chin which caused a bang of thunder beneath. She lifted her chin. "Cool, calm, collected," she chanted to herself.

She heard something, like a humming, that seemed out of place. Justyce turned to listen, causing the scales to bang. The sun shot up. Justyce threw her hands in frustration and walked away to find the sound. Below, the sun and moon both sat happily in the sky. *At least it's not a blizzard*, Justyce thought.

That sound again, like a mouse squeak. But words, maybe? She wasn't sure. Was it someone below? She kicked the clouds away, and they obeyed by opening a comprehensive view this time. Justyce grinned. She searched for something close. She only saw the two sky rocks hitting each other with rays in an epic battle.

Efra's lake got assaulted by massive waves from the unsettled gravity pull. She smiled on the inside, knowing that Efra would have no problem getting more building supplies now. Hordes of animals ran under the moonlight, then the sunlight. They basked in both.

She shrugged. It was OK for now.

Then she heard the murmur again. Words whispered in her mind, a send but a different frequency. She closed her eyes and focused.

Tell us what you need, was the send.

So distant.

Who is this? Justyce sent.

Atop the mountains surrounding the mines was a mass of Cattywampus vines. They tangled together, wavering to the sky. *A risky affair,* Justyce thought.

What else does someone chained want but a key? Justyce sent.

The vines closed into a box, then uncoiled and tangled again. When they opened, they held a golden key. The egotistical eagle from the labyrinth swooped by and plucked it from the vines.

The scream from Justyce's mouth surprised her and caused a burst of hail that shattered the tower of vines.

"No!"

A white bird with flesh dripping off his ribs swooped into view. Justyce clawed at the clouds to keep the picture. Red-stained talons attacked the eagle and snatched the key. Was he from Obscura?

He flew towards Equilibrium.

She stood, shocked and wide-eyed, as the Obscura bird came straight for her. Chamier, helping her? She felt confused, grateful but confused. The bird threw the key straight up into the clouds. It landed with a clang.

Too far from her.

Her heart collapsed. "Oh, wilds curse me."

The scales banged as the sun wanted to return without the moon. She felt the pull of the chain. She looked back at the sun. "What?" she snarled.

Keres had mentioned wanting to leave, but she never said the chains stopped her. But, of course, that could have been her hiding facts.

Justyce glanced over to the moon. It seemed to shake its face in a giggly double-chin way. She jerked her left arm over her chest and the moon spun. The dark side grinned. She clapped her hands together, and it skipped to block out the sun. It was an eclipse!

Justyce looked at the gems, which had no light, moon or sun, to sparkle. She ran, and it worked! The chains had disappeared for a moment. She snatched the key from the cloud floor and ran back to the scales. Doing quick work, she unlocked all the shackles attached to the scale tower.

The gems dropped off her arms and legs. Her chest felt lighter. She twirled the opposite direction, and the moon spun, showing his face, then sunk back into the clouds. He seemed satisfied. The sun settled, and the scales sat still.

How long it would last, Justyce couldn't guess. She fled past the fainting couch that was starting to dissipate on its own without Keres's magic holding it together.

She looked up, and with her whole heart, she sent, *Mother Nature, I need to leave. I have unfinished business.*

A clock appeared. It showed the numbers 24:11:05. She wasn't sure what it meant, but she took it as acceptance of her request. Then she ran for the exit.

CHAPTER 23

*H*ome, she thought and ran. *Mom.* She ran harder. She didn't care that Ruth wasn't her biological mother. Ruth was the only mother she wanted. Justyce's heart said if she showed up, a teenager with no home, a house would be offered as shelter. That's how big her mother's heart was. The rebuke of Mother Nature might be less severe once she was back on Earth.

Justyce skidded to the approximate spot where Keres had broken free. On hands and knees, she kicked and clawed at the clouds. She didn't dare look back at what she assumed was a clock. It was harder now to break through the cloud floor, which closed every opening she created. She shouted at the clouds to part, then saw a tear form, like a torn photograph. She jammed both hands through the jagged edges. They made a ripping sound as she pulled the clouds apart. Finally, she crawled to freedom.

Then she was falling. But slowly, as if in a dream.

Justyce hit the ground, and that felt nothing like a dream. The landing hurt. Justyce did a mental check, and it appeared every bone remained solid. She was sore when she peeled herself off the ground but managed to force her body into action. Her head overtook her and spun viciously. Justyce panicked. Did she have a concussion? She didn't have time for this. She had to get to Zavian's cabin and get through the door to Earth.

The forest tipped, threatening a mouthful of dirt if she fell. Sounds of an approaching stampede snapped Justyce out of the overwhelming dizziness. The ground shook. Justyce was in a forest she didn't recognize. She dashed behind a large fallen tree where bugs were chewing through the stump. She hunkered down to hide.

Wolf tracks were all around her in the mud. She hoped the sounds weren't wolves closing in on her.

The ground stopped shaking, and Justyce peaked over the tree. She saw a pack of wolves—no, more than that, it was several packs of wolves.

As she feared, one wolf twitched his nose and turned in her direction. He was massive, with black, green, orange, and blue fur that looked tie-dyed. He put his ears back and stalked straight towards the log Justyce hid behind.

I know you're there, he sent.

Justyce picked up a large rock.

There's no point in staying hidden. I can smell the human on you.

The wolf snarled as he stalked closer, snapping twigs with heavy paws. Justyce slithered away from the log to ready herself. She could throw the rock at his head when he came around the termite eaten log if there was enough room. Then she would run off and climb a tall tree.

Good plan, she thought, as long as he was the only one coming to check her out. Justyce knew she was losing valuable time.

The wolf's nose came around the edge of the log. Then his face appeared, and he lunged. Justyce threw the rock and watched in dismay as it missed. She turned to run, but he pounced on her back. Justyce screamed. She was shocked to realize no claws ripped her flesh open. Instead, the wolf pinned her down with the pads of his feet. Other wolves barked when they came to see the commotion.

I knew I smelled human, the first wolf sent.

Justyce squirmed under his weight. *I am not human. I was born of The Otherly*, she sent.

You stink of human, don't play coy with me, the wolf sent.

I once was human, but I am no longer!

Fancy dramatics. Do tell.

My whole world got ripped from me, but what's it to you? Justyce sent.

She struggled under his weight to get oxygen. Of all the ways she thought she'd die in The Otherly, a wolf crushing her was not one of them.

You have plenty of human left in you. I smell it, and it smells, hmmm, delicious, the wolf sent. He stuffed his nose against her shirt and inhaled deeply. *But, wait, you smell like the one Deryn wants.*

She's trying to kill me, Justyce sent.

She clawed at the dirt, trying to get traction.

He snarled. Justyce felt saliva drip on her neck.

Maybe I'll steal the pleasure from her, he sent.

Wilds, save me, Justyce sent.

She pushed energy behind the send and heard wolves whine in response.

She has keeper energy, a different wolf sent.

Pish. She's just a human girl. One that will gain me an Otherly seed, he sent, then lifted her with a mouthful of her shirt. Justyce hung from his jaws like a pup when the wolf took off to a run.

I need an Otherly seed as well! Maybe I can get it for you, she sent.
I don't trust human words.
I told you, I'm not human, Justyce sent. Her brain whirled around what to do. Then she remembered, *I'm Keeper of Equilibrium.*
Impossible.
It's true, Justyce sent.
Then why are you on the ground? the wolf sent.
Drool wet her shirt, but she was grateful it wasn't her blood.
I'm trying to get to Zavian's cabin, Justyce sent.
What's a Zavian?
He's a Memegwaan.
Mmmm, sounds yummy too, the wolf sent.
Either way, what would Mother Nature think if you sent the Keeper of Equilibrium to her death? Justyce sent.
The wolf slowed. *Prove it.*
Justyce lifted her hand. Nothing happened. The sky stayed a cool blue, telling Justyce the scales were perfectly balanced. She clapped her hands, and the wolf laughed in her head.
I knew it, another human trick, the wolf sent.
Justyce's cheeks heated. The one chance she had to save herself, and she couldn't even prove something as grand as being the director of the weather! What a useless task. Anger scorched her chest and produced lightning which snapped a foot away. The wolf yelped, released Justyce, and backed away.
He bowed to her. *You are a keeper.*
Justyce stood and brushed the twigs off her capris and smirked. *I told you.*
I'm so sorry. How can I help you?
Take me to the cabin.
Which way is it? the wolf sent.
Justyce walked right up to the wolf, no longer afraid. The weather was now her defence.
He gave me these clothes. His scent will be on them.

CHAPTER 24

Justyce held onto the wolf by the scruff as he ran. She was grateful for not being in his mouth any longer. Then, finally, she saw Zavian's cabin.

There it is, she sent.

And you won't tell Mother Nature about our, um, disagreement? the wolf sent.

No. Justyce climbed off his back and thanked him.

What's your name, keeper? he sent.

Justyce.

I'm Dragor, lovely to meet you. I hope for more snowy days, he sent.

His lips peeled back and made crescents at the edges. Justyce smiled when she realized Dragor was smiling at her.

I, she hesitated, *still need to learn.*

What she didn't say was "best of luck to the next keeper".

She waved her thanks to Dragor and took the steps two at a time. The front door swung open with the vine's help. They patted her on the shoulder, welcoming her back. She called for Zavian but found the house sat empty.

She walked straight to the room with the staircase. Her eyes caught on the newly constructed bookshelf. So, this is what the Cattywampus vines had been building. Justyce was mesmerized by the recently created whole-wall shelf, complete with Zavian's rock statues off the floor and in their new home on the shelf. There were leather-bound novels, recipe books, and atlases. The writing on the spines stared back at her wide eyes. She touched each book as she read the titles.

Herbs and Magic.
Journey to the Centre of Nothing.
Magic and Gardening.
Jarring for Dummies.
It's a Vine Life, Cattywampus.

Justyce pulled the last off the shelf. She cracked the book open to the middle and smelled that old book scent, basking in the aroma.

She read.

"While Cattywampus vines feel your aura, it's expected they will only aid the kindest souls. Evildoers can demand, string, and force vines, but they will not respond. The Otherly seeds instilled energy into vines. They breathe and cry as Memegwaans would. But they speak in a different frequency. Only enlightened, moral souls will hear the vine's voices."

Justyce heard a noise in front of the cabin. She placed the book back in its place and went to the front door. She quickly jumped off the steps and crouched when she saw all the wolves had followed. She couldn't see Dragor. They growled with high hackles at their prey in the centre of the pack.

She yelled an empty threat. "Go away, or I'll bring a tsunami down on your den."

The wolves turned as one to bare their teeth. Justyce felt the send among them, but the wolves didn't share. It was a secret send.

She kicked the wolves back as she ran into the centre, trying to keep them from attacking whatever hid there. What was she doing? The sane part of her mind told her it was a reckless move. She'd only just escaped a wolf. She assumed the new bold side was the keeper.

They backed away without a fight. Justyce squealed when she saw Zavian crouched in the centre. She ran and threw her arms around him.

"Oh wilds, I thought I'd never see you again." Her eyes welled with tears. Then joyful emotion spilt over her cheeks, and she squeezed the Memegwaan.

A smaller wolf stepped forward. Her fur was milk-white with a black line down her nose. *We were only having fun with the guy*, she sent.

Is that what you call fun? Does he think it's fun? Or only you think it's fun? Because then it's called bullying, Justyce sent.

She scowled, and black clouds drew overhead.

I told you the keeper was on the ground, one wolf sent.

The wolves barked and scattered like ants under a boot upon its descent.

"Is it safe now?" Zavian yelled.

Dozens of animals stepped out from the tree line. They wore armour and carried wooden spears with raspberry thorns as the spikes. Justyce faintly wondered what the time on the clock said now. Then an image appeared in front of her eyes as if she'd held a photo up—17:03:01. What are they, hours? Minutes?

Memegwaans marched out from behind the animals. They carried bows with arrows and had all sorts of creature hats. Justyce started to ask Zavian, but he was quicker to question.

"Are you OK?" he asked.

"Are you? I thought you were about to be wolf kibble."

The ferret wiggled his nose in a greeting.

"Didn't they smell my fear? Don't predators feed on the weak?" Zavian asked.

"You're not weak at all. Thinking of your kindness is what got me through The Otherly. There's so much I want to tell you," Justyce said.

A wave of relief came over her. Then a surge of anger. Before Justyce could control it, thunder and lightning crashed overhead. Animals charged through the cabin door for cover. Others darted to the trees. But the Memegwaans stood their ground like the ancient soldiers they were.

"You deceived me," she growled. "You lied."

Lightning clipped a tree in half. Zavian glanced to the sky, undisturbed by her accusation, then met her glare.

"Is this you?" he asked innocently.

Her words stung even her ears as she snapped, "Yes, it is. Keres didn't want to meet me. She never cared that I was her blood." Her tone wavered now. "She only wanted an out. So, she put the responsibility," then Luci choked, "of Equilibrium on me."

"She did what?"

"She said some words I didn't understand. Then the chains snapped off her wrists and locked onto me instead."

His voice was calm, "How would I know?"

The thunderstorm overhead dissipated. Justyce deflated. The vines responded like a long-lost family to Zavian, which was reason enough to trust his word. She hung her head, ashamed she had snapped at him. Keres deceived him as well.

Zavian took Justyce's hands in his own and stared into her eyes. The black faded to a crystalline blue. Then blossomed to a rose red. "Would I intentionally mean you harm?"

Justyce shook her head. "No, I'm sorry, I know you wouldn't."

"Have you had a hard day?" he asked.

She smiled. She was so grateful for this man. "I have to leave, but I don't know for how long. Zavian, I need to go home. To Earth."

He nodded, and the red crackled to royal blue. "Can you forgive me, Miss Luci?" he asked.

"I already have, and the name's Justyce."

"Don't you look strong with that name? Is it Keeper Justyce then?"

She smiled and squeezed his hands. "I have to go now. Will you walk me to the Earth door?"

"Would that please you?"

Justyce said it would, very much. His eyes bloomed red again, and they turned, hand in hand, towards the cabin.

"Do you want to shower before you leave?" he asked.

"Are you saying I stink?" Justyce asked. She laughed, and it felt good.

The white wolf poked her head up from the side of the stairs. *The fight has begun.*

"What's going on?" Justyce asked.

Zavian dropped her hand. His eyes spun neon pink. "Isn't it war?"

CHAPTER 25

Deryn wrapped the camera strap around her neck. Then she jumped on Toll's back and pushed him to full speed.

Are we going to find my brothers? Toll sent

They know their way home, Deryn sent.

Do you want the dandelion man back?

He's long gone.

Where are we going then? Do you need another tracker? Toll sent.

We failed that quest my son, Deryn sent.

Can I have a snack break now, then?

Soon, Deryn sent.

Secretly, she wondered if any of them would have peace again.

She used magic to project her voice for all the forest animals to hear. *Keeper Keres plans to steal all The Otherly's magic. To do that, she will have to kill everyone. But we can stop her tyranny. No longer will she rule us with the weather. Please,* Deryn sent. Her hair shifted to a lion's mane. *Fight with me for The Otherly. Gather everyone you can, far and wide. And I promise something better for you all.*

Deryn caught a side glance from Toll. He didn't need to send anything, as she already felt his questions. Was Deryn planning to kill her sister?

She watched eagles spread their wings to fly overhead as ground animals stampeded through the forest. Fire ants funnelled into lines.

Good, she thought. She would use any method possible to stop her sister. She had to protect the animals.

They, too, had seen friends and loved ones sent to Obscura to fuel Keres's magic. But, in contrast, the tough love Deryn used was to keep order, not do damage like her sister thrived on.

Toll slowed down. Deryn realized she hadn't been paying attention. A wall of animals lay ahead made of screaming monkeys and giraffes ready to charge. In front was one particularly angry hippopotamus.

Potamus, I apologize for the destruction of the mines, Deryn sent.

She climbed off Toll and knelt to show her regret. The thousand-pound beast took a step towards her.

He heatedly snarled at Deryn. *You've risked enough animals for that human girl.*

My motive is no longer about the human, Deryn sent.

The monkeys flung vines over Toll while screeching.

I don't trust you. I think you're tricking us into having everyone look for the girl, Potamus sent.

Keres is threatening an attack. She says she'll slaughter everyone and everything in The Otherly, Deryn sent. She crawled through the mud to her old friend.

I no longer believe your lies, Deryn, Keeper of Animals, he sent with venom. *So a new keeper has to be named.*

The request stung the heart she hadn't realized still existed. *If that's what you want, I will give my title away, but now is not the time.*

Madame, no! Toll sent.

The monkeys pulled down on the vines, forcing Toll to the ground. He grunted but continued his plea to Deryn. *We need your strength. Don't step down.*

What you did at the mines is beyond reconciling. Now is the time, Potamus sent.

The wolf pup was dying. I ended her misery. My heart aches for that too, Deryn sent.

Potamus stomped the ground, making Deryn crash into the mud. *I don't think your heart aches for anyone,* he sent.

No, you are right. I did shut down for a long time. When Keres changed you, it broke me to know the suffering you endured, Deryn sent.

She turned her face up to look at Potamus. He had always been a good friend, her once human nephew.

I'm sorry for what happened to you, Deryn sent.

Your words strung together are meaningless. I no longer mourn my animal form. Now, name a new keeper, Potamus sent.

The giraffes looked to Potamus with a secret send.

A scream emanated from the distance. Deryn knew who it came from. The monkeys dropped their vines in fear and shimmied up the trees. Potamus didn't seem to have heard the scream as he stomped to Deryn.

Deryn began, *do you—*

Another scream cut Deryn's send short. A few monkeys fell dead from the trees. Potamus looked back to his giraffe friends when a third scream killed them too.

Deryn reached up to warn him. She could smell her sister's greed approaching. Keres was using powerful magic to wipe the animals out quickly.

A shimmer of white appeared between the trees. Potamus turned and met Deryn's eyes. *Run*, he sent.

She felt conflicted. She couldn't leave Potamus to face Keres, but she had all the animals in The Otherly to protect. So, she jumped on Toll, and they ran. Deryn didn't look back.

CHAPTER 26

Deryn let Toll run without direction. What was she to do?
Why are the animals so angry, Madame? He sent.
Maybe I haven't been the best keeper, Deryn sent.

A rustle in the giant raspberries ahead made Toll slow. George and Boll jumped out, their noses stained red from snacking.

My sons, Deryn sent.

She smiled, not expecting to be so happy to see them. She allowed the three a moment of frolicking before she directed them to move with her.

They crashed through the next layer of bushes and ran straight into Gian Kaur.

The massive elephant was stomping raspberry bushes into spears. Hedgehogs collected the material and shuffled them to the next set of animals in the production line. Black bear cubs sat in a circle, wrapping vines around the branches to hold palm-sized thorns to make the weapons.

Gian's grey skin crawled with fresh magic. She was stronger being away from the labyrinth. Stick figures danced a war march over her wrinkled flesh as she worked at building morning stars and swords

"Deryn Moreth, how wondrous to see you," Gian said sarcastically.

Her tattoos shifted into hordes of stick figure elephants trampling a withering stick woman. Deryn rolled her eyes. She didn't understand the apprehension. Aside from Potamus, a scorned nephew transformed by Keres, this elephant was the only other animal in the lands that turned a nose at Deryn. Although she guessed, she could now add the wolves to that list.

Deryn suddenly wished she had time to contemplate these feelings. What had brought them up? Every creature in The Otherly would lose their life soon if Deryn didn't save them. That was her job. But there seemed to be something nagging behind the motive.

"And you," Deryn said courteously.

"It's too bad we meet during a war and not a celebration," Gian said.

"A celebration?"

The gem between Gian's eyes sparkled. Deryn shook her head, as she had no time for Gian's half-speaks. She knew what the elephant wanted but now was not the time.

"I see you have some hardy weapons," Deryn said as she jumped off Toll and bent to examine the spears. "I'm not sure they are strong enough."

She waved her hand over the twigs, and they turned to steel.

"Hmm," Gian said.

Her wide brown eyes blinked, but she said no more.

"Keres has escaped Equilibrium. She is already on her war march. I see no army behind her, but it is only a matter of time before she pulls the Obscurians up," Deryn said.

She looked back. Grateful the trees stood silent. The clouds boiled angrily in the sky. Deryn cocked an eyebrow and asked, "Who's controlling the weather?"

Gian shrugged. "The human girl you were looking for."

Deryn snapped her attention back to Gian. "You've seen her?"

A scream behind Deryn made her turn in time to see the same girl run, snatch a weapon from the bears' pile, and leap in the air.

CHAPTER 27

Justyce had heard the voices talking. She had just spoken to Gian in the raspberry bushes and had turned to go back to the cabin. She'd said her goodbye to the mighty elephant and was ready to leave.

When she was nearly back at the door, she recognized Deryn's voice. Saying nothing to Zavian, she turned and ran back. This woman had tried to kill her a few times, kidnapped Zavian the dandelion, and now threatened Gian? Justyce's fury at Keres, The Otherly, and Obscura all funnelled towards Deryn at that moment.

The raspberry bushes ripped gashes into her legs when she crashed through them. The animals sitting around building weapons all looked up with bewilderment. Deryn seemed to care the least, as she looked last. Justyce snatched a club from the pile and swung it at Deryn's head. It was a little low but still connected with her ribcage. The woman grunted, and Justyce jumped to make another attack.

Deryn caught Justyce by the wrist and hit her with a magic blow that felt like a truck tire to her guts, making her collapse. All her muscles turned to jelly. When Justyce lifted her arms, she screamed.

"You turned me into an octopus! Undo this now," Justyce said.

Deryn bent to pluck the weapon from Justyce's tentacle.

"You still have so much to learn," Deryn said.

Justyce spat ink at the woman. "Teaching is the last thing I want from you."

Deryn offered her hand to help the girl stand. "You want my blood spilt? Then get in line."

Justyce smacked the hand away with a floppy appendage. "You tried to kill me, and now you want to help? And why do you have my camera?"

Deryn genuinely looked shocked. What an actress, Justyce thought. But Deryn removed the camera from around her neck and placed it between them.

"No, I was trying to stop you from meeting Keres. I tried to prevent this from happening," she said and waved her hands around exasperatedly. "She's tried to make many take the position of Keeper of Equilibrium before. It always ended in disaster. Mother Nature imbued the keeper's magic within her. So the only way out was to put her responsibility on a child."

"How do I know you're telling the truth?"

Zavian poked his head out from the bushes. "Haven't I walked many of those children up the steps to Earth?"

Justyce looked at him, then back to Deryn.

"The lucky ones made it to stand in front of Keres to be

judged. She had a heart and sent them back to Earth, unscathed most of the time. There was always a chance she would be spiteful. If the children failed the trials, Keres sent them to Obscura. I always tried to intervene as early as possible when someone arrived. But every time was a risk. Sometimes it didn't work out as expected," Deryn said, her eyes dropping to her feet.

"I thought," Justyce started, then trailed off. She didn't know what to think anymore. Deryn swiped her hand again, and the girl's arms and legs reappeared. Deryn slumped to the ground.

Justyce stood. She didn't want to hurt anyone. Maybe she could just send Deryn to Obscura? She believed in the jail system. But then that would be condemning more souls to Chamier's torture.

"Alright, well, to begin with, my name is Justyce. You have one minute to explain everything, and then I'm leaving," she said with the calmest tone she could muster.

"I should properly introduce myself too," Deryn spoke carefully but genuinely in her tone. "My name is Deryn Moreth. I am your aunt."

"I already know this. Get to the good part."

"What's the part you want to know?"

"Why did you send a shark to kill me?" Justyce said.

Deryn laughed. "No, no, I was trying to chase you out of The Otherly. Scare you away, that's all. If he accidentally swallowed you, then he would have come straight to me. I never wanted to harm you, only turn you back to Earth."

"Grentsth said I couldn't leave without the trials."

"There is some truth to that, but there are other ways to get out," Deryn said.

She motioned to the ground.

"Obscura?"

Deryn nodded. "I never wanted any of this to happen. My sister became corrupt with power early on. Mother Nature no longer allowed her passes from Equilibrium, as she would come down, entice the Memegwaan king, birth a baby, and keep them in a cloud cage to grow to sixteen. It wasn't very kind. I don't know how we ever came from the same loving parents. Wilds rest their souls. I only wanted to scare you back to Earth."

"She told me that we had to go to Earth until we turned sixteen," Justyce said.

"That's partially true in that no one under sixteen is allowed in The Otherly. Keeping them locked up until their sixteenth birthday was no better. There were some she had integrated into human foetuses in the past."

Deryn's face resembled a creased page as if someone had viciously erased words. Her tightly clenched fists caused her finger tendons to pop up like starved spines.

Justyce wondered what Deryn was hiding. Justyce kept her eyes on the woman as she picked up her weapon. "I'll just hold on to this," she said. She also picked up her camera and placed it around her neck where it belonged.

"Yes, you'll need a weapon to fight."

Justyce glowered. "You can stay and allow Keres's evil to ruin you. I want no part. I'm going home."

She turned back to the cabin.

"This is your home," Deryn said.

"I want out of The Otherly. So, Mother Nature can deal with Keres and get her chained back in the clouds," Justyce said.

"Is that what your mother, Ruth, would want?" Deryn asked.

"Don't you dare bring her into this," Justyce said.

Clouds lit with electricity. They crackled with lightning which snapped along the treetops.

"Isn't being a keeper an immense responsibility?" Zavian asked.

Deryn held her gaze. "I want the same thing as you."

"How do you know what I want?" Justyce asked.

"Because I'm a keeper too. I can sense the like-minded. I don't want others to suffer."

"But you're cruel," Justyce said.

"No, I'm strict."

Justyce looked up to the clouds. A raindrop fell on her nose.

"I never wanted my sister to trap you, or anyone else for that matter, in Equilibrium. But that is her burden to carry." She looked to the sky. "She's almost succeeded in her plan."

"Almost?" Justyce asked.

"Now she intends to kill off all the creatures in The Otherly to absorb its magic. After that she wants to return to Earth with this magic. I couldn't even pretend to guess what she might want to do there. She's stronger already. I watched her wipe out some of my animals with a scream from afar. And quite possibly—" Deryn's voice dropped off. She wavered where she stood. After a long silence, Deryn continued, "You can go home now, avoid this whole fight. I will do my best to get a keeper in Equilibrium. That amount of magic might kill me, but then maybe I would have atoned for my wrongdoings."

"She stole magic from me as well," Justyce said. Then she remembered all the sad beings in Obscura. "I need an Otherly seed."

"I can manage that," Deryn said, "but be warned, at any time, Keres might find the strength to pull Chamier's chains from Obscura."

"Chamier's chains?" Justyce asked.

She thought she might have heard this term before.

"She holds them like a puppet master. Chamier cannot leave Obscura with Keres on the chains. If Keres needs Obscurians, she pulls on Chamier's chains, and the woman delivers the beasts. Chamier's bitterness created the chains. Like being addicted to sadness, she wallowed in the pain of others, and her own," Deryn said.

Justyce thought of the clock, and sure enough, it appeared in her mind—15:84:17. "Well, now it is me who might wallow in chains," Justyce said.

"Do you have to go back?" Zavian asked.

"Yes, I'm running out of time to get home," Justyce said.

Zavian blinked, his eyes green then royal blue. "Won't Earth always be there? What of The Otherly? Wouldn't Equilibrium crumble if The Otherly did too?"

Justyce looked at her palms. Freezing rain fell from the sky. She shook her arms out, and the clouds scattered. "I'm a prisoner, like Chamier. Unless I can get Keres back up there."

"We can't have Keres go back. She isn't what The Otherly needs. So I have to kill her," Deryn said.

Justyce allowed the woman's words to sink in for a long moment before replying, "Even with the horrible things Keres did, no one deserves death."

"You don't know enough of The Otherly to make these decisions," Deryn said.

She was right, Justyce knew, but something still felt wrong. The keeper's magic electrified the air around her. She looked to the ground, and the dirt bounced up, responding to her intensity.

"Go home," Deryn commanded. "I must stop Keres in any way I deem necessary to protect The Otherly." She turned to leave.

The puzzle-piece-marked horse lowered his head to the woman. Justyce heard his send.

Madame, please, that evil woman is strong. I can feel her energy from here. Don't go alone. I will take you.

A second horse, a Clydesdale, kicked at the grass then sent, *Madame, please listen to Toll. We don't want to lose you. Maybe he can help.*

My sons, this battle is too dangerous for you. Please, get the small animals out of here. Help where you can. Stay back from Keres and me. Deryn turned away.

Be safe, Madame, Toll sent.

Deryn turned back to the horses. *Maybe it is time you call me Mother. Everyone needs a mom at some point.*

The three horses looked at each other. Toll stepped forward.

Mother, Toll sent, *I want to stay to help you.*

Justyce felt his distress prickle through the air.

"Where's your army?" Justyce asked, looking around.

Gian trumpeted loudly, and a tribe of ruby-painted elephants crashed through the trees to their side. Potamus appeared in front of mountain lions and cougars. His head hung much lower than before. He looked desperately sad. Deryn ran to Potamus, hugged him deeply.

Justyce felt a wave of guilt when she saw the hippo. She walked over and lowered her face to meet his eyes.

Justyce of Equilibrium, he sent and bowed his head.

I'm sorry about your mine. And right now, it is simply Justyce of The Otherly, she sent.

I like it, he sent.

Deryn stood and looked at Justyce. "You know, there's an upside to a disaster."

"You mean like a silver lining?" Justyce asked.

She walked with Deryn and Zavian towards the pile of weapons.

"No, that fire was not silver," Deryn said.

"Ha, uh, I guess that one went over your head," Justyce said, smirking.

Zavian stopped midstride. "Do you need elbow space again?" he asked.

Justyce laughed. She couldn't leave. She didn't want to see these animals die or Zavian get hurt. Maybe Mother Nature would give her another pass in the future to return to Earth to see her mother. But, right now, The Otherly needed her to fight this battle. Then she could force Keres back into the sky.

Deryn's hair spiked like hedgehog quills. "I meant, now I know stibnite is explosive."

"I'll battle alongside all of you. Well, maybe not Deryn," Justyce said and shot a glare at the woman. "But with all of you, we will defeat Keres and get her back into the clouds where she belongs."

"No, we will destroy her. And you'll be the new keeper," Deryn said.

"I'm not sure I want to be the keeper."

"It's not like you have a home to go to now."

"That was mean," Justyce snapped.

Deryn cast her eyes to the ground. "I'm sorry. I think what I mean is, I may have an anger problem."

"Words are chosen, just as actions are," Justyce said.

Gian trumpeted. "That was very wise, young one."

Deryn nodded. "I know. I have some things to work on."

A flood of pygmy possums carrying explosives marched up behind the elephants.

"Nice to see you made good use of my stibnite," Deryn said.

I knew you enjoyed seeing my mine ruined, Potamus sent.

"No, I'm truthful. Maybe the fire in the mines wasn't all bad. We can rebuild your worksite and make it better, easier work. And the accidental fire showed us that crushed stibnite is explosive," Deryn said.

Justyce nodded. "It does add to our fighting power. Let's stop Keres before she uses Obscura. Then I can free those tortured souls."

"Is Justyce free?" Zavian asked.

She looked at her friend. She was surprised at how deep the question was to her. So Justyce sent a message to all animals that could accept it, *Let's make all of The Otherly free.*

CHAPTER 28

Justyce collected as many weapons as she could carry. Deryn asked her to call on the vines for protection. The girl beamed at the request. Shields dropped from the treetops into animals' grips, like worms to a hungry chick's open mouth.

Justyce heard drums beating on approach from Zavian's fields' other side. The raspberry bushes they had worked in were tall enough to conceal some of them. Other animals and Memegwaans hid, ready and crouched to fight in the forest.

Deryn sent the Clydesdale twins home to collect The Otherly seed. Toll argued they should stay to help, but Justyce agreed with Deryn for once. That magic power ball was critical.

A hawk sent, *Keres's flanks are herds of rock-formed horses. There are archers made of sticks strung together by magic. In the hundreds, they advance.* A sickness rose in Justyce's stomach, which caused a freezing rain cloud to rush over the area. Animals fell out of the trees from the slick branches. She called out sorry and steadied her emotions. *Clock*, she thought, and numbers appeared—07:59:01.

"Keep your emotions calm. We can't afford a setback by your anger," Deryn said.

Justyce turned and snapped, "Coming from the woman that has an anger-management problem."

Deryn dropped her eyes. Her hair slicked back into a tortoiseshell. "Maybe I do, maybe I do."

Arrows screamed through the air over the treetops.

"They're here," Justyce called.

Her knuckles were bloodless from clutching the shield and her sword. She was grateful it was steel now.

Deryn flew into the air and flung fireballs at the approaching arrows, making them disintegrate in the atmosphere. She swooped and rescued two hawks that nearly got impaled by a single arrow. Then she crashed hard into the ground, moaning, her magic spent.

Gian lifted Zavian onto her back. "Can we go fight?" he asked. Gian trumpeted and took off in a silent trot.

"Where's Keres?" Justyce asked anyone that would answer.

Animals scattered in every direction. Some were running towards the sounds, others away. A lone bear hobbled past with a shield on its back and a club in its mouth.

Where is Keres? Has anyone seen the front line? Justyce sent.

Keres is riding the skeleton horse. She pulls on her chains for Obscurians, the bear sent.

Justyce nodded her thanks. The bear trekked into the forest behind his fellow fighters. Trees cracked as Justyce watched the movement of the battle. Keres's first wave appeared: men made of gnarly sticks tied to stick horses with twine and stone men rattling around on stone horses. They all moved like puppets with too slack strings. The horses stumbled and tripped on their approach. Justyce swooped her hand and blew wind from the sky. Small woodland animals got blown away, but a dozen or so gnarly stick men went too. Justyce counted the hit as a win. The ground beneath her shook from the slaughter.

An arrow whistled past her head. The sky crackled but not from her emotions. Instead, Justyce looked up to see dozens of ravens carrying mice in their talons. The small rodents dropped bags of stibnite onto the stickmen, which exploded, and flames lit the sky.

An army of beasts from the mines marched past, led by Potamus. Justyce nodded to him. The animals funnelled by with vulgar howls, mean snarls, and threatening hisses. They marched through argent fields as the sky wavered between an obsidian brown and an apple-blossom pink.

Justyce chanted to herself, "Cool, calm, collected." Her footsteps matched the beat of her banging heart. "Wilds, keep us safe," she said.

A stone-formed horse skidded to a stop. The bowman pulled the string back with his arrow aimed right at Justyce's heart. She threw her body underneath, dragging her sword through the stones that built the horse's legs. He crumbled. The bowman fell to the ground next to Justyce. He swung his bow, which connected hard with her shoulder.

The Equilibrium scales tipped from her pained yelp allowing the sun to burst at an oven-cooking temperature above her head. Sweat dripped off her forehead. She held the shield up and swung the sword at the bowman's feet.

He jumped up to avoid the hit. Mid-air, he swivelled and landed on Justyce's shield. The weight pushed her into the dirt.

Justyce's adrenaline spiked, and a lightning bolt cracked through his body. Stones blew out in all directions. She bolted through several more waves of stick and stone warriors.

Justyce cringed at the devastation the battle created across The Otherly: broken trees, burning grasses, bleeding animals. She could no longer see Zavian or Gian. She'd left Deryn somewhere back in the fields, slowly recovering energy.

The hills grew in front of Justyce. At the top, soldiers catapulted boulders at the animals below.

Death lined the base of the hills. A Memegwaan, near his end, lay in the grass, desperately reaching for Justyce. She gave him her shield but had to continue to stop Keres. If she could find that woman, she could end all this.

At the base of the hills, Justyce ducked behind a mass of boulders to catch her breath. How could she end this battle without destroying the land? Any weather she pulled would injure her friends as well as Keres's army.

A scream from high in the sky tugged at Justyce's attention. She saw Deryn flying. It made her happy to see that Deryn had pulled together more energy. Even with Justyce's apprehensions, she knew she needed that woman to be a part of the fight.

Deryn flicked her arms, which collapsed waves of the enemy. Justyce saw Gian ahead on the hillside with Zavian still safely on her back. On the edge of the same hill stood a strange collection of boulders, a hastily made structure intended to be a barrier. And Justyce knew Keres would be coward enough to use that cover in a battle.

Justyce ran to the hill, but the heat from the sun was so intense she couldn't catch her breath. Anxiety crept up the back of her neck. She tried to pull cloud cover but felt the energy melting out. Animals fumbled to hide from the heat.

She lost control. Her heart beat erratically in her chest, and with each slam, the weather shifted dramatically between hail, freezing rain, and scorching sun rays. She tried to slow her emotions as she fought through stickmen, cutting them down with her sword. Rock horses faltered from the dramatic weather changes. Their rocks froze, cracked, and splintered.

Finally, she made it to the barrier.

Justyce lifted her sword as she crept around the corner, ready to attack.

Keres wasn't there.

Justyce heard crackling sounds like energy pulling from a plug that was about to burst into flames. She tried to slow her heart. Cool, calm, collected.

Justyce collapsed between two huge rocks and drank water that trickled into a stream.

It was warm.

She looked up to the sky but could no longer see where the sun shone. It was so bright, so hot. Keres's stickmen burst into flames from the heat. The rockmen marched on. Justyce needed a new plan. The heat was making her feel nauseous.

Justyce closed her eyes and concentrated on clear skies. She weaved her fingers together.

The heat dissipated from the air. It was easier to breathe now.

The wind picked up, and Justyce lifted her hands. She felt the rush of power through her. It pulled up from the ground like a comfy blanket wrapped around her shoulders. A growl. But she had no time for a distraction. She kept her eyes closed and pictured soft cooling raindrops.

A water droplet hit her nose.

The growl came again.

Justyce opened her eyes and unlocked her hands, swinging them out fast with energy.

A torpedo of wind rushed past her face, but did the trick of knocking back hordes of the rockmen. She felt warmth trickle down her face. Then saw blood. She had torn a layer of skin off her sunburnt face with the sudden gust. Droplets lifted in the air in front of her face. Justyce rained blood. But she still pushed the wind harder to clear the enemy that threatened her friends.

She lowered her hands, soaked in blood, and saw the hilltop was clean of soldiers.

"Good job," she said to herself.

A massive wolf knocked over the boulder where she stood.

"Dragor?" Justyce asked.

The wind blew dirt through the wolf's tie-dye-like hair, dirtying him and blinding Justyce. Her legs kicked against the loose soil on the hillside as she tried to run. She crashed instead.

The wolf exposed his teeth.

Dragor? It's me, Justyce.

Dragor leaped and sunk his teeth into her shoulder, causing her to holler. The clouds boomed into giant thunderheads, and there was a bang of lightning. Justyce pried Dragor's teeth out of her raw flesh, but a sharp tooth remained in her shoulder along with a bloody bite mark. She jerked it out and shakily stood.

Justyce held the sword in one hand and the serrated tooth in the other. *Don't make me do this*, she sent.

He leaped; Justyce collapsed.

CHAPTER 29

Dragor aimed for Justyce's throat. She eluded the bite, but his body smashed the sword out of her hand. She clambered for the blade. Dragor lunged again. This time, his teeth dug into her leg. A laugh interrupted her scream of pain.

It was Keres.

She sat on a skeleton horse, her hands, intertwined with colourful hair, making movements. Justyce glanced at Dragor and noticed missing patches of fur. Keres was controlling Dragor!

Justyce kicked at the snarling wolf who would chew her leg to hamburger if given a chance.

Dragor, she's controlling you. You're stronger than this.

A second wolf jumped on top of Dragor and dug its teeth

deep to stop him. Justyce took the opportunity to stand. Blood dripped down her leg.

The skeleton horse whinnied, and bones clattered. A pack of wolves circled the horse. Keres uncurled her fingers from the fur to keep her horse in position. Justyce noticed Dragor was himself again. He looked at her with sad eyes.

I didn't mean to, he sent.

Justyce didn't have time for apologies. She ran for Keres, but her run was slow and painful. It was a hobble that showed defeat. She refused to let her body quit or show weakness. She didn't care anymore if Keres killed her. She could at least stop this madness first.

Keres threw magic at the pack of wolves, breaking the group apart. More wolves appeared. Keres bellowed, but her shoulders sunk. Justyce realized the woman's energy must be dwindling. Keres flew in the air, away from the carnage.

Something wrapped around Justyce's waist as she attempted to run. It lifted her off the ground and placed her onto soft grey skin.

Justyce smiled and patted Gian. Her run was even slower, laboured. A trail of blood was left behind Gian, but it gave Justyce a chance to recover. She felt so weak. How does she pull energy up? She hadn't had time to learn how to use her magic. Justyce watched too much blood run down her leg and mix with Gian's blood. The elephant's trunk swiped a red tattoo off her leg and rolled it over Justyce's leg. Her leg felt instantly better—better than better. Gian tripped and stumbled to the ground.

Justyce's leg wounds were gone.

"Oh Gian," she began, but the elephant shushed her and climbed back to her feet.

Gian ran for the skeleton horse and crunched his body to dust with a swift kick and stomp. Then Gian swiped a giant rib bone off the ground and gave it to Justyce.

"A new shield," she said.

"Where's Zavian?" Justyce asked.

"He's fighting Ashier."

"Oh wilds," Justyce said.

Her heart dropped, and she only hoped that the bad Memegwaan wouldn't pull her friend into Obscura.

Obscura!

"Deryn!" Justyce yelled. "I need the seed now." She couldn't see her aunt but hoped the woman was close enough to hear.

Keres floated down closer to where Gian ran. "You won't get the seed. I'll send you back to Equilibrium before you touch that type of magic."

Keres lifted her arms, and chains burst from the clouds. They shot straight towards Justyce.

Justyce sent a secret request to Gian. The elephant steadied herself under Keres and lifted her enormous trunk for Justyce. The girl climbed up and reached towards Keres's foot. This woman had stolen her freedom.

Justyce threw her bone shield at Keres. Missed. The chains creaked closer from the sky.

"You were never much of an athlete, huh?" Keres asked.

Deryn flew in from the side, and Keres didn't notice.

The evil woman laughed, "I knew it—"

Then Deryn collided with Keres mid-air, and they fell. They hit the ground and tumbled past Justyce towards the giant hogweeds field.

Justyce ran. "I need her alive!"

Deryn threw punches that left tracers in the sky.

Zavian charged up the hillside, chased by a herd of white ponies with manes spiked high with blood paint. Obscura beasts. "Can't someone send help?" he yelled.

"Go help him," Justyce told Gian.

Then she jumped off the elephant's back and turned towards Keres. Justyce held her sword high and hid Dragor's tooth securely in her back pocket. Keres was on top of Deryn, throwing mighty punches, causing blood to spout from her aunt's mouth.

Justyce bolted down the hill to where they fought in a heap, Deryn now on top slamming Keres with her energy-formed spheres. Keres laughed. Justyce watched a failed magic attack drop from Deryn's hand. Her aunt was weakened.

Keres took the opportunity to catapult Deryn into a boulder. Deryn's head lolled to the side. Then she didn't move again.

Keres stood. Panting and bleeding, but still, she stood.

Toll appeared over the hill. His send was desperate, *Mother! Mother!*

Gian returned. She charged in front of Justyce and grabbed her with her heavy trunk. "Stop," Gian said, holding Justyce back from intervening.

Potamus bowled over the ponies.

Keres walked to Deryn and smashed her hands together. Then she pulled bright-red magic into her hands and smacked her hands down on Deryn's chest, causing her whole body to jolt. Deryn woke. She kicked Keres away.

Keres hollered, with a voice full of rage, "Sister."

An echo hit Justyce with power, even on the edge of the hill. Deryn could only open one eye. The other was swollen shut.

Keres slapped Deryn.

Justyce screamed and struggled to get free from Gian. "Let me go."

The elephant looked at the girl sadly and moved her trunk.

Justyce ploughed through rows of stickmen that stood between her and her family. She needed Keres alive. And, though it looked like Deryn was the one about to die, she wanted Deryn alive as well.

Justyce swatted the remaining Obscura ponies away with her sword, then ran towards Keres. Unfortunately, the blade caught the light of Keres's fireball smashing into Deryn's chest. Justyce screamed for Keres to stop. But, instead, she ignored the girl and pulled a thread of energy from Deryn's jolting body.

Keres glared at Justyce as she drew closer. She flicked her fingers, and Justyce got hit backwards as if a horse had kicked her. She flew back and landed in a heap.

Flames crept up the hill. Then the fire lifted into a perfect wall that locked all parties in a hell-circle with Keres.

Toll arrived at Justyce's side.

New keeper, he sent.

Justyce felt exhausted as she dragged her sword towards Keres.

Hey, new keeper, Toll sent again.

Justyce's eyes trained on her aunt.

"Keres, stop this insanity," Deryn moaned.

Her hair faded to grey, and her face sunk and wrinkled when Keres pulled another thread of magic from her torso.

The elephants trumpeted behind her on the other side of the firewall, a friendly reminder that she was not alone. The allies outside the ring of fire outnumbered Keres.

"You left me to rot in a cloudy hell," Keres yelled in her sister's face.

Deryn's lips moved, but Justyce couldn't hear her words. She was too far away, and wished Zavian was nearby. She was so tired. So weak.

Toll followed close behind Justyce. *New keeper*, he sent again.

Not now, Justyce sent.

Deryn's horses helplessly watched on the outside of the ring of fire. Stickmen parts lay on the ground. A few animals staggered around the field, but all eyes were trained on the two centre women.

Justyce knew as soon as the wall of fire came down, the animals would slaughter Keres. But Justyce wanted her put back in the sky. She almost thought *clock* but quickly sent it away so it wasn't an ask to Equilibrium. Time seemed unimportant right now.

Toll snorted behind Justyce.

Keres acted chaotically, flying up with a surge of magic then crashing down to scream into Deryn's face. She hollered of betrayal, and Justyce felt her pain. Someone wronged all three inside the fire circle for them to be in this position.

Justyce was close enough now to hear her aunt's voice.

"No, you closed those shackles on your wrists when you sent your children to Obscura. Death would have been a better option for them," Deryn said.

"This war is your fault. All this death. Look, dear sister, it's all your fault," Keres said.

Deryn's voice was weak. "It is your doing, only you."

Keres's voice cracked with emotion. "What else was I going to do? I had no one. You left me."

Keres flew over the ring of fire. Zavian had appeared, hunched over and bloody but alive. Keres ripped the ferret off his head. He screamed a blood-curdling howl. Keres crushed the animal with her hands, and Zavian collapsed to the ground, still.

Justyce cried out, "What have you done?"

Keres held her gaze for a moment, then turned back to Deryn.

"Time to finish the task at hand," she said. Then she flew over and grabbed Deryn by the hair. "I guess you won't be coming back to Earth with me after all."

"I'm sorry I didn't visit," Deryn breathed.

"What?" Keres said. She dropped the handful of hair.

New keeper, Toll sent.

Justyce shook her head. Fat tears rolled down her face as she stared at Zavian through the flames.

Toll kicked Justyce in the back of her thigh, which caused her to yelp and turn on him. He interrupted her cuss with a send.

You will need this, Toll sent, and spat an Otherly seed onto the ground.

It looked like a giant pearl. Justyce stared at the swirling object. The outer shell seemed separated from an inner layer, and they spun in opposite directions exposing many layers of magic.

Give it to Mother. It will heal her, Toll sent.

Justyce nodded. She gently picked up the seed and her sword. She crept along the blind side of Keres. She was so close now.

Deryn grasped at Keres, desperation painted on her face with blood. Keres shook free.

Justyce picked up into a sprint. Horror blossomed in her chest when Keres skated a hand laterally down her arm, producing a burning blade. She brought the edge down on Deryn.

"No!"

Justyce's arm stretched out, impossibly trying to reach the last distance.

The blade connected and cut deep into Deryn's leg. She was too weak to scream. Instead, her head dipped to the side, and blood dribbled from between her lips.

The world went silent for Justyce. She saw the wrinkles of stress crease Deryn's forehead, then release as she accepted fate.

Toll suddenly charged past Justyce with silent hooves. He slammed into Keres's side, pushing her through the dirt. Silence.

Then Keres sprang up and swung hard at Toll with the magical fire blade. It connected. He fell over, bleeding.

Justyce bolted at Keres.

The ground shook from some unseen cause. Justyce felt the heat of the fire grow dangerously close. A send from Deryn in her mind made Justyce look back at the woman who inched near death.

Keres yelled something.

Justyce saw the grey moth fly out between the boulders and over the firewall. He threw pebbles that exploded with grey ash.

She realized in horror that Ashier was attempting to force all the animals into Obscura. Justyce ran to Deryn.

"I'm sorry I doubted you. I thought Ashier was your ally," Justyce said through a muffle in her ears.

She couldn't hear Deryn's reply.

Deryn touched Justyce's ears, and the sounds of battle rushed back. Metal crashing, people crying, and animals howling between the crackles of fire and the rumbles of thunder Justyce caused by her unintentional emotional turmoil.

The moth morphed into Ashier mid-flight.

"How do I stop him?" Justyce asked.

Deryn's eyes rolled to the back of her head, and she went silent.

The ash spread on the ground, seeped into the dirt, and tore black seams into Obscura. Then a white hand emerged from one.

Justyce watched in amazement as Zavian pulled himself off the ground as if forced back from death when presented with the threat of Ashier. She commended his strength. But what was she to do? She held an Otherly seed, which she could use to save Deryn or destroy Keres. But she could also use it to close Obscura.

Zavian ran straight through the flames. He lunged at Ashier, knocking the bag of grey ash to the ground. At least he had stopped any more holes to Obscura from opening.

Deryn put her hand on Justyce's arm. She looked over, but Deryn didn't say anything.

"Come on! Put the flames out already!" Keres challenged.

Justyce shook her head. Anything that Keres wanted would not benefit The Otherly. She knew that now.

"Fine, I have to do everything myself, do I?" Keres asked.

She flew up and threw mighty wind over the flames, which doused them easily.

Keres landed near a black hole where Obscura creatures crawled out. They attacked. Keres knelt on the ground, yanking lengths of rusty chains out of the earth. Then Chamier's dusty face appeared. In the daylight, she looked weary. Depressed. Keres pulled a thread of energy from the woman, then kicked her back down the hole. The clang of iron beds echoed. Obscura beasts poured out by the hundreds.

CHAPTER 30

Chamier's scream drowned out the battle cries of the Obscura beasts. The battle intensified. Even the weak, twisted human forms staggered around, hitting and biting, the need to fight forced into their brittle bones. The holes in the ground pulsed with power as they controlled the beasts.

Lightning illuminated her surroundings. Justyce saw Toll crawl to his mother. Her face sunk as she stood and looked out over thousands of twisted Obscura forms. She had to stop this.

Zavian fought Ashier viciously by hurling himself over Ashier and knocking a hard blow to the evil Memegwaan's head. Ashier spun and elbowed Zavian. He retaliated by sticking his leg out and tripping Ashier. Justyce heard his arm snap. When Ashier stood, his arm had a wide U shape in the middle. Zavian seemed to be holding his own quite well, even without his ferret.

Thunder banged, and lightning crashed, closer to Justyce this time. Again, Gian's army charged at the cascading Obscura demons. Again, Justyce cringed from the sheer number of animals ploughed down by the Obscura army.

The Otherly was absolute mayhem. Is this what Keres wanted? Justyce thought about what it would mean for the animals if she did force Keres back into the sky. Maybe Justyce could be a better keeper. The idea sunk her heart but lifted her soul.

Another bolt of lightning hit a tree near the front of the Obscura army. The tree burst into bright orange flames. Justyce ripped a rain cloud over to douse the fire and help her allies attack the Obscurians. She could get used to this weather control.

Tabit, the bear, appeared, bowling through a collection of twitching white demons. He threw the creatures in every direction and away from the Otherians. He roared and seemed happy, hitting foes and not friends. His mighty strength cleared the field.

Justyce ran through the clearing. The fight was getting dangerously close to the scorched hogweed fields. She yelled to Gian Kaur, who stormed past. Gian led her herd of stampeding elephants straight into the hoard of Obscura demons, who jumped and bit at the elephants' gold bangles. Gian swung her trunk and toppled a pile of thin, bony brutes like bowling pins. They fell with ghastly cries and crumbled into the dirt beneath them.

A blood-curdling shriek commanded the attention of all the warriors in the field. It came from Justyce when she threw a strike of electricity straight into a running line of attackers. Next, she threw a tornado at the hogweed and tore it from the roots. Finally, she cleared more room for her friends to battle the enemy.

She threw another shot of lightning that smacked through the Obscura beings' thin bones. It devastated their bodies and disintegrated their skin. Justyce sobbed as she ran. She didn't want to kill all those innocent creatures forced into battle. This war was all Keres's fault. Justyce funnelled her anger into a wall of hail but stopped short when she saw the woman encircled by hundreds of pygmy possums crawling over her body holding stibnite-created explosives.

Justyce was close enough that she could hear the sizzle of the fuse. She no longer cared if Keres died, but the possums didn't have to pay for Keres's evil. Justyce threw a monsoon and washed the animals away, diffusing the bombs. Keres grinned at Justyce, her silk dress flapping in the pelting rain. Her power had grown massive from the death lying out in the field. She pointed at Justyce, and an unnaturally sized Obscurian ogre climbed out of the ground and stomped towards the girl. His clumsy hands groped at heavy chains that held his crooked neck to his torso.

Justyce fell to her knees among the dead. Her tears blurred her vision. The stench of ash and death filled her nostrils. She looked down to see a wide slit that opened into the dark.

The light from the bland sky above lit up Obscura through the numerous seams that had opened in the ground. Justyce could see every wall, and she gasped at all the empty beds. The tile floor splintered, the daylight hit, and the concrete walls crumbled. War should never be the reason for one to see light.

"This isn't right," Justyce said.

War was how the Obscurians finally received freedom.

An answer came from someone she didn't even realize was nearby. "How sentimental," Chamier said.

She lay in a soot pile between two iron beds, her face in her hands.

"Chamier," Justyce said.

The woman glanced over. She showed no emotion.

"Come, take my hand. I'll pull you out," Justyce said.

"Did you bring me the seed?"

Justyce patted her pocket. Sure enough, it was still in there. But suddenly, she remembered Deryn. The ogre lumbered closer. What would Chamier do with the seed? Justyce tried to read her face. All she saw was pain. Finally, Chamier sat up, her crumpled nurse hat in her hands.

"I only wanted to help, I swear," she said.

The number of bodies piled up into horrendous stacks of death, and Justyce still couldn't decide. First she looked to Chamier, then to the possums who had resumed their charge at Keres.

Justyce had to do something, quick.

The Obscura ogre grunted. He was too close now, causing Justyce to scramble back. The wolves intercepted his approach. The ogre slaughtered half the wolf family with one fist.

Justyce cried out, "Enough!"

No one even looked.

"Give me the seed. I can help," Chamier said.

She had moved so close that the breath from her words pushed the hair from Justyce's eye.

A crate of stibnite detonated, pelting Justyce with shrapnel. Metal bits stabbed into her side. She cried out in pain.

"Give me the seed," Chamier insisted.

"I don't know," Justyce said.

The ogre hit the ground. Glass propelled by the explosion cut his throat. He clawed at the wound, stuffing dirt into the torn flesh to stop the bleeding.

Keres lifted her arm in a rage, and all the stibnite, attached to animals or not, exploded at once. A cougar leaped from between the burning bodies and attacked Keres. The ogre stood, wavered, and turned around to face Keres. The red-taloned eagle that had brought Justyce the key in Equilibrium sat on a small tree that bent under his weight, behind Keres, watching silently.

A bone-white sabretooth cat appeared from a seam in the ground and snarled as he leaped at the cougar. The ogre slammed the two cats together, instantly killing them. He dropped their limp bodies. Gian's tusk impaled the ogre. The Obscura creature turned his attack against Gian by using the embedded tusk to lift and throw her high. The ground rattled when Gian landed.

Snowflakes fell from the sky. Justyce felt so torn on what to do. The snow melted as soon as it hit the ground and mixed with blood. Crimson red and metallic smelling, it choked Justyce and pained her soul. They were losing the battle. She had to do something.

She looked to Chamier and pulled the seed out of her pocket. "Don't make me regret this," she said and dropped the seed into Chamier's open palm.

The spinning sheen on the seed spread over Chamier, enveloping her in a pearly aura. She floated out of Obscura.

Justyce screamed, "Obscura, seal your gates!" The words burst from deep in her being with such energy the ground shook.

The last few souls ejected from Obscura seams before the ground shuttered and stitched closed with long strands of scorched grass. Chamier floated higher above the ground, her body wrapped in the cocoon of light emitting from her palm.

Justyce forced her tired muscles back into action. If Chamier turned traitor, she would find out eventually. She was torn, tattered, and broken-souled, but this battle had to end. Even the Obscura creatures paid horribly. They all deserved to be free of Keres's wrath.

Justyce stepped into the clearing as Keres rose to her feet at the opposite end. Justyce smacked her hands together and shot a lightning bolt at the woman. It missed the direct hit Justyce had hoped for but did the job of knocking Keres over. The woman scrambled into the willow forest, where Justyce lost track of her.

The red-taloned eagle screeched and swooped down onto the ogre to pin him to the ground. Justyce ran across the field as The Otherly fell oddly silent.

Ominous faces like she'd seen at the river and in the cobweb tree appeared with a low fog along the ground. The mouths moved with words that Justyce could just barely hear. She threw the mist and the faces away. The willows dropped their limbs low to cover the space where the fog disappeared.

"Your tricks won't work anymore, Keres," Justyce yelled.

"No tricks. I decided to teach you how to control the weather so there wouldn't be spontaneous tornadoes ripping our lands. Surely you've killed more with this wild weather than what your silly battle cost."

"This is not your land or my land for that matter. And I don't want to ever share anything with you, so do not use the word 'us'. Also, I don't think you're welcome here anymore." Justyce said.

She followed Keres's voice when she answered.

"I've changed my mind. I was thinking of staying and being the new Keeper of Animals. Then it could be our land. The animals could forever source my magic. And the Memegwaans too! Think of the wonders they could supply. It would be brilliant. You and me, queens of this land."

Keres's voice seemed to bounce off every tree in every direction.

"I renounce you as my mother. I give all-loving rights to Ruth," Justyce said.

"I don't think you can do that, my child, and besides, your Ruth will never know who you are. You've missed more than a decade now on Earth," Keres said.

"That doesn't matter. My mother will still love me. She's a kind, good person. Besides, I've changed my mind too. The Otherly is my new home. Equilibrium is my fortress," Justyce said.

She didn't decide before verbalizing it, but hearing her voice say the words made it real.

"Perfect, you can have Equilibrium," Keres said, "but I want The Otherly," she growled the last words.

"I didn't say you could have anything."

"Ha! What are you going to do to me? You're just a child. A weak, insignificant girl," Keres said.

Justyce pulled up a hurricane, ripping the tops off the willows. Keres tumbled across the sky. Justyce slammed the force of the wind down, causing Keres to smash to the ground.

She slowly walked to Keres, like a leopard to a lizard snack. "You're right. I am just a girl. But if you had raised me, then you would know I'm a little different than most."

Justyce stepped over the mess of trees. She waved the hurricane away. Keres took the opportunity and flew up again, but Justyce knocked her back down with hailstones the size of her fist. They hit right on target. But Keres stayed in the sky.

"I'm still more powerful than you," Keres said.

"You stole that magic."

A vine slithered along the ground. Then more. Cattywampus pulled out of the wreckage to Justyce's rescue. They followed Justyce like pets, ready to bite an intruder.

"I never wanted to hurt you," Keres said.

"You're right. You just wanted to hurt everyone else." Justyce pulled thick fog walls around Keres, enclosing her in a box. "Now I want to hurt you."

Justyce's rage made her rush Keres blindly, swinging the sword. The blade connected. She felt the twang of the sword cutting bone. Success!

Keres mumbled something and simply waved her hand over the wound, making it heal in an instant. Failure.

"You might want to be careful with that stolen energy. Like friends, it too will run out," Justyce said.

She stepped back into the fog cover and sent multiple lightning bolts down into the middle. Keres caught the brunt of several volts before jumping out from behind her veil. And right into Justyce's trap. She swung the sword for the woman's head.

Keres ducked but lost a chunk of her scalp. Her fingertips grazed the end of Justyce's sword, turning it into a snake. The girl threw the reptile at Keres, which sunk long fangs into her cheek. Keres ripped it off, leaving two perfect puncture wounds. Black poison lines spread over her face quickly. She waved her hand over the damage, and it disappeared. Her stance wavered.

Weakness. Justyce saw the woman falter. Justyce pulled the wolf tooth from her pocket, screamed like a banshee and lunged at Keres.

Keres caught Justyce's hand mere inches from her heart. The tooth flapped into a butterfly and flew away, leaving her weaponless. Justyce kicked Keres in the stomach rapidly, venting all her desperation for her mother into her legs.

Keres fell to her knees. Justyce lifted her arms and brought more hailstones. One slammed into Keres's skull with a sickening thud, but the woman just shook her head. Justyce felt a small victory when she saw her eyes swim. Keres tried to get back up but couldn't. She lifted her hand to heal the damage, but Justyce intervened, jumping on the arm and breaking it at an awkward angle.

Justyce kicked the woman over. Then she threw a tornado that slammed Keres into a heavy log.

"I will lock you in an iron bed," Keres snarled.

A twig snapped, both Justyce and Keres looked over to see Chamier. Deryn was hanging off the pale-faced nurse who suddenly looked years younger. Chamier's long straight brown hair dragged along the ground, collecting leaves. Her tattered clothing exposed smooth, glowing flesh. Her high cheeks lifted higher when she stuck her tongue out at Justyce. The disturbing teethy bumps on her tongue were gone. She looked the exact age of Justyce.

"I will force you to stay alive and be tortured for an eternity!" Keres threatened.

"No, you won't," Chamier said. "You will never lock any being in an Obscura bed again."

Chamier lifted Deryn and threw her near-lifeless body at Keres, which collided with a sickening thud. Keres tried to drag Deryn off her.

Keres began, "That's just pointless—"

"No, sister, you are the pointless one now," Deryn said.

Deryn placed her hands over her sister's heart. Chamier slammed seed magic into Deryn's hands, and Justyce lunged to add her love for Ruth into the energy. A dandelion seed floated overhead.

Keres screamed, and magic rushed out of her into the air above them.

"This is the end of the tyranny of Keres Moreth," Justyce said.

Keres half laughed, half choked. Her body caved into insignificance under Deryn's hands. Justyce gasped when her aunt's silver hair began to fall out in clumps. She felt the drain through her body. Chamier was forcing every ounce of energy the three had into collapsing Keres's evil into itself. Like the collapse of a mighty star. Keres's flesh became a hard exoskeleton. Then she shrank until she was no longer visible beneath Deryn's hand.

Deryn rolled away, exhausted, and Chamier stood, satisfied. Justyce scrambled back, curious.

Keres pulsed with a heartbeat. She had changed into an insect—a trivial termite.

CHAPTER 31

Justyce patted Chamier on the back and walked over to Keres the bug. "I guess you get to stay in The Otherly after all. You can live long days and never hurt anyone else. For so many moons, you can watch The Otherly thrive, not from sight, but from the pheromones of how much we love," Justyce looked to her new family, "each other."

Deryn rolled over and stared at Keres. Not a word or send came from the bug. Her mandibles twitched. Justyce's aunt smiled, put her thumb and pointer finger together, and flicked the bug into the trees.

Zavian appeared on Gian's back. Justyce was happy to see him alive and well. Without the ferret, his eye sockets were a ghastly white. "Was Ashier too strong for me?" he asked.

"Maybe," Gian said, "but his moth body wasn't very vigilant against my teeth."

Justyce looked at Gian quizzingly.

The elephant grinned from ear to ear. Then she snapped her jaw. "I ate him."

Toll limped in with help from his brothers. He knelt near Deryn, and his brothers helped pull her body on his. *You'll be OK, Mother. Just need some rest is all. I will make the snacks.*

Take me to the elephant, Deryn sent.

It was a feeble send, but Justyce heard it all the same. She watched Deryn closely. The horse took a few stumbling steps towards Gian. Deryn reached out. Justyce was about to intervene when Deryn simply placed a warm hand on the elephant.

Deryn smiled, a strained smile, but it was there. She struggled to voice the words, "Mother Nature bear witness, I pass Keeper of Animals to you."

The red paintings on Gian's skin of people and mazes shifted to birds flying gracefully among treetops.

"Oh," Gian said. "Oh, oh, oh!"

Then she happily stomped. Zavian desperately held on so as not to be flung off.

Justyce smiled. "That was mighty big of you. Will you be OK without absorbing the power of a keeper any longer?"

"Time will tell," Deryn said.

Chamier bounced around like a child with a bag of candy, clapping her hands. "This is all so exciting! Let me try something too, since I am, after all, the most powerful one here."

She placed one hand on Gian, and the other she opened and closed in a fist, like pumping a stress ball. The elephant's tattoos expanded to cover every inch of her body, then danced up Chamier's arm, to her shoulder, then out to her other hand.

Chamier tossed the tattoos into the air. The two-dimensional hearts flew over the devastated field with a whistle.

As if an ice bucket of life was thrown in the air, the dead and injured bolted up shrieking. The heart tattoos from Gian's magic shattered into millions and rained over their bodies, healing all wounds. They erased the destruction of the battle. Animals stood, shook, and wobbled on their feet. Some gathered around Justyce and her family. Others wandered back into the woods. Dragor walked by and smiled widely as the cub that had died in the mines hopped around him in circles.

The Obscura creatures peeled off the ground. Justyce yelled no, but stopped mid-syllable when their bodies filled in with stunning colours. Humans of every race were granted their souls back, erasing all the tortures of Obscura. As they initially were, humans and animals walked to Chamier to give their thanks before wandering off into The Otherly.

Justyce grinned wide. She brought warm raindrops from the sky to extinguish any remaining fires. A wide rainbow bloomed over the top.

The ferret ran out from under a boulder and climbed Zavian's head. His eye sockets snapped to the black Justyce was used to seeing. Then blinked to green. "Who's that?" Zavian asked.

Justyce turned to see the mighty Obscura ogre lift his tarnished chains. He moaned a horrible sound that made everyone jump except Justyce.

His muscular arms snapped out to the sides as if pulled from his body. The war wounds on his thick torso faded. Gashes filled in with brown spurts of long fur. He shook the chains off and flicked his gnarly head to the sky. When the Obscura beast brought his head down, his torn ear lobes stretched into a set of long antlers with dozens of tines. Tendrils of swinging flora sprouted and flowed along the ground.

His hands and feet curled into hooves with toes.

"It's the forest spirit," someone whispered.

The beautiful creature considered Justyce, then bent his neck in thanks. He stepped lightly towards the tree line. Each footprint sprung purple crocuses from the ground.

"If I ever saw one in real life, that would be a wild thing," Justyce said.

"My sons and I need to return to fix my gate. Oh, and the mines," Deryn said.

"Yes," Justyce said. She thought *clock* and saw the last few—seconds? minutes?—tick down to 00:08:22. "I must return as well."

Deryn cocked an eyebrow. Justyce was happy to see the humour in her face once more for some strange reason. "You've decided, then, to remain our Keeper of Equilibrium?"

"I suppose I could make you do it," Justyce said.

Deryn turned Toll to leave, "That's our cue."

Justyce laughed.

Then Deryn had a more serious tone. "I hope you'll consider visiting me on my farm. Since Mother Nature seems so happy with you and all, I'm sure you'll have many day passes."

"I would like that, thank you," Justyce said.

Zavian waved to Deryn. "Can I come too?"

She smiled and nodded.

He slid off Gian and hurried to walk beside the woman.

"How do I get back?" Justyce asked no one in particular.

"You'll know. There is no crawling for a keeper," Deryn said.

Her hands moved to her head, maybe to adjust her hat that was no longer there. Then she winked, and Toll took off.

Justyce looked to the clouds. "OK, Mother Nature, bring me to Equilibrium."

Clouds appeared then billowed downward, a spiral staircase unfolding. Justyce wasn't sure if Mother Nature or she herself had done this. She figured she had lots of time to learn.

Justyce stepped on the first cloud stair.

"Justyce," Gian called.

Justyce glanced back. Chamier, Gian, Tabit, and about a dozen mine animals stood waiting along with a few humans. For something, she supposed.

"Thank you, everyone. You've all done miraculous work to free The Otherly," Justyce said.

Gian laughed. "Great speech. But what I wanted to tell you was you need a better outfit."

Justyce looked down at her clothing. It was a mash-up of the stained blue capris and tattered tank top from Zavian, as well as a few scraps of the cloth and gem suit Keres had thrown at her. She closed her eyes for a moment, sent to the Cattywampus vines, and spun on the cloud steps.

She wore pink flats, jeans, and a Wonder Woman long-sleeved shirt when she stopped spinning. *Like home*, she thought. She lifted her hands over her shoulders and pulled on a cloak made of dandelion seeds turning with gems.

"Lovely," Gian said.

"No," Justyce said, "strong like a nutritious power punch hidden in a weedy little yellow flower."

Gian shrugged, confused.

Justyce climbed the cloud stairs to Equilibrium. Home. At the top, she adjusted the scales and sat down to click through the photos on her camera.

EPILOGUE

Justyce was mildly impressed when Mother Nature granted her a pass the next day. She quickly pulled cloud stairs down to Zavian's cabin.

The Cattywampus vines opened the front door and held out an impressive display of bouquets. She hoped they weren't flowers from Deryn's garden.

"Isn't it a lovely day when Justyce the Keeper comes to visit?" Zavian asked.

He set two mugs on the table, both covered with leaves. Steamy shapes crept out of the corners and danced above the table.

"Keep them warm for when I get back," Justyce said.

She'd waited too long for this. She walked straight to the room that held the staircase. The same trapdoor, with a golden lion handle, glowed from the ceiling.

She stepped on the first stair, and Zavian asked if she would take long. "Just long enough for the tea to cool," she said and stepped on the second stair. The trapdoor creaked open and exposed a collection of trees in the distance.

The climb was twelve stairs. Justyce counted. She stuck her

head cautiously through the exit and smiled at the beach. She walked through without so much as a creak on the stairs.

Her house stood there waiting for her arrival.

Justyce wondered if her mother would recognize something in her. Maybe the way she spoke? Her mom had to see something, or at least she hoped.

Her camera sat on the scales in Equilibrium to hold them at a balance until she returned. She had considered bringing it as proof, but the story would be too crazy for anyone to believe, especially someone whose daughter had already returned. So instead, Justyce wondered if they'd noticed Luci's blonde hair colour. Or if love would overlook the change. Or maybe it was part of the magic of The Otherly.

Justyce felt the crackle of power on her skin when she walked across the sandy beach in front of her house. It felt strange. Tip toeing around the corner of her house to approach the front door also felt odd.

She didn't hesitate to walk up the steps to her house, but she did pull her hand back before instinctually opening the door. Her skin felt like it was on fire, and her heart banged erratically in her chest. *Cool, calm, collected.* She knocked. Justyce wondered if she would look older. She felt ancient, even though the reflection of her face on the glass had the youthful glow of a teenager.

She heard footsteps, then suddenly wished she'd thought of what to say before the door creaked open.

A cat poked his head around the corner. Earl! He had never liked her much, but he had never appreciated anyone much. She moved quickly and snapped the hissing cat up.

The door opened. Ruth smiled with her face radiant as always. She looked older, many more wrinkles, but they were still beautiful tree lines adding to her age rather than taking away. Her glasses were gone, replaced by contact lenses or corrective surgery. There had been lots of changes. Justyce felt the weight of time that had passed. She felt happy to see her Ruth, but sad at the same time. She smiled to force back any unwanted emotion in the moment. What she wanted to do was jump into her mother's arms and squeeze her tight. But she kept herself calm. Her mother smiled back. "Hello," she said.

Relief warmed Justyce when she heard her mother's voice, like the sun's heat emerging from behind clouds on a long cold day.

"Hi, um, is this your cat?" Justyce asked.

She chuckled. "Yes. What kind of trouble has Earl caused this time?"

Justyce shrugged. "He was chasing a ferret."

Her mother rolled her eyes. "Of course he was." She laughed. Justyce fought back the urge to throw her arms around her mother. She wanted to bury her face in her shoulder and cry and tell her everything. "Funny buggers, aren't they? That cat hardly even lets us pick him up, but a stranger ..." Her mother squinted at the girl. "Have I met you before? You certainly look familiar."

Justyce handed over the angry cat. "Yes. I mean no. Well, here you are."

"OK, thank you," her mother said.

Justyce turned to leave with the answer she'd sought. There was recognition on her mother's face, causing her heart to fracture.

"Mom? Who's at the door?" a voice called.

Justyce turned back to see Luci bouncing down the stairs. It was strange, like seeing herself in a video she didn't recall recording. Luci was older too. Her blonde hair was straight and silky. She had a splatter of freckles around her nose and a single mole beside her eyebrow, just like Justyce.

A little black truck pulled into the driveway. Justyce suddenly felt like a boxed mouse. She wanted to run, but the truck door opened, and a tall, lanky man climbed out of the vehicle.

"Hey, Mom," he called.

It was Lane. He was taller than Justyce now. She turned

and smiled at him before she remembered she was technically a stranger here. But Lane returned the smile and nodded before he walked into the house. "Am I late for dinner?" he asked.

"No, it's still an hour or so out," she said.

"Hi," Luci said.

She wrapped her arm through her mother's arm. Justyce lived the moment vicariously through Luci.

"She was returning Earl," her mother said.

"Do you go to Pambina High?" She stuck out her hand. "I went there years ago. I'm the local paper's photographer now, but I've been meaning to come by the school and get pics of the addition. Maybe you could give me the low down?"

Justyce shook Luci's hand. An electrical shock passed between the two women.

"No, I'm, uh, homeschooled."

Luci nodded.

Justyce nodded. The moment became stale and awkward.

"Do you want to come in for a tea? Or some dandelion cake?" her mother asked.

Justyce heard her father speaking to Lane. She looked to Luci again, who matched perfectly to her family. She wasn't sure she would fit in any longer.

"Mom, it's so weird when you mention that. Most people don't cook with weeds!" Luci grumbled.

Justyce's cheeks hurt from smiling. "I've heard they're very nutritious. I would love to try some."

Then she remembered this home was no longer hers. She turned to leave, "I have to go. Thanks for the invite, though."

"Wait, what?" Luci came down the stairs after Justyce. Where are your parents? You're all welcome to stay for dinner," Luci said.

"Thanks, but my mother just bugs me now. So, I'd rather not bring her." The two walked down the sidewalk past the sandy beach where the door to Earth had produced Justyce. Her eyes rolled over the sands to find a sign of the door. Nothing. She kicked a pebble on the sidewalk. "I don't want to intrude on your family dinner either. Because my mother is such a nettle," Justyce said.

The words tumbled out. Justyce felt guilty that Luci even kept pace with her. Luci should go home to her family, leave Justyce alone to return to Equilibrium. But that felt wrong.

"I get it. My mom annoys me sometimes too. When I was your age, she pressured me to do her hobbies. Collecting driftwood." Luci huffed. "Who wants to pick up stinky seashells and stones? Then to spend hours buffing them. It wasn't until I got into a university that she was interested in my photography. We're all different. That's what makes us a strong family. One day your mother will find your originality, and she'll love it all the more because it's different than her own."

Justyce realized she'd walked to the bridge at the end of the road. It was down here where she'd learned to take pictures of her daymares. Photos that helped her discern between truth or a waking nightmare.

"Thanks," Justyce said.

She tossed a stone into the stream.

"I have felt a little lost lately."

Luci put an arm around her shoulder, "Then come for dinner with us."

"What time?" Justyce asked.

"Usually six," Luci said. "What's your name, by the way?"

"Justyce."

"I'll see you at six then?"

Justyce gave a thumbs up before Luci turned and left. Justyce watched the water flow- destined for the ocean. She stepped under the bridge, where hidden graffiti greeted her.

Deryn called from The Otherly. "There's hail pelting the farm!"

Justyce sent back an acknowledgement and turned to leave. She could fix the scales in Equilibrium and still make it back in time for supper. She took a few steps, but one graffiti sign caught her eye. It was a black dog with concrete holes for his eyes. The black spread from his body, taking over the side of the bridge. The lines blurred, and colours blended until everything was black. Finally, an ominous seam tore through the concrete wall, and a grey veil burst free. Justyce screamed as Obscura pulled her back.

CPSIA information can be obtained
at www.ICGtesting.com
Printed in the USA
BVHW091338010922
645662BV00002B/7

9 781665 722810